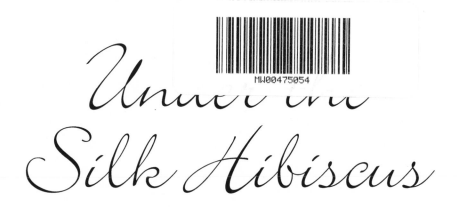

Under the Silk Hibiscus

by Alice J. Wisler

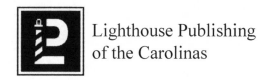

Lighthouse Publishing
of the Carolinas

UNDER THE SILK HIBISCUS BY ALICE J. WISLER
Published by Lighthouse Publishing of the Carolinas
2333 Barton Oaks Dr., Raleigh, NC, 27614

ISBN: 978-1941103302
Copyright © 2014 by Alice J. Wisler
Cover design by writelydesigned.com
Interior design by Karthick Srinivasan

Available in print from your local bookstore, online, or from the publisher at:
www.lighthousepublishingofthecarolinas.com

For more information on this book and the author visit:
http://www.alicewisler.com

This is a work of fiction. Names, characters, and incidents are all products of the author's imagination or are used for fictional purposes. Any mentioned brand names, places, and trade marks remain the property of their respective owners, bear no association with the author or the publisher, and are used for fictional purposes only.

Scripture quotations are taken from the HOLY BIBLE The Authorized (King James) Version. Rights in the Authorized Version in the United Kingdom are vested in the Crown. Reproduced by permission of the Crown's patentee, Cambridge University Press.

Brought to you by the creative team at LighthousePublishingoftheCarolinas.com:
Courtenay Dudek, Eddie Jones, Rowena Kuo, Michele Creech, and Brian Cross

Library of Congress Cataloging-in-Publication Data
Wisler, Alice J.
Under the Silk Hibiscus/Author Alice J. Wisler 1st ed.

Printed in the United States of America

Praise for *Under The Silk Hibiscus*

Alice Wisler is courageous in her storytelling and compassionate in how she unfolds the truth of the past. *Under the Silk Hibiscus* is all at once stirring, beautiful, and thought-provoking.

Tina Ann Forkner
Author of *Waking Up Joy*

Under the Silk Hibiscus is a skillfully crafted novel set in a Japanese internment camp. The picturesque writing transports the reader to another time and place where the story unfolds in layers of history, driven by memorable characters.

Deanna K. Klingel
Author of award-winning books for young-at-heart readers of all ages

Alice has done a wonderful job of capturing the thoughts and worries of a 15-year-old in a war-time situation, much like *The Diary of Anne Frank*.

Sally Jo Pitts
Private investigator, inspirational writer

Alice J. Wisler's *Under the Silk Hibiscus* is an unforgettable fictional journey, filled with history, romance and hope. Wisler draws on her firsthand experience of growing up in Japan to deliver an authentic tale. The way she strings words together is a beautiful expression of storytelling in a book not to be missed. Enjoy her newest release, one I give 5 stars.

Dianna Benson
Award-winning author of *The Hidden Son and Final Trimester*

DEDICATION

This book is dedicated to those who lived through

the Japanese-American internment camps of World War II.

And in memory of those who died there.

"In any moment of decision, the best thing you can do is the right thing, the next best thing is the wrong thing, and the worst thing you can do is nothing."

Theodore Roosevelt

Acknowledgements

This work of fiction is a result of reading books, watching documentaries, having conversations with some who lived in camps, listening to taped interviews, and my own creations. The message I hope to convey is that we never want anything like this to happen in our country to any of our citizens again.

Special thanks to Artie and Elizabeth Kamiya, Terri Takiguchi, and to John Tateishi for his invaluable book, *And Justice For All, an Oral History of the Japanese American Detention Camps*.

Gratitude goes to my agent, Chip MacGregor, to the staff at Lighthouse Publishing of the Carolinas, and to my invaluable beta readers.

PRELUDE

Ten weeks after the December 7, 1941 Japanese attack on Pearl Harbor, President Franklin D. Roosevelt announced that the United States West Coast was a potential combat zone. Living in that zone were more than 100,000 people of Japanese ancestry. A third of them were aliens; two-thirds of them were American citizens. With the president's signing of Executive Order 9066, Japanese-Americans were told to leave their homes, sell their businesses and possessions and move inland. First they went to assembly centers and then by September 1942, ten internment camps had been built. Each of the ten camps were in remote locations, fenced, and guarded by the War Relocation Authority (WRA). Tule Lake and Manzanar camps were in California, Topaz in Utah, Poston and Gila River in Arizona, Granada in Colorado, Minidoka in Idaho, Jerome and Rowher in Arkansas, and Heart Mountain in Wyoming. About 110,000 evacuees ended up living behind barbed wire in wooden barracks during World War II.

This is the story of a family who was sent from their home in California to barracks in Heart Mountain, Wyoming.

PART I

Heart Mountain, Wyoming

Chapter One

A s an afternoon wind blew over the camp's sagebrush terrain, I wiped dust from my face with a handkerchief that once belonged to Papa. Frustration, like the surrounding barbed wire fences, taunted me. At breakfast, something vile overcame me; I'd demanded to know if anyone knew about Papa. I targeted my aunt because she was the easiest to bully. As I continued insisting that she tell me what she knew, the families at the nearby tables lifted their faces from bowls of dry rice. *Shut up*, I could read from the older men's and women's expressions. *We're at war; this is no time for you to become hostile. Besides, you are only a child.*

Since there had been no communication from Papa after that fateful day in February when two FBI agents entered our home in San Jose, I was certain he was dead. They had taken him away in handcuffs. "Spy," the tall one with a crew cut had called him. "We know you are working with Japan's military."

As the memory of that day burned in my mind, I trudged toward the camp's latrine, bucket in hand. Yesterday afternoon, Lucy had smiled at me; I'd nearly danced across the dirt road. Today, I felt almost as despairing as the day Mama, my aunt, my brothers, and I were told we had forty-eight hours to pack up for relocation.

"Relocation," Mama had cried, the word obviously foreign to her. "We don't need to go anywhere. We are happy here."

But happiness had not been the point. Fear seemed to be. Was it the picture of Emperor Hirohito on our living room wall that made Caucasian men tremble? Did they think that Mama was sitting under her knitted grey shawl at the kitchen table, sending messages across the Pacific to the enemy?

My thoughts sprang, one bouncing off another. An army truck sped past toward the mess hall, creating a blanket of dust around the row of bleak barracks. The roar of its engine brought me back to reality, and I increased my pace. If I weren't careful, I'd wind up like my ten-year-old brother, Tom, who seemed to live in his own world of poetry books and fantasies. Tom could get away with it on two accounts. One, he was only ten, and two, he'd had polio, so was lame in his right leg.

But I, Nathan Mori, was able-bodied and must not dilly-dally. Dilly-dally, that had to be my aunt Kazuko's favorite word. She used it as often as she could. When I'd set out with a bucket just moments earlier, she had called out, "Don't dilly-dally."

At the communal lavatories, I hoisted the metal bucket to the sink and watched it fill with water. I splashed some of the tepid liquid onto my forehead, cheeks, and nose. Using Papa's handkerchief, I wiped my face again. *Papa, where are you?*

"How is your mother?" an elderly woman stopped to ask as I made my way back to our barracks. She was one of the few who wore a kimono. Today, she was dressed in a charcoal one, the color of Heart Mountain at dusk.

I wanted to give her a hug for showing concern, but that would probably set her off. She was the same woman who complained in the mess hall that we should have seaweed. How, she'd shouted, was she supposed to eat steamed rice without a piece of *nori*? Aunt Kazuko had warned me not to tell this woman too much about our family affairs because she was a busybody. She'd been known to spread gossip quicker than sagebrush blew over the campsite. However, after my outburst this morning, keeping our family concerns a secret was over. Everyone now knew that I was angry. What did I have to hide?

"Your mother?" the woman asked again. "I didn't see her at breakfast or at lunch."

I felt the weight of the bucket in my hands, almost as heavy as the thoughts of my mother. "She's all right."

It was a lie, and something told me that Mrs. Busybody knew it. For a second I thought she was going to accuse me of not telling the truth; it wouldn't have been out of her character.

She shielded the sun from her face with a thin hand pocked with liver spots. "Well," she said, and gave a deep sigh. "Well." With a nod, as though she had just recalled what to say next, she added, "I think she needs ginger root. My grandmother swore it helped her when she was pregnant. Is she sleeping at night? She needs her sleep."

I didn't want to go into all the details of how Mama had spiked a fever and moaned last night, keeping all four of us in our living quarters awake until the sun broke through the dark Wyoming sky, its broadcast of a new day. Only then had she calmed and settled into sleep.

"I can come over. I'll have tea with your aunt."

I nodded, tried to smile, and said I had to go. As I took a step toward our barracks, the woman called out after me.

"You know, your father is not a spy."

At her words, unexpected tears swarmed in my eyes. "Yes." I drew a breath. "I know he isn't."

"He's just in a camp. Like this one. No seaweed there either."

Suddenly, I was aware that time had slipped, and I was late. The wrath of Aunt Kazuko was near, I could feel it. I hurried toward our barracks, allowing myself one last glance over the plains at the limestone mountain that emerged from behind the camp's barbed wire fences. That was Heart Mountain, a strange name for a mountain by a camp that seemed so heartless. There were days I wished I could run to the mountain's knobby peak and hide out until this war ended. But with looming guard towers strategically placed around the facility, there was no hope of that happening.

Once I stepped inside our family's one-room unit, constructed of wood and insulated with tarpaper, my aunt rushed toward me like a military Jeep. "Where were you? I am dying here." She had a robust face and stocky body to match, and I doubted she was anywhere near death.

At the lone table that stood in the middle of the room with cots to the left and right, Aunt Kazuko removed a glass and steadied it as I carefully poured water into it. This was a ritual we were familiar with, and no words were needed.

Aunt Kazuko carried the glass to Mama, who lay in one of the cots, a cotton sheet pulled over her protruding belly. As she helped Mama up, my aunt barked at me, "You need to go to hospital and tell them to come here. Your mother need medicine."

I dismissed her choppy orders, spoken in a language she had not quite mastered. Yesterday, I made a trip to the hospital and, after waiting for fifteen minutes, a nurse came to my aid. She followed me to our barracks to check on Mama. She probed and asked a few questions while Aunt Kazuko and I stood around Mama's bedside, trying not to appear anxious. The nurse told me that the baby would be here any minute now and to make Mama as comfortable as I could. She's going to be fine, I said to myself, recalling the nurse's words from yesterday.

Lifting a wobbly chair, I placed it closer to my mother's bed.

I smiled at her, remembering how she used to button my sweater on winter mornings and, with a playful smile, tell me that I was her favorite son named Nathan. "Hey, Mama."

With Aunt Kazuko supporting her, Mama took a few sips of water before easing onto the uneven mattress filled with hay. She gave a weak smile. "Nathan," she breathed. "My favorite Nathan."

Aunt Kazuko moved to the table, poured her own glass of water and nibbled on a sugar cookie, one she had stowed away in her sleeve after dinner last night. She was always hiding morsels of food. If anyone ever wanted a late night snack, digging through my aunt's sleeves would be a good move. I was grateful that my aunt gave me some time alone with Mama. Usually, she was flittering about, interjecting her worries.

I took Mama's hand in mine, noting the slender fingers, the simple gold ring that signified her union with Papa. Papa, who was somewhere, but had not been heard from in over six months.

Stroking Mama's palm, I wished. It is a scary thing to wish when you know the wish can't come true.

Nevertheless, I wished that she could play the piano like she used to. It seemed that no matter what was going on in my life, when Mama played Chopin or Beethoven, the world was a tranquil place. I was about to form a prayer of asking. In my opinion, people usually pray on one of two occasions—to ask for something or to thank God for something. I had no time to offer up a prayer of asking because my mother interrupted my thoughts.

"You work too hard." She spoke as though the words sapped all her energy. I wanted to hear her voice, yet at the same time, I wanted her to rest and not tire herself by talking.

"Are you too warm?" Before she could nod yes, I picked up a silver and red silk fan that rested against the top of her leather suitcase under the foot of her cot. Opening it, the scent of sandalwood permeated the air. I moved it across her pale face. The breeze from it fluttered strands of hair into her eyes.

I brushed the black strands, smoothing them with my fingers over her scalp. I'd seen my father do this once and was captivated by what an act of sacrifice it was. He had taken time, time away from the business, time away from a game of chess—his love—to spend time with my mother and do something for her. The thought of that scene made it hard to swallow.

I needed to get a grip, as Ken, my seventeen-year-old brother always told me. Recently I'd been plagued with too many tears.

"I ask God to give you some time for fun," Mama said, pausing between each word. "You need fun."

"Not everyone can run around and play," I wanted to say, but I was sure if I said it, she'd accuse me of being too hard on my older brother. Ken felt life should be a playground and neither work nor household chores seemed to get in the way of him doing what he wanted.

She winced and closed her eyes. "Nathan," she said after a moment. "I want you to make a promise."

I leaned in closer as her dark eyes looked intently into mine. "The watch . . . You keep it safe."

Immediately my view shifted from her face to beneath her cot. Inside her leather suitcase was the family heirloom, the gold and diamond pocket watch my grandparents had brought over on the freighter from Hiroshima. Of course, I knew of its importance, of the story that was behind that expensive piece of craftsmanship. I'd heard Papa tell how a member of nobility had requested a local craftsman to design the watch. When my grandfather saved the nobleman's daughter from a raging river, the watch had been presented to him in appreciation for his act of valor. It had been in the Mori family ever since.

Mama gasped for air, coughing. "Nobu?"

I sat straight. It was seldom that she called me by my Japanese name. "I will," I vowed, recalling the Boy Scout promises I once held important. "I'll keep it safe."

Moistening her lips, she closed her eyes. "Good," she whispered as the sun vacated the sky, casting shadows through the window onto her blanket. "Good. I know I can count on you."

After dinner, Ken, Tom, and I walked from the mess hall over to the Yokota's barracks which was parallel to ours, just across the dusty dirt road. Ken matched Tom's slower pace—slower than most due to Tom's right leg brace. The two conversed about baseball, recalling a game some of the boys had played at the camp when we'd first arrived. I hadn't played or watched as I'd been searching for spare pillows for Mama so that she could sit comfortably in her cot during the day. She liked having pillows propped around her back and belly.

"That was the first time I'd ever seen you get a home run," Tom said to Ken.

"Just call me Babe Ruth." Ken laughed.

"I bet you were beat after that. I know I'd have been. That was a lot of running."

"Ah, when you're that happy, you don't feel tired."

I lagged behind, feeling a little sick, as the noodles and chicken I had just eaten thickened and soured in my stomach. The searchlights scoured the camp, I watched their beams and then looked beyond them over the barbed wire fence toward Heart Mountain. The mountain seemed close, like if I reached out, I could touch it, but I knew it was miles away.

At the entrance to the Yokota's barracks, Ken paused and turned toward me. "Aren't you coming?"

"Nah. Can't," I mumbled. Of course I wanted to hear Fusou Yokota sing. To my ears, her Japanese name of Fusou had to be one of the most beautiful names. And it matched everything else about her. Ken argued that Fusou wasn't that great of a name. "It's just a name. Nothing else." What did he know anyway? I bet he'd never taken the time to repeat it several times in a silent room and watched how that name filled every dark corner with light. He didn't know how it sounded as it pushed over his lips like a puff of air. He called her by her American name, Lucy, which was not nearly as special. In fact, everybody called her Lucy. Even she went by Lucy.

That evening, although I wanted to join my brothers, I rushed into our barracks to check on Mama. Someone had to be responsible. I hoped that the bowl of rice I had for her was still warm enough for her to enjoy. I entered our living quarters and shut the front door.

Seated next to Mama, Aunt Kazuko removed an object from her pocket. As I drew nearer to her and to Mama's cot, I saw that it was a small sugar cookie. "I need a little pep," my aunt confessed as she chewed. "Dinner was too small. A little pep for pep-me-up."

Mama groaned. "Kazuko, you will turn into a cookie."

I laughed. Ever since she'd been bedridden, Mama had been uncomfortable, but when her words showed that she still had her humor intact, I knew that she couldn't be suffering too much. I handed her the bowl of rice as my aunt scurried around the barracks for a pair of chopsticks.

Wanting to hear Lucy, I opened the wooden front door. Immediately, dust flew into our quarters, burning my eyes.

"You always forget to open slow," my aunt chided. "Slow is best way."

I also knew that quiet was *best way*, but now was not the time to pick a fight with my aunt.

Aunt Kazuko complained about not having shampoo that she liked. "My hair is like dried shrimp when I use that green stuff."

"You should head over to the salon," said Mama, referring to the hairdresser two barracks down who cut hair for fifteen cents. "She might have some better shampoo."

My aunt finished her cookie and wiped stray crumbs from her lap. "I need hair color, too," she said and then explained in her native tongue about how her roots were looking grey.

We were forbidden to speak Japanese inside the camp. All the signs reminded us of this. Yet, there was something comforting about hearing the language of my people spoken. There were words for which English had no equivalence like *gambare* and *gaman,* words of encouragement and endurance.

Suddenly, my aunt stopped talking. From across the camp we heard the sweet voice of Lucy. Tonight she was singing about God watching over us.

"Go on," Mama said to me as my aunt lifted a bite of rice on wooden chopsticks to Mama's mouth.

"Go on what?"

She chewed the rice, swallowed and then shifted in her bed, her large belly protruding underneath the sheet. With a weak gesture, she brushed back hair from her forehead. "Go over to her house."

My whole being lurched into one word: YES! Yes, I would head over there, yes, I had Mama's blessing and yes, yes, again, yes, this would be my chance to get Fusou Lucy Yokota to notice me.

Inside the Yokota's living quarters, men, women, and children were seated on mats on the floor. To the left of the stove hung a rope with an assortment of garments on it—a man's shirt, a woman's skirt, a hand towel, and a blouse.

Lucy stood near the table; cots had been pushed to the walls to make room for the crowd. I found a spot on the floor crammed between Tom and my classmate and friend from San Jose, Charles. Lucy had finished one song and was preparing to sing another. I was just in time! Charles's elbow accidently jerked into my side, but I didn't care. Pain didn't matter, I was in the presence of Lucy!

All conversation stopped as Lucy nodded at the gathered group, the cue that she was about to sing. Her song was one I had never heard before, something about a lost canary finding sanctuary in a hollow log.

We were confined to a camp, away from all we knew, many of us separated from family members, but to hear her voice, that soprano timbre that was distinctly hers, made the smile stay on my face during her entire song.

When she finished, we clapped. A man in the front, with a boy on his lap, asked if she could sing a song in Japanese for his son, one about the rain.

Ken rose to his feet, stepped over seated bodies, and moved toward Lucy. He poured water into a cup from a metal bucket that sat on a birch table, a table identical to the one we had in our unit. Gently, he handed it to her.

Why couldn't I have done that? The answer was simple—that thought never crossed my mind. Whenever I saw Lucy, all I could think of was how pretty she was, how I couldn't wait to hear her sing, and how I hoped that she'd look at me. I couldn't think about actually doing something more.

She thanked him, her lips then pressed into a tiny smile.

Ken winked at her and then slipped back to where he had been seated.

Why couldn't I be more like my older brother? I'd prayed to be, feeling that it must be all right to ask God to make a person more suave. After all, the Bible said somewhere that God opens His hands and satisfies all His creation with their desires. Ever since we'd come to camp, Lucy had been my desire.

When I drifted off to sleep that night, the sound of Aunt Kazuko's snores penetrating my thoughts, I wondered how I could get Lucy to notice me. Dreaming about her was easy; it was the actual communicating that left me in a quandary.

In August, after we first arrived at camp, I saw her walking on the road, the wind in her long hair, a pensive look on her face. I decided I could do it and summoned the courage to speak to her. I'd seen her at the assembly center in Santa Anita, but had never said a word to her during our months there. Here was my chance! Standing in her path, I waited for her to approach me. She stopped, cocked her head to the side and said, "Hello."

My throat was as dry as the summer air. "Uh . . ."

She waited, a smile on her lips.

I'd almost forgotten what I'd wanted to say.

Looking me in the eyes, she asked, "You're Ken's brother, aren't you?"

Borrowing strength from somewhere, I blurted, "Why do you want to be called Lucy?"

For a moment, her hand toyed with the silver barrette behind her ear. I was afraid that she wasn't going to answer. "We are Americans," she said at last. "Fusou is the old name for Japan. I can't be associated with Japan now."

"But you can still use that name," I protested. "Your mother and father gave it to you. It's . . . it suits you."

The smile she flashed made my heart quiver. How could one person cause another to feel such . . . such tenderness toward her and affection? I swallowed and kicked a rock with my shoe, just for something to do, just because I didn't want to be caught staring at her.

Chapter Two

Early the next morning before faint sunlight crept through our billet's slats, Aunt Kazuko screamed. "The baby is coming! The baby! Somebody help us!"

Ken wasn't in our barracks. His cot was empty, untouched; in fact, both the pillow and wool army blankets were still in place as though he hadn't slept there at all.

As usual, it was going to be up to me. I scrambled out of my own cot as one of my blankets fell onto the floor. From the back of a wicker chair, I pulled off a checkered shirt and then grabbed a pair of trousers that were in a heap at the foot of my bed. Once dressed, I worked my feet into my shoes and looked for my jacket. I didn't wait for Aunt Kazuko to tell me not to dilly-dally. Sprinting toward the clinic, the frosty autumn air didn't bother me. By the time I reached the clinic, my face was damp from sweat. The main door was locked. I banged on it.

Mekley, one of the uniformed soldiers assigned to the camp, appeared from the clinic's vicinity. "What in tarnation are you doing?" he cried.

"I need a doctor."

"Well, I need a million dollars." He spoke with a drawl. Everybody told me it was Southern. I didn't know for sure. I'd never heard a Southern accent before. I just knew that he was ornery. That characteristic had nothing to do with accents. "I need a good woman, too." He winked, but it wasn't a wink like Ken's; it made me feel dirty to have witnessed it. "Know where I can find one?" he asked.

Thirst cloaked my throat, and I tried to swallow to ease the dryness. Mama needed help and it was up to me. "Where's the doctor? Where's Doctor . . . ?" My mind suddenly became like a boarded-up window. *What was the doctor's name from San Jose?* "Yamagata."

"Ya-ma-ga-ta?" he said, drawing the surname out like it were a piece of taffy, the kind you got at the fair. "What happened that you need a doctor?"

"My mother's having a baby."

He grinned. "A baby, huh? Another one?"

I wasn't sure what he meant by that. I knocked on the door again and then heard a strong and familiar voice from behind. "Are you looking for me?"

Turning around, I tasted relief. Dr. Yamagata stood before me, a Dunlap hat on his head.

"You have to come. My mother is in labor."

"Can't she come to the hospital like all the other mamas?" asked Mekley.

"No," I said. I didn't need to say anymore because I knew that Dr. Yamagata had said that when it was Mama's time to give birth, he would come to us. He knew that Mama was too weak to get to the hospital on her own.

❀

"Go outside. Shoo, shoo." No sooner had I rushed back to our barracks with the doctor when Aunt Kazuko commanded me and Tom to get out.

Dr. Yamagata pulled the covers off of Mama and asked her a few questions.

With brisk movements, a nurse entered our living quarters, her shoes stamping off the frost that clung to the heels. In her hands she carried towels and a basin of water. Over her shoulder, a bag swung. She placed the basin and towels on our table and from the bag pulled out a pair of gloves.

My aunt muttered in Japanese that we needed to hurry and something about children needing to mind adults. She grabbed our coats off of pegs on the wall and flung them into my arms.

Tom hobbled outside and I followed, purposely letting the door slam against the frame.

Why did I have to be treated like a child?

I was fifteen. Not a baby. Since our arrival at camp, I was the one who did all the work. I fanned Mama's perspiring face, held her hand, got her water, and read to her. Why was I now told to shoo?

Tom didn't seem annoyed at all. And that annoyed me even more. He eased himself onto the top stair, his back against the door, his polio leg sticking straight out with the strap wrapped below his knee, causing his trousers to bunch out like balloons. "I hope it's a girl," he said with a smile. "Wouldn't it be fun to have a sister?"

A sister? I'd never thought that Mama could actually have a girl. What would it be like to have a sister? As Tom and I put on our coats, I thought of the words I'd overheard months ago before the train took us from the processing center to Heart Mountain. It had been a rainy evening in early February, and I'd woken to the sound of rain pattering against my bedroom's windowpane. I went to the kitchen to get a glass of water, and on the way back to my room, I heard my parents' muffled voices across the hallway.

Mama had said to Papa, "I know we don't need another child."

Papa had said, "We'll make do. The boys are older and can help out."

"I am too old to be having a baby."

"You are still that young girl I fell in love with the moment you stepped off that freighter in San Francisco."

Mama giggled, and her lightheartedness made me smile in the darkened hallway. "Really? All those years ago."

"All those many years ago, my sweet picture bride."

That was the first I knew that Mama was pregnant. Three weeks later Papa was taken from us. I only thought about Papa and saw her worry, all of which made me forget that she was going to have a baby in about eight months.

It was not until we had to make our home in horse stalls at the Santa Anita assembly center that she told Tom, Ken, and me why she was feeling so sick. I acted like it was my first time hearing the news, letting my eyes grow wide and saying, "Really? Wow!" over and over until Ken told me to shut up.

Now I watched the sun rise into the grey Wyoming sky and wondered what was happening back home, back in San Jose. What were the kids doing in my school? Did they miss me?

Tom shivered, bringing me back to reality. "Let's sit on the rock, Nathan," he said.

"What rock?"

"My rock. I found it and put it there." He pointed to the right of our unit's entrance and, sure enough, there was a large, flat rock, about the width of two army helmets. He limped over and sat on it.

I slipped down next to him. A wind whipped around us, making it colder than any wind I had ever felt in San Jose. Tom huddled against me, he rested his chin on my shoulder, a gesture he had done for as long as I could remember. I patted the top of his head, and we both smiled. I supposed I had been patting his head for as long as I could remember, too.

From inside, the moans and cries increased. The nurse abruptly shut the door.

Tom started to hum, perhaps to drown out the noises. He hummed "You Are My Sunshine," a song Papa often sang to us. Then he hummed a few lines from "Away in the Manger." It didn't matter that it was only September; Tom loved Christmas songs anytime of the year.

To further distract Tom from the painful sounds coming from our billet, I pointed toward Heart Mountain. Today, only the top of it could be seen, the base was covered in thick clouds. "I wonder what it feels like?"

"I think it feels like cotton candy. The kind you get at the fair."

Cotton candy. I had never thought of that. I was thinking more like dirt or pebbles or maybe sand.

"I wrote a story about a spaceship landing on the top of the mountain."

"Really? A spaceship, huh?"

We stopped talking when suddenly there was a distinct cry, the sound of a young cat.

Above the cry, we heard my aunt. "Oh, now, now. *Yoshi, yoshi*. You are here. It's going to be all right. You are here at last."

"Get the children." Mama's strained voice made me jump. I pulled Tom to his feet.

Dr. Yamagata opened the door to our billet. His smile assured me that everything was all right. "Go on inside," he said. "You have a new family member."

Tom limped after me toward Mama who was seated in her bed, her face flushed, her hair matted. In her arms, she cradled a small life, swathed in blankets.

I smiled into the face of my new sister. Her eyes were shut, her skin as smooth as the silk that was wrapped around our gold watch, hidden in Mama's suitcase. And her fingers, they were barely fingers, just about the size of matchsticks.

"She's got fuzzy hair," said Tom, edging his way around my shoulder to see the baby. "She's the size of a turtle I saw on my way to school."

"Emiko," said my mother. "That is her name."

I waited to hear more. After all, each of us sons had English first names as well as our Japanese given names. Mine was Nobu, although ever since I was five, I had opted to go by Nathan. Which American-sounding name had Mama given to her daughter? When Mama started to moan, I wiped her brow with a towel we'd brought from our home in San Jose. "Do you want some water?"

She kissed the top of my sister's head and closed her eyes. "No, not yet."

"What is her American name?"

"Emi."

"Emi?"

"Emi." Mama sighed as though she was too exhausted to be bothered coming up with an English-sounding first name for her newborn.

"Do you think she has piano playing fingers?" I asked, hoping to see a smile on my mother's lips.

But before she could reply, she clutched her neck and was taken over by a deep cough.

Aunt Kazuko quickly gathered Emiko from Mama and said, "Boys, wash your hands."

I didn't want to have to leave our billet yet again. I wanted to stay close to Mama.

Mama took a few raspy breaths and then closed her eyes. Her voice was as soft as a distant train whistle, way in the distance. Just as I thought she hadn't heard my question, Mama replied. "She does. You will teach her how to play, won't you?"

I wasn't the best piano player, not at all like my mother, but I supposed I could teach my new sister a few songs.

As my aunt once more told Tom and me to go wash our hands, I wished that my father were here. If he were here, he'd be singing one of his favorite Bing Crosby songs. After he exhausted all he knew, then he'd hum a hymn or two from the Second Street Church's hymnal. He would probably start with "Praise God from Whom All Blessings Flow" and then let that one ease into "Blessed Assurance" and end with "Rock of Ages."

People would be sure to ask how he felt about having a girl now, and I imagined that his reaction would be something like, "Well, bless us all, a girl to add some class to this family. It's about time, wouldn't you agree?"

With Papa on my mind, Tom and I trailed out of our unit for the latrine. If I closed my eyes and breathed in, I could almost smell the air that surrounded our fish market, that lovely salty aroma I had grown up with. Way back before Japan decided to change our lives and drop stupid bombs.

Chapter Three

Everyone wanted to see the new baby. The news of my sister's birth spread across the camp. In the mess hall, women eagerly approached me, asking how my mother and the baby were doing. Small knitted socks and caps were handed to me for Baby Emiko.

Women knocked on our door and then entered, congratulating Mama, who was usually asleep. They made their way over to Aunt Kazuko who proudly showed them my tiny sleeping sister, nestled against her, inside a flannel blanket. The women's comments were endearing.

"She is beautiful."

"A Heart Mountain baby."

"She's so alert."

"Look at that smile. Did you see it?"

"You must be so happy."

"Feed her some ginger root." Mrs. Busybody was adamant about her advice.

Yet Mama, even when awake, barely acknowledged their congratulatory remarks. I could tell she was tired. I knew that she should rest and, with people entering our billet, she was not getting the sleep her body needed. So I placed Emi in a wooden crib that Mr. Kubo had made for us out of scrap wood. I set the crib to the left of my cot and, while at first I responded to the visitors, after a day I chose not to answer the door.

As Mama slept, I sat on my cot and watched Emi. I watched her eyelids flutter and her mouth open and close as she slumbered by my side. When she woke and inevitably cried, I gently picked her up, the way I'd watched both Mama and my aunt do. Emi was so tiny; she couldn't have weighed more than a mackerel. I felt huge. Yet her lungs had this tendency to expand and let out cries that made me wince. When she didn't stop crying, I carried her to Mama.

One afternoon, as Mama nursed Emi and Aunt Kazuko went to the washroom area to launder cotton diapers, I lay on my cot and prayed one of my begging prayers. These always started with, "Please, please, God." I thought of all the things I wanted, all the things that were not right, all the things I missed from home in San Jose. When my muttered prayers stopped, I silently prayed for better food and for Lucy to like me, for Papa to return to us, and for the war to end.

The only man who came to visit besides a brief stop from Dr. Yamagata, who brought two glass baby bottles, was Mr. Kubo. Mr. Kubo asked us what we needed.

Aunt Kazuko said, "Cookies are always good."

Mr. Kubo said, "I meant for the baby."

"Oh. Oh. Diapers and pins. Always more diapers and pins." And with that remark, she went over to my sister to change her diaper.

As Mr. Kubo got ready to leave, I asked how his wife was doing.

He didn't mince words. Taking his hand off the doorknob, he said, "Let's see . . . Her recent grievance is that she doesn't want to be around anybody who uses Jesus or God in every other sentence."

"Why not?" I'd seen her in church with him, both in San Jose and here at the camp. I didn't think that she was opposed to Christianity, but perhaps I'd been wrong.

"She's just bothered by all of this, Nathan. She doesn't want anybody telling her that all things work together for good. She's basically very tired."

I looked around our quarters and knew we were all tired of being confined to these surroundings and to this wasteland. My aunt tried to console Emiko, who was not too pleased at the moment. As Emi wailed, it seemed that, even as new as she was, she was already tired of this life.

"*Yoshi, yoshi,* Emi-chan." Aunt Kazuko drew my sister close to her breast and patted the small of her back.

Over Emi's cries, Mr. Kubo said, "My wife worries about everything. She misses her boy. When we were told to move out of our house, she wanted to go to Chicago to live with him."

"Why didn't she?"

"That's never going to happen. She loves our son, but his wife . . . she's hard to please."

More so than my own aunt, I wondered. I didn't need to ask, Mr. Kubo volunteered, "John's wife only eats egg whites—whipped. No pork fat. Wants her milk steamed for her coffee."

"Where is she from?"

"Kansas."

I tried to picture where the state was located. I was pretty sure it was either near Colorado or Oklahoma.

"She's a farm girl, but very sophisticated. She went to Wellesley College and wants us to believe that she's highly educated, too."

"Is she *Nissei?*" I asked, wondering if she, like me, had been born in the United States.

"No, she's French. Her grandparents emigrated from Lyons. They are down-to-earth types. She thinks they are regular hicks."

"Well, please tell Mrs. Kubo that she can come visit us here. Aunt Kazuko doesn't say God or Jesus in every other sentence, and she eats all parts of the egg." I supposed that wasn't really true, so immediately added, "Except for the shell."

He rested his hand on my shoulder. "Keep your sense of humor, Nathan. And your faith. Both will serve you well here."

Later that afternoon, the one light bulb we had fizzled and popped, leaving us without any light in our barracks. I was assigned baby and Mama duty while Tom and my aunt went in search of a bulb. I said I'd go, but I think that my aunt wanted to get out of our quarters and have some time to chat with others.

As I sat on my bed, keeping one eye on a sleeping Emi, there was a knock on the door. I peeked out the window to see Lucy. Hallelujah, my heart cried; one of my prayers had been answered.

Lucy, dressed in a grey skirt and blue blouse, stepped inside our barracks.

I breathed in the sweet floral scent that entered with her. Her long hair hung over her back and the urge to reach out and touch it to see if it felt as smooth as it looked overcame me. It was like being caught up in a ride at the circus, both fun and intoxicating at the same time. I fought for words to say. I wished I were like my older brother, never at a loss for the perfect sentence. At last I stuttered, "H-hh how are you?"

"I'm all right."

She handed me a blanket, saying that her mother had knitted it. As I held the soft yellow gift, I waited. Something told me that this was going to be my moment; this was when she was going to tell me that she liked me, that she thought I was a great person. Glancing up from the blanket, I let myself look into her eyes.

But all she said was, "Can I see your sister?"

After she stroked Emi's cheek and commented on how sweet she was, she said that tonight's song would be dedicated to Emi. "So when you hear me sing, know that it's for her."

"Thanks," I said and then wondered if that was the right thing to say. Perhaps if we both sat down, I could think more clearly and come up with some topics to talk about. I looked over at the one chair that was behind the table. I'd offer it to her, and I could sit on the end of Tom's cot.

As I devised my plan, Mama sat up and adjusted a pillow behind her back.

"Hello, Mrs. Mori," Lucy said. "You have a beautiful daughter."

"Thank you." Mama pulled the covers across her abdomen, and as she did, one of the pillows fell to the floor.

Lucy picked it up and handed it to Mama.

"Thank you." This time Mama's gratitude sounded weak. I wondered if she should sleep instead of staying seated.

"Mama?"

"I'm fine, Nathan." She looked at me; I knew she was trying to reassure me. In a moment, she'd tell me to go outside and get some fresh air, have some fun. But she merely closed her eyes and mumbled, "Thank you for the blanket, Lucy. Please thank your mother."

"I will." Lucy flashed a smile that made my heart spin. Turning to me, she asked, "Do you know where Ken is?"

Snow whirled from the thick clouds over Heart Mountain and covered the ground. We had never seen snow, and the elders commented that it was only September. A few of the *Issei* men (those born in Japan) said that where they were from in northern Japan, sometimes the first snow fell in early October, but never in September.

The cold whistled through the cracks in each of the barracks. Mr. Kubo said that the barracks had been built too quickly and without any insulation. He was a carpenter by trade, and from the moment he'd stepped into his new living quarters last month, he had studied the structure and had shaken his head.

When Lucy sang the night of the first snow, we were all inside our unit because my aunt had put us to work. Under the single light bulb, with the stove hissing as it burned coal, we worked to string fabric against the windows. Next, we used wads of paper, and pieces of cotton and flannel, to stuff into the cracks of the walls. Mama smiled from her cot and called us wonderful interior decorators. Emi seemed attentive to Lucy's voice as it swayed across the crisp camp air.

But even though 24-F, our *camp house*, as Tom called it, was now insulated, the wind still found its way inside. Mama still coughed. Emi and the others slept in spite of Mama's labored breathing. I lay awake and thought of summer back home when the days and nights were so warm that we kept the windows opened and still needed an electric fan to draw away the heavy air.

I must have dozed off. When I woke, Ken was kicking off his shoes. Still fully dressed, he slid into bed. Once I asked where he went at night, but he told me not to worry. I knew he was forming some sort of a gang with other boys from San Jose. They called themselves The Samurai. There was another gang, a rival group of boys from Los Angeles. They called themselves The Warriors and wore grey headbands made from burlap bags.

Aunt Kazuko said that they looked ridiculous.

Tom thought the Heart Mountain Aliens was a much better name for Ken's gang, but then again, my younger brother thought anything extraterrestrial was impressive. His teacher read his stories with interest and said he certainly had "the active mind of a young boy." Tom took his teacher's words as encouragement, and continued to create.

As I walked home from school, I hoped to run into Lucy. The roads were pools of melted snow. The sky held thick bulky clouds, and more snow was predicted.

When I entered our barracks, an eerie feeling came over me. Silence. There was no chatter from the radio my aunt often listened to. There was no talking, no cries. Quickly, it became obvious; no one was there. Mama's cot, which always held Mama because she had been too weak to go anywhere, was vacant.

"Mama?! Aunt Kazuko?" My words echoed in our billet. No one responded. Emi's crib was empty except for the yellow blanket Lucy's mother had made for her. I pulled back the dark piece of material my aunt had strung up to provide privacy for undressing.

Rushing outside, I hoped to see someone who could help me. A few classmates trailed to their barracks, but they wouldn't know anything. Where was Tom? Ken? I scanned the road, and suddenly I saw Mrs. Busybody strolling along the side of the road.

Running toward her, I cried, "Have you seen my mom?"

She pointed behind her. "Hospital. They took her this morning."

Panic gripped my throat and burned like hot oil throughout my veins. I ran.

At the hospital, I asked a nurse where my mother was. "Mrs. Mori?" I repeated until at last I was ushered down a corridor and into a room where metal beds, all occupied, lined the walls. At the end of the room, Aunt Kazuko and Tom sat beside a bed that held my mother.

"What happened?" I looked at my mama—in between the sheets she appeared frail, tiny. Her eyes were shut, and the lids looked as pale as the Wyoming sky before snowfall. I wanted to rush over to hug her, but I was afraid she might break like glass. So I compromised by standing near her feet. "What's wrong?" My voice was hoarse, as though I had been shouting at a baseball game.

"I overheard the doctor say that she has pneumonia," said Aunt Kazuko.

"Pneumonia? What does that mean?"

Tom supplied the answer. "That means she has fluid in her lungs."

And all I thought was wrong with her was that she had a cough.

"Go to the pharmacy and ask for milk," said my aunt.

"Milk?"

"Formula for Emi," whispered Mama.

"Who has her?"

"Mrs. Kubo," said Tom.

Mama reached out for me, and as I edged closer to her, her fingers rested against my hand. "You will ... be sure to ..." Her strained words were hard to hear over the conversations of other patients around us. I bent closer to her face. "Take good care of Emi ... won't you, Nobu?"

"Of course," I said. "I'll take care of everything. I'll get the milk now and then I'll get Emi from the Kubo's."

In Japan, the *chonan*, the eldest son, is supposed to be the one to carry on the family affairs. Since our family's eldest was most likely flirting with the girls or scheming up some gang prank against The Warriors, it was up to me. I, Nathan Mori, would be the hero.

Later, as I stood in line at the store and waited my turn for the powdered milk, I knew that Papa would be proud of me. I was the good son, the honest one, the noble Nobu. Just like the man who had saved the drowning girl and received the prestigious gold watch with the bamboo and crane etchings as a token of appreciation.

But I was only fooling myself. There would be no heroes. There would be no saving lives.

The next day, Aunt Kazuko told me that the angels came in the night to take Mama away.

Chapter Four

Accompanied by a bamboo flute and a *shamisen*, Lucy sang "Amazing Grace" at Mama's funeral. Her voice rang effortlessly over the camp, and at one point when she started the last verse, I could have sworn that she was an angel sent by God, straight from Heaven.

At first, Mama's service was to be held in the church, but then one of the block leaders, Mr. Higashi, felt it was best to have the service out in the open on a makeshift wooden platform that seemed to be hauled out from nowhere.

Minutes before the service started, the area around the platform filled. From each of the barracks, people in coats, gloves, scarves, and hats, trickled out and down the wet roads, dodging potholes.

"See?" said Mr. Higashi to me and my brothers. "If we had the funeral in the building we use for church, it would have been standing room only." He nodded as if to say that he had made the best decision.

I bet the church wouldn't have been this cold, I thought as the October wind whipped over the camp faster than a horse swinging his tail to swat a fly. Also, at least inside, some of us would have been able to sit. Here, we huddled together, our hands in our pockets, with nowhere to sit. I couldn't help but look up to see that the guards were at their towers, guns visible. Even at a funeral we were reminded that we were confined. But not Mama anymore. Mama was free. No more cold or dampness for her. No more visions of guards, army trucks, and guns.

After Lucy sang "Rock of Ages," there was a prayer. I couldn't concentrate on any of the words and had no idea who was praying. I held Tom's hand, looked straight ahead, and focused on nothing.

When the service ended, people greeted me with soft voices and solemn faces. Some approached me so that they were close enough to pat my hand. Others stood at a slight distance, as though I was diseased. Perhaps, they thought, that if they got too close to me, they might die like Mama.

"She will be missed."

"She was the best."

"She was so young and beautiful."

"God take care of you."

"My prayers are with you."

"You will see her again soon."

"She is in Heaven where there is perfect beauty."

When I let myself look out at the crowd, it was a sea of sadness. Each face, every person, acknowledging Mama's death—it was too much to take in. I felt my knees grow numb; I gasped for air. Rocking on my feet, I released Tom's hand and thought, I am going to fall. Teetering back, I felt arms catch me.

"Hey, little bro. Lean against me." Ken's embrace was tight as I crumbled into his grasp. "It's all right, it's all right," he repeated.

But it wasn't. Mama was dead, and none of the Mori boys were crying. Others were crying into handkerchiefs and here we were her children—stoic—no different from Heart Mountain. Later, much later, I would learn that sadness is not measured in tears. There are many tears that never reach the eyes, but take harbor in the heart until they feel safe enough to let loose.

After a few moments, I let go of Ken, stood on my own, and reassured Ken, Tom, and my aunt that I was not going to fall again.

Before the mess halls opened for lunch, we returned to our barracks where Mrs. Kubo was taking care of Emi. "Too cold to take a newborn out," she'd told us that morning as we prepared for the funeral. "I'll care for her here."

As the four of us entered our billet, we greeted Mrs. Kubo, who was seated at the table with Emi in the crook of her arm. Shivering, we went toward the coal stove to warm our hands.

Emi let out a gurgle and then sneezed.

"Oh, my," said Mrs. Kubo. "You are so sweet." She drew my sister tightly against her bosom.

"Is her diaper all right?" asked my aunt. "It might need changing."

Mrs. Kubo turned from Emi to glance up at us. "I heard the Yokota girl sing. Just now. She has a beautiful voice."

"Yes," said my aunt, "she has nice voice."

Mrs. Kubo stroked Emi's head, smoothing down my sister's soft hair. "They always talk about funerals being lovely. How can it be lovely knowing that beloved people are gone from us?"

None of us knew how to respond, so we said nothing.

"I always wanted a girl." A faraway look filled Mrs. Kubo's eyes.

"I don't have any children." My aunt rubbed her hands together and blew on her fingertips. "I think my sister wanted me to come to America so I could help her with hers." She chuckled as though that was a funny joke. "I tell God that I am too old to do this. He could have made me beautiful, given me a husband, and my own children, but instead I am who I am."

But it seemed that Mrs. Kubo had no interest in what my aunt was saying. She still had that expression on her face, and when I studied it more closely, it felt to me that it was a mixture of sadness, regret, and something else that I could not decipher.

Chapter Five

A lthough I wanted to pretend that she was still in the hospital, I knew that Mama wasn't in any of those beds there. She wasn't coming back to us. Her breathless body had been placed inside a pine coffin and would be buried in the ground once the soil softened in the spring. Gone. Dead. I hated the sound of those words as they slammed inside my head.

Why didn't I sit with her every night? Why did I fight with Ken? What kind of son was I? What would Father say? Where was he? If only he'd been here, he could have stopped this madness; Mother wouldn't have died.

When Lucy sang that evening, I could not listen. Her words about God's love and mercy sounded out of place, void of any ability to soothe. I turned onto my stomach and covered my head with my pillow.

Where was God? What kind of God didn't hear the cries of His people?

A faint murmur from Emi had me up and attending to her. Mechanically, I changed her diaper as I'd done only once before with the aid of Mama. I gave her a half-full bottle my aunt had prepared for her from evaporated milk.

"Oh, Emiko, what are we going to do?" I said as she sucked the milk into her small mouth.

I wanted to cry, but no tears came.

Two nights later in the mess hall, someone dropped a plate. It was as though each of the broken pieces took off in a different direction. The plate would never be whole again. A member of the kitchen crew swept all the pieces, all the jarred fragments. Into the dustpan they went and then he took the dustpan and emptied it into a large waste bin. Gone.

My heart and that plate had a lot in common.

"We need to let Papa know," I said to Aunt Kazuko.

She brushed her lips across Emi's head. "I love the smell of a baby."

Had she not heard me?

But she had. "You can write to him."

"A letter?"

"No, a note in the mud. Yes, silly, a letter."

What would I say? I had already written to him many times and had not heard back.

As I pondered, my aunt said, "Tom writes to him often."

"He does?"

"Yes, I took peek into his notebook."

"Snooping?" I raised an eyebrow and waited to see how she would get out of this accusation.

She laughed. "I don't snoop, just make sure he isn't writing anything too crazy."

I guess she meant one of his stories. Once he wrote about a boy who had special powers and could fly and burn through buildings with his supernatural vision. He would often read them to Mama, and she never laughed, just told him to continue with his "talent."

"Why don't you write a love story?" asked Ken one night as he combed his hair before heading over to the adjacent barracks to hear Lucy sing.

"Love?" Tom made a face similar to the kind he made when my parents insisted he eat Aunt Kazuko's fermented soybeans.

"Yeah, something racy." He added a dollop of some smelly tonic to his hair and ran his comb over the sides.

"Ugh," said Tom. "Yuck."

"We need coal, lover boy," Aunt Kazuko said to Ken.

Ken smiled at his reflection in a slice of a mirror he kept on a shelf that he had built over his bed. "Coal?"

"Yes, this stove won't fill itself."

Ken placed the mirror back onto the shelf. "Doesn't the truck come around and deliver it every Tuesday, or is it every Saturday? We can get it then."

"We will be out before morning. Go."

"I'll get it after—"

"Now." Aunt Kazuko gave one of her piercing looks which usually made any one of us do as we were told.

He actually took the bucket we filled for coal and said he'd be back soon. After he left, we all hoped he was searching for coal. With Ken you never knew.

"Write a letter and send it to your papa," my aunt said to me the next night as we huddled around the stove. I wondered if we needed more coal and where my older brother was. He had found some coal for us last night. My aunt had taken one look at him upon his return and exclaimed, "Well, well, look who is capable of work after all! I am flabbergasted."

Tonight, he was out again per usual. Clearly, for him, there were more important things than family.

My aunt took a morsel of chocolate from her pocket. "God knows that your papa needs mail." She looked at me before placing the chocolate into her mouth, "I only have one piece," she confessed. "Sorry." With a handkerchief, she wiped a smudge of chocolate from her lips. "Write to him. Cheer him up. But first fetch water."

I recalled when I'd been Tom's age that my aunt had been much quieter and less assertive. Heart Mountain had made her heart as tough as shoe leather.

Even though she appeared to be strict and tough, I knew her heart was broken.

I sat in our billet at the wooden table listening to the evening news. As the commentator on the radio spoke of General Sato and the Japs' propaganda, the water in the kettle on top of the pot-bellied stove hissed. Steam escaped from the spout.

"Water's ready," I called out to my aunt. I'd filled the kettle for her earlier while she'd opened a fresh container of loose tea, some Mrs. Kubo had given her. Bending closer to the radio, I listened to hear the words I longed for: The war is over. But there was nothing to indicate that, just talk about a rocket destroying a Nazi battalion in Stalingrad.

The newscaster took a break from the current events and announced the familiar spiel about Mobil Gas and Oil, both with *flying power*.

The kettle hissed louder.

I thought the kettle might have power to fly off the stove; the sound was vehement. Turning my attention from the radio, I scanned our apartment for my aunt.

She was seated on her cot with Emi in her arms, her back to me.

The water continued to boil, the noise, irritating. I had to turn the volume up on our radio. "Water's ready!" Seeing that she was not going to take the kettle off of the stove and pour the liquid into a cup, I tried using the tactics she used on me. "Don't dilly-dally! Get the kettle off the stove!" When she didn't move, I stood and stormed over to her. "Do you want me to make your tea for you?" I asked.

My aunt just sat there with her head down, as though unable to move.

"Aunt Kazuko. Did you hear me?" When she didn't reply, I took Emi from her embrace, and immediately felt how wet the blanket around my sister was. "The blanket's wet," I said.

Aunt Kazuko raised her head, sniffed twice, and said, "Well, don't know why it would be wet."

But her face gave me the answer. It was drizzled with tears, tears that had made their way onto her chin. I knew she was crying about Mama.

The next day, Aunt Kazuko was no longer crying, but back to her insufferable ways. She complained that the billet was too cold, that we were lazy boys, and that there was no money for milk for Emi. "I don't know what we do." She looked at Ken's bed, and not seeing him, sighed in despair. Over the months, I could classify my aunt's sighs into three categories—disgust, despair, and determination. That night she found me seated on my bed reading for my history homework.

"Nathan, you find out what we need to do to get milk."

I knew that the camp received its milk from a creamery in Powell. I'd seen a truck deliver it. But what happened when we needed more than what was supplied at meal times? Who did I need to talk to about that?

When I asked Ken what we should do, he seemed more consumed with flirting with girls. I watched as he'd edge close to a girl, his eyes never leaving her face. With a quick glance, he'd move his gaze across her body, her shoulders, her chest, and down to her waist. Then he'd take her hand and say, "Doll, let me tell your fortune." With fingers caressing her palm, he'd add, "Ahh, I see some great stuff."

"Like what?" Most of the girls were curious and would ask.

"Your future looks bright. You're going to be a movie star." And he'd flash his movie-star smile as though he were Clark Gable.

I'd seen him do this same routine over and over. I knew the lines he used, the way he looked at each girl as though she was the only one. But she never was. He had been saying he was a fortune teller since middle school. Mama warned that telling fortunes was not a good practice. Ken had merely shrugged off her apprehension with, "It's just a line, Ma."

He knew it was just a line, but there had been girls who really believed. It wasn't that they believed he could really see their future, but they did trust that he cared about them. There were those who thought his words and gestures meant he liked them. Yet, truthfully, I doubted that he carried a torch for any girl. He wasn't after an intimate relationship with one; he was out to be put up on a pedestal by all.

Ken was equally good with males, befriending his peers and making them believe that they had what it took to be whatever they wanted to be. Charisma was the word a teacher once used to describe my older brother. "Filled with charisma," the teacher had written on his report card. While teachers wrote, "Studious" about me, Ken got the more charming superlatives. "A team leader, one of a kind. Destined to go far." I would have added Flirt to his repertoire. It was a good thing that I wasn't one of his teachers. I think he liked girls from the day he was born, and even as an infant found a way to charm my parents' friends.

Now it seemed that he wasn't affected much at all by our mother's death. He carried on as usual. He would be out late conducting *business*—as he called it. Although I asked him once what that entailed, he never explained it to me. I didn't care anymore to learn what he was up to.

But we still needed milk.

"Check the Ohashi's shop." Ken pulled a clean shirt off the rope that was stretched overhead—our indoor clothesline.

"They're out. Apparently, all the other families with babies need milk."

He buttoned his shirt, leaving the top buttons undone to expose part of his chest. "A milk shortage?" Sitting on his cot, he rolled up each leg of his dungarees, producing the tailored cuff-look so many of the boys liked to sport. "I guess Heart Mountain needs to buy a cow."

"Be serious for once."

"Ask the mess halls. Go around to all of them. I gotta go."

"She's your sister, too!"

"I know. But you're the smart one." And with that, he left our billet.

Chapter Six

My heart, though pained, was not gone. Whenever Emi let out baby gurgle noises, I felt a tinge of life come back to me. And, gradually, I was able to listen to Lucy sing again.

When she sang, she secured her long hair on top of her head, a tendril or two floated around her neck. On most nights, she wore a rose-colored kimono with a simple *obi*. During the summer, she slipped into a pair of sandals. Now with winter's arrival, saddle shoes with socks were her choice. Some of the older women thought it disgraceful to wear saddle shoes with a kimono. I overheard Lucy telling Ken she hadn't brought any proper *tabi* or *geta* to camp because her suitcase had been full of more important things—movie star magazines.

Whether it be in her barracks or inside the rec room, whenever she sang, she looked at no one, yet her message spoke to everyone. Even Aunt Kazuko stopped whatever she was doing, took a seat, and listened.

I worried about my sister growing up under such damp and sorrowful circumstances. I worried for her health; I woke from nightmares that had her in a casket, identical to the one Mama was placed in. Yet when she turned her head toward Lucy's tender voice and would fall asleep, I counted my blessings. At least she had the privilege of being soothed to sleep by the most beautiful person and voice ever to enter the camp.

One night, when Lucy sang the song about the canary finding safety, an idea came to me: Forget going to school every day. I should get a job. While plenty of the internees now worked within the camp in the mess halls or administration services, I knew of a few people who worked outside the camp. If I could get a job outside this place, perhaps I could find a way to get our whole family out. Perhaps a Caucasian store owner would want me to help out or run a business with him. I'd helped Papa at our fish store; I knew more than most people, especially my aunt, gave me credit for.

As Lucy finished her song, I prayed one of my "Please God, help me" prayers. I hope God heard it; Aunt Kazuko once said that God hears every prayer, even those of boys who dilly-dally.

❀

By midnight I was praying for quiet. Usually Aunt Kazuko's snores and Emi's cries didn't disturb my sleep. Usually, when Ken crept in around two in the morning, I wasn't bothered, I just turned over in my cot, and resumed my sleep.

But that morning, sleep would not befriend me. Every sound irritated me. I stretched out on my back, but that was uncomfortable; I turned over onto my stomach, but my neck felt cramped. I tried to close my eyes and dream of my nice bed in San Jose, and that only made things worse.

By the time Ken entered our apartment, I had had enough. As he dropped his shoes onto the floor, I yelled out at him, "Why do you have to make so much noise?" Then for emphasis, I threw my pillow onto the floor. That was silly. I needed my pillow.

As I bent down to retrieve it, Ken said, "Don't worry, little bro. It will all be all right."

❀

The War Relocation Authority wanted to pay Aunt Kazuko nineteen dollars a month to work with the project director, ordering food for our block's mess hall. The job had been filled by one man, but he had to leave the position when he developed bronchitis. The director spoke with my aunt, impressed by her mathematical skills and work history in Japan. "We could use a good accountant," he said.

This flattered Aunt Kazuko. "He said I am just what he looks for." She beamed as she told me the way he had asked her.

"Great!" I gave her a hug. "We can have more money to buy things."

"Buy more? No, we save. Always save. Save for a rainy day." Playfully, she bounced Emi against her knee, waited for her to smile.

"When will you start work?"

Emi gurgled, produced a wide smile and laughed.

"Will you start Monday?"

"Not going to happen."

"Why not?" I asked. "Why don't you want to work?"

She stopped bouncing Emi and drew her to her chest. "My obligation is to care for her. She is full-time job."

True, Aunt Kazuko's days were filled with caring for Emi. Between feedings, nap times, and diaper changes, I knew Emi was a lot of work.

I wondered if Mrs. Kubo would care for Emi during the day so that my aunt could earn the cash we needed for coats, hats, clothes, milk and toys for Emi, and other items that the War Relocation Authority didn't provide enough of. "Do you think that she would babysit Emi?"

"Who? Are you thinking of Mrs. Kubo?"

I realized I hadn't said the woman's name. "Yeah, her."

"She isn't strong enough to take care of a child."

"What do you mean?" Mrs. Kubo didn't seem weak to me. She could change a diaper without any fuss and seemed to enjoy being around my sister.

"She is not strong in her spirit. She is not suited."

"Not suited?"

"Don't make fun of my English."

"I wasn't. I just thought that maybe Mrs. Kubo could take care of Emi." Sometimes I wondered if it was language that kept us from being able to understand each other or my aunt's stubbornness.

"No. Answer is no."

I suppose that settled it. Aunt Kazuko would not take the job helping the project manager with ordering food for our camp. Ken was too busy with his affairs, and of course, Tom was only a little boy in a leg brace. Getting a paying job was up to me.

Filled with determination after lunch on Saturday, I begged to work with the coal. I knew I could haul it from the gondola into the delivery trucks which then took it to the barracks so that it could be used to light our stoves. Yet the men said that I was too young. Mr. Kubo told me that I was needed at school and at home. "You have a new baby and must care for her."

"But we have to have more money. No one else in my family works."

He looked me over. "I know." He started to say something else, but was taken from my side by a woman who said her barracks' roof leaked.

I lingered at the scene and continued to watch the men loading the coal onto the trucks. I listened to their conversations, sometimes a word or two was spoken in Japanese, especially by the *Issei*. Some of the words I knew, thanks to my aunt and parents. Other words left me clueless. As they worked, a man with a dusty bucket pocked with dents approached one of the parked trucks.

"We are out of coal," he said. "Can you fill my bucket for me now, just enough to last until your truck makes its deliveries?"

His bucket was filled by a thin man in a wool cap, and the man with the bucket acknowledged gratitude. "They sure have kept us from the rest of civilization here," he said, placing his bucket on the dirt and wiping his face with a gloved hand. "We are in no man's land." His gaze stretched over to Heart Mountain, and when his eyes met mine, I saw a vacancy, one I was seeing more and more in the eyes of my elders. Then I recognized this man. I wasn't used to seeing him in a coat, but I knew who he was. Once, he had been a successful businessman, selling furniture to Caucasians, but today there was no way to tell that he'd ever worn a pressed suit. He was just like the rest of us—hanging onto frayed threads of hope.

"I don't know how we are going to be able to accommodate more people in the camp," another man admitted. Whispering, he confessed, "At first, I welcomed the newcomers and wanted to be helpful, but now, I wish so many wouldn't come."

"They make it more crowded, taking up more places at the lavatories and in our mess halls," the businessman said. "I think we should protest."

The others looked at him and said nothing. The businessman picked up his bucket and walked away.

I wanted to call after him, but I didn't know what to say. I hated seeing him in such despair.

When Mr. Kubo returned, he told me to go back to my barracks. Unlike me, he always knew what to say, even if it was harsh. As he got into one of the trucks, he barked, "Go home. I'll be delivering coal to your barracks soon. You need to be there to carry it inside."

Chapter Seven

B ut I didn't want to go back to our living quarters that reeked of soiled diapers and unfulfilled dreams. I wanted to hop on his truck and head out of the camp's perimeters. I wanted to sail down roads until the camp was so far away that I would never be able to find it again. I wondered what the town of Cody was like and the other town called Powell. I wanted to see how the real people of Wyoming lived, what they ate, how they worked, and what sacrifices they were making because of the war.

As snowflakes fell, I wandered around the roads between the rows of barracks, passing a few people hurrying to get inside their apartments to warm their hands by their stoves. They acknowledged me with greetings, but I only nodded. I stopped at the edge of the camp, right by the long barbed fence that separated us from the rest of America and stared in the direction of Heart Mountain.

She was draped with endless clouds, but every few minutes, I caught a glimpse of her rocky build. I thought of the verse from Psalms about looking to the hills for help and help coming from God. I wished God would come to my assistance, but I was probably beyond help. Buttoning my jacket up to my chin, I ambled away from the fence, my eyes on the ground.

After about half an hour, I found myself in front of the hospital.

A soldier, a toothpick hanging out of his mouth, was leaning against the wall; three girls were next to him. The girls laughed, and the soldier joined them.

The laughter grated at my nerves, and I knew I had to get away from the scene. But before I walked away, I heard, "Hey, there!"

Not to be impolite, I replied. "Hello."

Mekley, the solider, winked at me. "Look at me, Mori. I'm with three beautiful girls today."

I had no words for him. I cut away from him and the girls, away from the hospital where my mother had died, and, increasing my pace,

I headed back to our barracks.

Just before I stepped onto the stair leading up to our unit, a woman's voice in the distance caused me to pause. Her voice sounded so much like my mother's. If only. Inside, I flung myself onto my cot and heard Mama's voice in my head say, "You are my favorite son named Nathan."

When the first sob came, I made no attempt to muffle it because I knew I was alone. I recalled my aunt saying earlier that she, Emi, and Tom were invited to tea at Mrs. Kubo's. Who knew where Ken was. Probably with his gang members doing whatever worthless acts they did. Lenny Tanaka had begged to join the group, and I'd overheard Ken say that, in order to be a gang member, Lenny would have to be initiated first.

A rap at the front door broke my thoughts. I hoped whoever it was would go away.

The knocking continued.

Finding my voice, I called out, "Come in."

The door opened, and there stood Lucy. "Hi, Nathan."

"He's not here."

"I was actually looking for you."

I shot up then, ran a hand over my hair, smoothed out my cowlick. "Oh, come in."

She entered and sat on the cot beside me. She was so close, too close. I looked at her shoes, her bobby socks folded neatly around her ankles. Nervously, I shifted from her. Don't do that, I told myself. Stop being so afraid of everything. With courage borrowed from somewhere, I looked into her eyes. Briefly. Those round and dark eyes, filled with specks of light.

Quizzically, she studied my face. "What's wrong?" Concern laced her voice, causing my heart to tear a little bit more.

"What do you mean . . . ?"

"Have you been—"

"No," I said forcefully. "I mean, no." This time I removed the edge from my voice.

"But . . ." Placing her fingers against my chin, she lifted my face. "Really?"

"Dust," I said and turned away. "That dust gets in my eyes every day."

"I hate the dust." She placed her hands on her lap.

I didn't want her to leave; quickly, I thought of something to ask.

"Are you going to church Sunday?"

"Yeah." She smiled. "I'm singing a solo."

I tried to smile. Mama sang a solo once, I recalled. I felt my lip quiver.

"Nathan, are you all right?"

"Oh . . . yeah . . ."

I knew that I was not, and that she knew it, too.

"Why?" The word echoed against the walls. "Why?" This was the question I wanted to ask, and for so long it had sat in my mind like a stone in a brook that could not move.

Her face softened. "I don't know. I don't understand. All I can say is that God loves you, Nobu."

I didn't realize that she knew my Japanese name. "I know He does."

"God is watching over us. Even here."

"Why?"

She looked at me and started to say something and then looked deeper into my eyes. "I don't know why," she said after a moment. "I don't know why your mother had to go."

Emotion clawed at my chest; I had to look away.

"Nathan, she is in Heaven. That's what my mother tells me. But you know what I tell her?"

"Wh . . . what?" Why couldn't I be more like Ken? He never stuttered and tears never plagued him.

"Her being in Heaven now does your family no good, does Emi no good."

"What does your mother say after that?"

"Nothing."

"Nothing?" I thought adults were supposed to have all the answers. "Nothing to say?" I asked.

"Once I overheard her say that we don't understand God's ways."

"Well, that's true."

"I don't understand any of what has happened lately. Your mother . . . this war . . . us being pulled away to live here."

I glanced around the walls and saw the opening between two slats of wood above Mama's bed. *Did the cold air blow in and kill her?*

Why?

Lucy took my hand. My vision blurred and my face felt damp. From her jacket pocket, she handed me her handkerchief, but I pushed it away and wiped my cheeks with my shirt sleeve. "You are a good brother," she said. "I see you with Tom and Emi. You are so strong for them."

But later, at bedtime, as the wind howled like a roaming coyote, and Emi woke with a cry, I didn't feel like a good brother at all. As I held my sister in my arms and wrapped an extra blanket around her small frame, soothing her until she settled, my thoughts were far from good.

I wished that God had never let this baby steal Mama's life. If Mama hadn't been pregnant, she would have continued to be strong and healthy. The pneumonia wouldn't have crept in. She would still be here with us, with no vision of Heaven's perfect beauty. Emi wouldn't have come into our lives, but Mama would be here.

The thought was a terrible one, I knew. I would never confess it to anyone. When the wind blasted through the camp early the next morning, I felt it was the loud booming of God's punishment to me for thinking such a horrible thing.

Chapter Eight

Bing Crosby sang, "I'm Dreaming of a White Christmas," but we saw no romanticizing of snow. Snow, along with the penetrating winds that brought it, made our hands and feet raw and feel like slabs of ice.

Christmas arrived. Despite the wind, the tinsel we hung on the outside of our door didn't blow away. Inside, we cut paper angels with scissors and taped them to the walls. We wrapped gifts in brown paper with strings. The gifts were meager, but I didn't care. Christmas was just another day without my parents.

What was Papa doing? Why couldn't he come to see us?

For nights after Christmas, I dreamed about him. In one dream, there was the sound of a horn and then the camp's gates gently opened. Proudly, with his head held high, Papa walked through them. He smiled as his children and Aunt Kazuko ran out to meet him.

The summer sun was hot against our skin, the air as dry as coal dust. And we were happy.

Papa scooped us up in his arms, laughing. There was so much laughter.

I handed his daughter to him, and he kissed her cheeks and drew her to his chest. She touched his face with a pudgy finger and nestled against him like she knew exactly who he was and that she belonged to him.

As much happiness as I felt, I knew that something wasn't right. Mama wasn't in the dream. I so wanted her to be, and as the dream played out, I kept hoping to see her.

Tom said, "Mama wanted to be here, but she's with Jesus."

Papa seemed to understand. He told us he knew about the angels who had whisked her off, and he was sure that Mama was playing the piano in Heaven right now.

I said, "She's coming back here, you know. She is, she is."

But they all looked at me like I was one of Tom's imaginary aliens, and then the sun stopped shining and it started to snow. Without any warning, Papa was gone. One by one, the rest of us made our way back to our barracks through the snow, back to our home that was as cold as the day.

❀

As we anticipated a new year, we hoped it would bring the end of the war. In our confined humble surroundings, we did the best we could to get through the season. We listened to the radio every morning and evening. Ken and a few others said that they would like to join the military to fight against our enemies. I wanted to tell Ken that, while that was a noble thing to do for our country, once in the army, he would be far from any females. I doubted my older brother could function without an entourage of girls.

By March, Emi was sitting in her crib, and when we moved her to the floor on a blanket, she was even able to sit on her own there. Tom often knelt down to be with her, a notebook and pen in his hands. The alien stories still prevailed in his mind. Sometimes he read portions of them aloud to Emi. Like Mama, she never laughed at them.

My desire to get out of the camp to work was still with me as signs of spring showed in minute ways. I wanted to get out to see what was out there as well as earn some money for my family's needs. I wanted a job, but it seemed that no one wanted to hire me. Every week I asked our project director, several block leaders, and even the women working at the salon when I went there to pick up bottles of shampoo for my aunt. Everybody just looked at me and said they were sorry that Mama had died.

Some left camp. As long as you left for someplace away from the West Coast, you were free to go. The WRA even encouraged families to leave. Like the Kubos, those in our block had family elsewhere. But unlike Mr. and Mrs. Kubo, once in Chicago or Milwaukee, former internees got along with their daughters-in-laws.

Perhaps we should move. But where would we go? We had no family anywhere else except for relatives in Papa's town of Hiroshima, and Mama and Aunt Kazuko's village in Nagano. We were stuck here. Papa was stuck in Tule Lake.

I wanted to hear Papa's voice. I wanted to hear him tell me the family story of the gold watch with the bamboo and crane etchings on the back. I wanted to see his eyes light up with the warmth of excitement as he shared the story. No matter how often he relayed to us

46

how the Mori family was honored with this watch, I never grew weary of hearing it. It was our family's story, and Papa said every family had one, but ours was the most special.

After school one cloudy afternoon, Charles entered our apartment to tell me that a sheep farm needed help. "Their hired hand got sick so they need someone to replace him. I asked if they could use us both. Apparently, they want a few of us to work there."

"Great!" I said. It was as though sunshine had found its way into my day.

"Do you know anything about sheep?"

"No." *How hard could it be?* I'd heard that sheep were dumb; I was pretty smart.

"We have to feed them, take them out to graze, and then clean their pens."

"Do we get to shear them?"

"I wasn't told that." He pushed his glasses up onto the bridge of his nose.

"When do we start?"

"Do you have a pair of boots?"

"Like rain ones? Or cowboy?"

"Probably ones that can get dirty."

Under my cot was a pair of rubber boots. They had leaked the last time I wore them, but what was a little water on my socks? I was going to work and earn money!

Charles told me that a bus would come this Saturday morning to take us to the Towson Farm.

"Only on the weekends?" I asked, making sure that I heard correctly.

"They know we go to school."

"Forget school." *Really, was I learning anything?* Ever since the school opened last October, classes had been only a shadow of what they had been like in San Jose. There weren't enough text books or desks. The chalkboard was a piece of plywood painted with black paint.

"The block leaders say we need to be in school. We can get plenty of hours in on the weekend. Saturday morning the bus comes at five a.m."

"Five?" I swallowed hard. *That early?* But I pretended that it was no big deal. "All right. How long do we work?"

"Till about five."

I was glad that this was just going to be a one-day a week event.

"In the summer when we have no school, we can work every day," said Charles.

Emi whimpered, and I went to her crib. The air around her was sour and stunk; I knew a diaper change was eminent, but I didn't want to have to do the task in front of Charles.

"Don't you want to know how much we get paid?"

I nodded and then tried to console my sister who was expanding her lungs. Her wail grew louder until finally Charles yelled, "I'm out of here!"

He left, leaving me to wonder how much the pay was going to be for taking care of sheep.

A rickety white bus, covered in dust, was at the camp entrance when I got there. Charles was already on the bus and waved to me from one of the windows. He seemed excited, and I could understand that; I was, too. Two men from another block boarded, and I followed.

I sat in the seat next to Charles. Charles rubbed a gloved hand over his nose. "This farm is cool."

"Have you been to it before?"

"No, but Mr. Yanagi has, and he said it was a good place to work. They pay every day after you work. We are going to get a whole dollar today."

The bus rattled, shook twice, and the driver announced that we were on our way.

As we rumbled down the road, I shifted in my seat. The seat was lumpy and reminded me of our mattresses at camp, which were filled with hay.

I hoped I was dressed right for the job and that no one would care that there was a hole in the knee of my dungarees. These were the only pair I had that fit me. A nicer pair I had passed down to Tom because they were too tight in the waist. As I studied Charles, I saw that he, too, had on a pair of blue dungarees, boots, and a cotton jacket. I supposed no one would mind if we both looked a bit worn, after all, we weren't on our way to church.

We rode in silence for miles, passing wide vacant spaces. Dawn was just about to break when the bus slowed at a stop sign.

I turned to my left, and immediately my attention was grabbed by a sign on the front entrance of a women's clothing shop. With the help of the street light, I was able to read: *No Japs Allowed*. The print was black, bold, and angry.

Japs. Whether I read it in the newspaper or saw it on a sign or heard it spoken, it always cut at the core of my heart.

"I bet they've never met a Jap," Charles said over my shoulder. He pushed his glasses over the bridge of his nose and blinked. Apparently, he had seen the sign as well.

Once we got through town, the bus picked up speed. Charles and I viewed miles of barren terrain. I wished that the bus would never stop, just continue on and on toward freedom. I wished that the driver would forget how to return to camp and take us on a journey where we could live as real Americans, in houses with white fences instead of in barracks surrounded by barbed wire and soldiers with rifles.

A few lone farmhouses dotted the landscape like buttons on a shirt. I saw sheep grazing in the fields, the bodies round from their fluffy white and grey coats.

When we pulled into a gravel driveway beside a milky-white house with green trim, the driver said, "This is it. The Towson Farm!"

Alice J. Wisler

Chapter Nine

A few hundred yards from the farmhouse sat a rust-colored barn
with a silo, surrounded by acres of fields as far as the eye could
see—some green, most the color of straw. Wooden fences zigzagged
over the land. Horses grazed at the edges of the fences. The peaks of
the mountain range beyond the farm were sprinkled with snow and
cumulus clouds. It was a scene straight out of a Western; no wonder
this state's nickname was The Cowboy State.

Apparently, Charles had done farm work before, and I realized that
it was because of his skill that we got the job in the first place. I didn't
know that he was a farm boy; his family had tended to a fifty-acre plum
orchard in Vacaville, California. They'd grown a few rows of tomatoes
and lettuce, too. Now I knew why Charles missed fresh produce so
much in camp.

Mr. Towson, a middle-aged man in a checkered shirt and baggy
dungarees, greeted our group. He assigned Charles and me to feed hay
to the horses and clean the sheep pens. I was glad I wore boots. The
two other men that had been on the bus with us were told to assist with
plowing the fields.

Charles and I used rakes and shovels to clear out the sheep poop. We
added new hay to the stalls and feed in the troughs. The stench was strong,
but I suppose no worse than the odor from one of Emi's diapers. "How
much are we getting paid?" I asked, as a blister formed on my thumb.

"Enough to add to my piggy bank," said Charles. "I'm saving up for
a ticket to San Antonio."

If I was correct, that was a city in Texas. "Why there?" I asked.

"I want to own a cattle ranch," he said. "I figure that I lease one at
first and then buy one."

I looked at this squirrely boy with stiff hair and a rosy complexion.
I pictured him in a cowboy hat, but the image seemed too far-fetched
to believe. A professor at a university, yes, or perhaps a scientist finding
the cure for polio, but certainly not a ranch owner.

At noon, we were told to enter the farmhouse, where we were seated at a long wooden table in an alcove off the kitchen. A woman, who introduced herself as Mrs. Towson, placed bowls of hot chili in front of us, and we were told to take half an hour for lunch.

I was excited to eat something other than camp food, and as I spooned the chili into my mouth, I was reminded of how real food tasted. Spoonful after spoonful, it was hard to slow down, but then I burned my tongue and stopped to guzzle a glass of water.

When Charles wiped his mouth with a napkin, I decided I better remember my manners. I took a sip of water and made sure that the next bite entered my mouth slowly. As I chewed, I also wiped my mouth with the napkin placed by my bowl. When I finished my lunch, I looked around the kitchen.

A boy in a striped shirt with a red ball cap sat at the kitchen table with a box of crayons, a few pencils, and a sheet of white paper. He picked out a blue crayon, colored with it and then put it back inside the box. At one point, he put his hands above his head, cupping his fingers. "I want to go for a ride," he said. "Clippity-clop, clippity-clop."

I gathered that he was pretending to be a horse, his cupped hands were the ears.

Mrs. Towson filled a glass with milk and walked over to him. "Put your hands down, Henry," she said.

Obeying, he dropped his hands to his sides and then picked up the glass. He downed the milk in a few gulps, and in a flash, his hands flew back over his head, this time two fists against his temples.

She seemed used to his antics and calmly refilled his glass. "Drink up, Henry."

"Not now, Mama. I am a horse now. Clippity-clop."

Curious, I listened more intently.

"What color is the horse?" she asked.

"Grey."

"Who else is with the horse?"

Craning my neck, I looked over at the sheet of paper to see a grey horse behind a white picket fence.

"Who did you draw with the horse, Henry?" asked his mother.

"Me," replied Henry. Sure enough, he had penciled in a figure of a boy, lanky and thin, just like Henry. He added a cowboy hat and a pair of black boots. "I colored this. I did it all by myself."

"Nice, Henry," she said. "I need to make a few pies now. You keep coloring and working on your masterpiece." She wiped her hands on her apron and turned toward the pantry.

The next Saturday, our lunch was a bowl of chicken stew with yeast rolls and butter. Charles ate two rolls before he touched his stew. I tried to take small bites, but after about six of those, I gave in and shoveled spoonfuls into my mouth. Then I buttered two rolls while Charles popped half of another one into his mouth. It was amazing how farm work made people hungry.

Henry was drawing at the same table again. "Look, I made a pig," he announced.

His mother walked over to his side. "Good work," she said.

"Do you like my picture?"

"Yes, I do. Now let me make some cobbler, Henry. We have army guests staying over."

When I later asked Charles who those guests might be, he said that the Towsons served as a guesthouse for servicemen on R and R.

"They have two nice bedrooms in the back that men can stay in. You ought to see them. Double beds. I'd forgotten what one of those looked like. They have their kid's artwork all over the walls in frames. That kid seems stupid, but he can draw."

"I guess he's pretty good."

"One picture is of a man in a straw hat sheering a sheep. I think he must have drawn that of one of us."

"One of us?"

"You know, a Japanese. He made the man's eyes narrow and used a yellow crayon for his skin."

"Yellow?" I bellowed. "We aren't yellow."

Charles didn't seem disturbed by my outburst. Calmly, he stated, "Yeah, well, people say we aren't white. And we aren't black."

"I just never thought we would be considered yellow."

I wondered when Charles had been invited for a tour of the home. I must have missed that. I was curious to see what the rest of the farmhouse looked like, but for now I kept to the kitchen.

One Saturday, Mrs. Towson gave me a paper bag with cookies. "Take them home for your family," she said.

I thought about stashing them away from the others in our apartment and eating them all myself, but Aunt Kazuko had eagle eyes. She called to me from across the road. Emi was strapped to her back, and I figured that they'd been out on a stroll. "What's in the bag?" she asked.

I swore that my aunt could sniff out food no matter where it was.

"Nothing," I lied.

"Is it heavy?"

"What?"

"The bag?"

"Not really."

"*Nothing* is not really heavy?"

That night, she kept saying how she needed a pep and that her blue container was empty. She opened her container, rattled it and then said, "Nothing. Nothing."

I couldn't stand it anymore. "Here," I cried, pulling the bag from under my pillow. "Take a cookie."

She smiled. "You so good for me."

"It's you are. You *are* so good for me!"

"What?" she said, her mouth filled with the oatmeal cookie. "You don't need to complain about my English. Everybody understand me."

All I could do was groan. One day I'd be out of this camp, far from here. Maybe I'd go to San Antonio and join Charles on his ranch, maybe I'd go up north to Chicago. Wherever I went, it would be a place where I didn't have to share cookies with Aunt Kazuko.

Chapter Ten

"**A**re you going to the dance?" Charles asked on the bus ride home one Saturday night, just before the bus made its way into the camp gate.

I rubbed my knee; it throbbed due to hitting it against a fence post earlier. At least the skin on my hands had grown tough, and I seldom got blisters anymore.

"I might go," said Charles. "How about you?"

"What?"

"The dance."

Dance? I let the word conjure images of my brother flirting with girls while I sat on the sidelines. Why would I want to put myself through that torture? Yet, my hope that Lucy might dance with me prevailed. Ever since our last conversation, when she came into our barracks to console me, I thought I just might have a chance.

After exiting the bus, and telling Charles that I would be at the dance, I showered at the communal washroom. As the soap lathered, hope ran through me; tonight just might be the night to dance with Lucy.

In our barracks, Tom sat on his cot reading a book of American poetry, and Aunt Kazuko played peek-a-boo with Emi.

I slipped behind the makeshift dressing room and put on a clean flannel shirt I'd bought last week at the co-op's clothing store and zipped up a pair of black trousers that Ken had outgrown.

"You going to dance?" asked my aunt when I pushed back the dressing room's curtain so that I could be seen.

"Yeah." I walked toward my cot, got a smile from Emi, and a glance from Tom. Yes, I would go and I would find Lucy.

My aunt studied me for a moment. "You look like meow of cat."

"Cat's meow," I corrected her.

"You going to be the best looking boy there."

I hoped so. I searched for my shoes and a clean pair of socks.

"Have a good time," she called, as I swung open the front door. "Don't be gone long. The bucket of water is nearly empty."

Following the music, I walked over to the building where dances were held. Glen Miller songs wafted throughout the perimeters of the barracks. A few teens were seated on the steps outside. I recognized two of them, Ken and Lucy.

"How were the sheep?" asked Ken.

I thought of how I'd hit my knee against a fence post when I was chasing after a disobedient sheep who was about to escape through an open gate. Just thinking of how my kneecap had banged against the wood made it sting even more. But forget pain, I was with Lucy. "They were good." I smiled at Lucy.

"What do you do on the farm?" asked Lucy. "Is it hard work?"

I was about to answer when, from behind me, I heard a familiar voice. "Well, it's the Mori boys."

I turned to see Mekley. He was in uniform, and while he usually looked clean, I noticed dirt on his boots.

"The Mori boys," he said again. "And with such a pretty girl. Very pretty for a Jap." He let out a burp that filled the air with the stench of beer.

"Hey," said Ken, as Mekley staggered toward us. "You need to stay away."

Mekley didn't listen; he came forward. "I can do whatever I want."

Ken sprang to his feet and marched over to the soldier.

I strained to hear what my brother was saying to the man, but couldn't make out any of the words. I looked at Lucy, her arms were wrapped around her waist and a fearful expression filled her face.

After a few minutes, Mekley grinned at us, looked Lucy over a few times and said, "Whatever you say, Ken. Whatever you say." He released a light laugh, burped again, and left, heading in the direction of the hospital.

"Let's go inside." Ken reached for Lucy's arm

Lucy took his hand and sprang to her feet. "He is too creepy."

Ken placed a protective arm around her, and the two entered the rec room.

Chapter Eleven

I followed them inside. If ever I felt like the fifth wheel, this was the time. The music was loud, and couples were dancing to Glen Miller's "Don't Sit Under the Apple Tree."

A girl walked from the other side of the room toward me. She was Lisa, a small girl, a few years younger than me. Her hair didn't flow; it was always in pigtails. She made me think of how Emi might look at age five. "Hi, Nathan," she said. "It's nice to see you."

"Yeah. Thanks." I realized I was mumbling.

"Would you like to ask me to dance?"

She was cute to some, I suppose, but no beauty queen. Her eyes didn't have that way of finding mine and making my knees grow weak. But she wanted to dance, and how could I deny her? Just because my heart was hurting didn't mean that I had to hurt somebody else.

We danced the jitterbug, but my eyes were hardly on her. I kept looking over the floor to see where Lucy and Ken were. I saw a guy and girl huddled in the corner kissing. It wasn't them. The girl had short hair, cut and curled, not at all like Lucy's long locks.

After the music stopped, I tried to smile, tried to join in the debate among those congregated in chairs by the door. But it all seemed so pointless. They talked of the war and Roosevelt and how we were Americans and needed to be treated better, not stuck out in this forsaken land in the middle of nowhere. I knew that their thoughts were important; knew that Papa would have wanted me to contribute my ideas. But I was not in the mood for trying to appear knowledgeable and thought-provoking. Besides, the room was too warm, and the smell of aftershave and hair tonic was making my nose run.

When I couldn't find Lucy or Ken anywhere, I felt it was futile to stay. Feeling defeated, I walked back to our barracks. Who needed girls? Who cared? I would go to sleep. I would forget that Lucy existed. I would work and forget that there was a life other than feeding sheep, cleaning out stalls, and eating Mrs. Towson's homemade chili.

Two days later, there was a letter for us. I recognized the immaculate cursive writing right away. My heart did one of those happy jumps, and a smile spread across my face and stuck.

I carried the letter from the post office to our apartment and was glad that no one was inside so that I could read it alone. It was postmarked sixteen days ago. The envelope was a simple white one. There was no need to open its seal; someone had already done that. I believed that there were Caucasian Americans whose only job was to make sure that every letter that arrived at each relocation camp had been scanned for pro-Japan propaganda. Mr. Kubo said that full paragraphs from one of the letters from his son had been marked out with black ink.

In the quiet of our living quarters, I sat on my bed and carefully took the letter out from the envelope. The letter was one page. Not one word had been blotted out. Unfolding the sheet of white paper, I read:

Dear Ones—Etsuko, Kazuko, Ken, Nathan, Tom, and my daughter, Emi,
Thank you for your letter, Etsuko. I realize that it was written many
months ago. Forgive me for not writing to you sooner. It is hard to put
words together and you know I have never been good with words. I
miss you all and love you. Please do your best under these unfortunate
circumstances. Please know that my lack of communication does not indicate
my lack of concern and love.

It was not signed, as though he had either forgotten to write his name or had not wanted to for whatever reason. I read it again. He had included all of our names, even Emi's. So he did know that Emi had been born. He'd included Mama's name, too. He didn't know that she was gone.

I wanted to share the letter with the others, but wondered if it would make them too sad to read his words. The letter was for all of us, addressed to each one. Was it selfish not to share it with everybody else?

Charles found me as he often did and asked about a paper. "Have you finished it, Nathan?"

"Which paper?" I pulled myself up from my cot.

"The one for English about Walt Whitman."

"No. When is it due?"

"Tomorrow."

"Due tomorrow?" How could I have missed out on hearing that? I sighed and tucked the letter under my pillow. It looked like I was going to have to work all night to get that paper written.

Exhausted, it was midnight when I finally completed it and slipped into bed. Everyone else was already asleep, even Ken had made it home. As I listened to all the noises my family made during sleep, I was relieved. Not only was my paper completed, more importantly, Papa had written to us.

I wondered what his camp surroundings were like. Like ours, had they been built quickly from green lumber that shrunk, producing large gaps in the walls? I wondered about the food he was served, if he got meal tickets like we did here, if he had friends. But most of all I wondered if he was able to smoke and play chess. Along with fishing and running a business, those two had been his favorite pastimes. I knew they weren't letting him fish, but even if they still thought he was a spy, I hoped that they would let him have a few puffs of a cigarette in the evening as the sun went down.

Chapter Twelve

The next morning, I woke from a dream about Mama. Immediately I knew that I had experienced something grand, better than any piano performance, even the one in sixth grade when I had my first standing ovation in that dank auditorium that smelled of kerosene. The dream clung to me like a soft cotton blanket, the kind we had back home in San Jose. I didn't want to move for fear the warmth would slip off and leave me. In my dream, Mama had whispered, "I want you to be strong, Nobu. It will be very hard on you, but you must persevere."

I lay in bed listening to the snores of the others as they slept; the warmth from the dream still present. I opened my eyes, although I knew I shouldn't. Rolling over and closing my eyes in the hopes of continuing the dream would have been best. But Emi was stirring in her crib, and the reality of having to eventually get up and face the day began to take command. Before some of the dream could fade, I played it over again in my mind. Emi would have to wait.

In my dream, Mama had been seated in our house in San Jose on the piano bench. Bright sunlight entered the living room through an opened window, lighting her face and every part of the room. Mama had been wearing a teal dress with a pair of pearl earrings. I was somewhere in the same room, but of course, typical of dreams, I had not seen myself. When I walked over to the bench to sit beside Mama, she again whispered, "You must persevere, Nobu."

As Emi gave a few gurgles, I knew I had to get up. The notion to slide over to Mama's bed became strong, and I was compelled to act. It was as though the dream was taking on a persona, one that was pushy, forceful, even asking me to do something. So, slowly, I eased out of my cot and went over to the empty bed where Mama had once spent three months of her life.

I didn't like seeing the cot unoccupied. Last week, I'd asked my aunt if we could move it out of our *camp house*. She merely frowned, shook her head, and said we didn't need to move it out.

"But it will give us more room," I'd said.

She'd shrugged and said that we might need it when Emi grew up.

I had walked to school that morning wondering how tragic it would be if we never got out of this prison. Were we doomed to live here forever? Were Emi and the rest of us going to grow up inside this confined barbed wire region of the world?

Now, as a strong feeling overcame me, I crouched by Mama's cot and removed the suitcase. Along with my suggestion of moving this cot out of our barracks, I'd also wanted to suggest that we go through Mama's suitcase. In the six months since her death, I had not said anything about doing this; part of me was afraid that Tom might become distressed. I suppose that I wanted to protect him. I unlatched the case and opened the lid. Swallowing hard, I let my fingers touch her light blue cashmere sweater. Under it was a book, a leather Bible, and then to the left was a white cotton shirt, a lacy scarf, and a small wooden jewelry box. Opening it, I saw the pearl earrings that Papa had given her one Christmas. I smiled—these had been the earrings Mama had on in my dream. But when I drew out the piece of silk crimson fabric, panic set in.

"Where is it?" My words came out not in a whisper, but in a demanding tone as though I was asking the brown case a question.

Emi whimpered. Aunt Kazuko rose from her bed, repeating in a tender tone, "*Yoshi, yoshi.*"

I dug through the suitcase, no longer using gentle fingers. As I took out each item and placed it on the floor, my mind pulsated with fear. "Where is it?" I ran my hands over the inside of the now empty suitcase.

My aunt, with Emi in her arms, stood over me.

"It's not here!" I cried.

I didn't need to say anymore. The look on my aunt's face showed that she not only knew exactly what was missing, but was also worried. "Perhaps she put it some other place," she said.

"Where?" I shot a glance under the bed, but there was nothing else there. "Where is it?" I fought to breathe.

I couldn't wrap my mind around it. The watch was gone. Fueled by frustration and disbelief, I stood, scanned our room, my eyes stopping at the curtains my aunt had made, the floor, the table with her teapot. Where could it be? Had Tom perhaps taken it out to look at? To write about? To describe, perhaps, for one of his classes?

"Tom," I said, shaking him awake. "Tom, where's the watch?"

He had to have it. He probably unlatched Mama's suitcase, opened the case and went rummaging through it, saw the watch, liked it, took it out to hold, or to sleep with. My reasoning made sense, and I resumed normal breathing once again.

As Tom sat up in bed, I searched through his covers and pillow.

"What are you doing?" he asked. "Hey, stop!"

No watch. My stomach sank. "Sorry," I muttered to Tom as he gave me an exasperated look.

Ken! The wool blankets on Ken's cot were rumpled, so maybe he had slept here last night and left early to go out to the dining hall for breakfast. What time was it? I opened the door to see if I could spot my brother walking over to our barracks from the dining hall. In the chill of a new day, the sun was barely peeking over the horizon.

Aunt Kazuko, who had seemed concerned, suddenly went back to her business-as-usual manner. Using Mama's cot, she placed Emi on her back to change her diaper. "We need water." My aunt sounded like a soldier, one of the tower guards. Give her a rifle and she would have fit right in with them.

I pulled on my shoes and without thinking, grabbed a container off the floor.

"Wrong one," said Aunt Kazuko.

I looked down at it and saw two soiled diapers. The one to carry water from the washroom to our barracks was over by the table.

Suddenly, Ken entered our living quarters. He was dressed in a wool cap and coat.

I cornered him as he removed his cap. He reeked of alcohol and cigarettes. "Do you have our watch?"

"What?" He slipped by my side and made his way over to his cot. From his shelf, he grabbed his mirror and studied his hair in it.

"Do you have our watch?" I asked again.

"No."

"Then where is it?"

"I don't know."

"What do you mean, you don't know?"

My aunt carried Emi over to the table, sat on one of the chairs and from a tin can, pulled out half a cookie. "It has to be somewhere," she said.

How could she be eating at a time like this! This was no time for a "pep." "Where?" I asked with force.

"Calm down, little bro," said Ken. "We'll find it." He walked over to the stove, opened the door and added coal from another bucket into it.

My aunt said, "This camp is crazy, who knows who might steal it."

"Steal?" The word took my breath away. I slumped onto the foot of my cot.

Aunt Kazuko said that she must go get breakfast, she was feeling faint, she had to eat something right now, and for me to join her.

How could the watch be gone?

"Get water," she said, standing to warm her hands over the stove. "Then you must eat."

"Not feeling like it," I muttered.

A knock at our door brought Mrs. Kubo into our barracks. She greeted each of us and then joined my aunt to warm her hands over the stove. "Cold today," she said. "End of April, but it's still a frozen wasteland around here. I miss San Jose."

"I miss the flowers," said my aunt. "I miss the red hibiscus."

Mrs. Kubo took Emi and cuddled her to her breast as she and my aunt conversed in Japanese. I figured Mrs. Kubo had come over to take Emi so that my aunt could eat breakfast in peace and then do the laundry.

As my aunt dressed behind the long curtain at the back of the barracks, she said, "We need detergent. Who has some?"

"Ask the Ohashi family," said Mrs. Kubo. "They seem to have everything."

"They have pretty good prices," my aunt said. "But I never got laundry detergent from them. How much you think it costs?"

But Mrs. Kubo was too busy studying my face to respond. "You look pale," she said. "What's wrong?"

I was not sure how to phrase what was going on, but I didn't want to be rude and not reply or my aunt would surely give me grief over that. "I'm just not feeling well," I said, and as I said it, I realized that it was not at all a lie. My skin was clammy; my heart pounded.

"You should eat something," my aunt said from behind the *dressing curtain*—the name she had given the large piece of material.

"It's time for school," I said.

"Not yet," said Tom as he attached his leg brace. "Breakfast first. I'm hungry."

"Go with him," said my aunt, coming out from behind the curtain, now dressed in a skirt and blouse.

Tom was dressed, too, having mastered the art of getting both undressed and dressed under the covers. He wiggled to the end of the bed and then rose.

"Go with Tom," Aunt Kazuko repeated.

Didn't she realize that I had to find out what happened to the watch?

The door banged shut; Tom had left; he was always eager to get to the dining hall.

Aunt Kazuko chatted with Mrs. Kubo as she buttoned her coat and fastened a scarf around her neck. Then, with a disdained look at me, my aunt headed outside.

I watched Mrs. Kubo change Emi's diaper. Only twenty minutes ago, my aunt had done the same thing. How many diapers did Emi go through in a day? How could something so small make so many messes? After school it would be my job to wash out every dirty diaper and hang each one up to dry.

But before school, I needed to fetch water. This time I picked up the correct bucket.

After school, I was at it again, asking if anyone knew where the watch was. Tom sat on his rock with a notebook and pencil, dreamily looking out over the mountain range. "I don't know where it is," he said as he scribbled a word and then resumed his stare ahead. "I hope you find it."

Inside our house, Aunt Kazuko fed Emi her bottle. "I know you are worried," she said, as she turned from my sister to look at me. "Me, too. I don't know why the watch would be gone. I am flabbergasted."

"You aren't flabbergasted," I said.

"I am so."

"You aren't. Flabbergasted means you are shocked or surprised. You act like you don't care about the Mori watch."

"I am indeed shocked and surprised."

The way in which she enunciated made me want to applaud. Had I been in a different frame of mind, I would have.

Ken entered the room, smelling clean, like he'd just showered. "How is everyone?"

"You need to wash out the diapers," my aunt said.

He held his nose. "I'm busy."

"Too bad," she said. Standing, she burped Emi and then laid her in her crib.

Ken picked up his comb, added some hair grease to his thick locks and looked proudly into his mirror.

With one quick motion, my aunt grabbed the comb from his hand. "Other boys help their family."

"I'm busy."

But our aunt would have none of his excuses this afternoon. "You must do more than run around like a crazy monkey with your gang."

We were silent. Had we had a wall clock, we would have been able to hear it tick.

Ken glared at Aunt Kazuko, motioned for the comb, but she did not hand it back.

I tasted fear. I'd never seen our aunt stand up to Ken like this. Unable to handle the silence any longer, I blurted, "Does anyone know where the watch is?" Ken acted as though he hadn't heard me, and so I asked again.

Lifting the metal diaper container over his shoulder, he said, "Be glad that I'm doing your job for you, Nathan."

"My job?" The words stuck, and I wasn't able to say anymore. Weren't we all supposed to be helping out? Isn't that what Papa had written to tell us? Help each other. Take care of each other. But of course, no one knew what Papa had written because I had yet to show his letter to anyone.

"Everybody works here," said our aunt. As Ken left the apartment, she called after him. "Tomorrow you can get us coal and help the other families get their coal." To me she muttered, "He's a big strong boy, and old people here need his help." She puttered around the apartment, taking dried clothes off the overhead lines, folding them and mumbling words in Japanese I couldn't fully understand.

"English only!" I called out, to which she threw a sock at me.

"Mother language is best for when complaining," she retorted. Then she said something about needing a miracle.

I tried to focus on my math homework, but after five minutes, I gave up.

Outside, the wind from earlier in the day had died down, and the sun streamed across the camp.

Tom was still seated on his rock, writing on one of the pages of his notebook. He looked up at me.

I sat beside him, and it was then that I noticed he had a strange look in his eyes.

"What's wrong?"

"Can I ask you something?"

"What is it?"

After a moment of deliberation, he asked, "What if an alien came into our house and took our watch from Mama's suitcase?"

Here I was worried sick, and he was talking about something from his active imagination. I moved closer to him and decided I'd let him engage me in one of his stories that he made up in his head. "So tell me what this alien did."

In a whisper, Tom said, "I was sleeping."

Was Tom going to tell me about a dream? Again? He recently told me in great detail his dream about a Martian and a classroom of toads.

"Well, I'm pretty sure I was." He bent toward me, his face just inches from mine. "I was thinking I needed to get up to go use the john."

"And?"

He glared at me, clearly taking the role of a storyteller, one who needs to set his own pace and one who needs a cooperative audience.

"So I was about to get out of bed to use the john."

Irritation grated at every nerve. "Just tell me what happened."

Tom gave me a bewildered look. "I am," he said empathically.

"All right then, go on."

"I turned over from my left side to my right side. But before I could sit up, I heard something. I listened over all the other usual noises and then I heard something different. I was sure that it was a noise beside Mama's cot."

"A noise? What kind?"

"The noise sounded like footsteps and then it stopped." He paused and waited a few seconds before continuing. "The door opened, and I saw a person leave our house."

"A person?"

"Yeah. He was short and slim and—"

"He was leaving our house?"

"That's right."

"Who was he? What was he wearing?"

Tom paused. "I was getting to that. He had on dark clothes."

"Who was he?"

Tom leaned back. "I don't know. It was too dark to see."

I didn't know what to believe.

Why would someone come into our barracks to steal? We were all confined to this camp, all united, weren't we? All of us brothers and sisters—alleged enemies of the United States, but never of each other.

As Lucy sang that evening, I lay on my bed and recalled the story of the watch. In between her songs, I could hear my papa's strong voice inside my head. "The gold watch was first crafted in Osaka, Japan, in 1888. It was gifted to the patriarch of the family for his act of nobility in saving a young girl from drowning in the river. With the family's relocation to the United States in 1919, it was part of their belongings, safely tucked inside a suitcase in the folds of a scarlet silk kimono."

Along with bedtime stories of Peter Pan and biblical accounts of Joseph and his coat, I'd been well-versed in our family legacy of the watch. "Not everyone has such an heirloom," Papa often said. "We have been given a story that will never be forgotten."

How could someone steal our history?

In the night, I woke from a dream and tiptoed over to Mama's suitcase. The silk that protected the watch was still inside, but the watch was still missing. Our prized treasure was gone.

I must have been dreaming, I realized, as I slipped back into my warm cot. In my dream someone had put the watch back where it belonged.

Chapter Thirteen

There was a dance three nights later. Posters were plastered around the camp to announce that the event would be held in the recreation room from eight to eleven p.m.

My aunt informed me that we were out of evaporated milk and powdered milk. "You go get now," she told me. Sometimes she gave my sister evaporated milk diluted with water, and other times she would feed Emi powdered milk.

"But what about water? And cleaning out those diapers?" I opened the diaper pail and even though Ken had emptied it yesterday, today it was full again.

"Never mind that," she said. "Milk first. Food and drink always come first when you are in tough situation. Hurry. No dilly-dally."

The co-op on the premises was closed, but I knew that Mrs. Ohashi had items for sale, letting all of us know one night in the mess hall that she was open for business. When I stopped by the Ohashi apartment, sure enough, even though it was past seven, this shop was still open.

She sold evaporated milk, throat lozenges, chewing gum, Kellogg's cereal, stationery, candy bars, and antacid. Where she got those, I was not sure. The prices were less than at other places in the camp. I supposed what she was doing was legal as far as the block leaders were concerned; after all, Mr. Ohashi was our stern leader. I'd never seen a smile on his face.

Tom's theory was that they both were in on some highly-sensitive operative and every day had a secret package flown in from a spaceship.

Of course, as she conversed with me to ask about my aunt and Emi, frustration and worry occupied my mind. *Who took our watch?* I started to suspect everybody. I bought two cans of evaporated milk. As I paid for them, my eyes roamed the Ohashi barracks. I noted their clothesline that held shirts and socks, focused on their floor, covered in throw rugs. The gaps in their walls were crammed with newspaper and wadded-up cereal boxes to keep out the cold; could one of those gaps be the hiding place for our watch?

I felt like a detective, minus the trench coat.

A woman in a jacket, hat, and a pair of knitted gloves, entered the barracks and greeted me with a pleasant smile, as though we were old friends. "I miss your mother," she said. "She shouldn't have died. My husband said that if the hospital had been one in San Jose, it would have been better supplied and would have saved her."

My face froze as though it had just been whipped by the Wyoming wind.

"Nonsense," said Mrs. Ohashi to the woman. She handed me two packs of spearmint gum. "Here, take these," she said warmly and then casted a look of disapproval at the other shopper.

With affirmation the woman said, "Well, my husband is a doctor."

"Yes, well, we all do the best we can." Mrs. Ohashi gave me a forced smile. "You have a good day, Nathan."

Feeling she wanted to get rid of me, I wondered why. Was it something I said? Was it Mama? Or perhaps, she was the thief who had taken our watch?

At school, I'd looked over at Charles and wondered if he had been the slim figure who'd come into our barracks. Lucy? Mr. Kubo? Mrs. Kubo? I thought of all the people who had come to our billet. All the women who helped take care of Emi. Would they steal?

When I returned to our barracks, Ken acted frustrated, too. "I'll kill the guy who took it," he said, his tone biting with anger. "I'll get the Samurai after him." Ken flexed a muscular arm. I supposed his new task of lifting buckets of coal for our stove and for the stoves of other residents was paying off.

Glad that he was showing some concern about our family heirloom, I said, "Do you have any idea who would have come inside to steal it?"

"No," he said. "But I will find out, you can count on me."

He left with great momentum; my aunt thought he'd knock the front door out of the frame. But later that night at the dance, when I approached him, he was nonchalant, unmoved by my anguish. Girls surrounded him, and he stood to dance with one. I waited till the music stopped, and when he stepped off the dance floor, I asked if he had found out anything. He acted as though he hadn't heard me.

He jumped up to ask another girl to dance; by this time I counted that he'd danced with ten different girls.

As the lively music continued, couples sprang up to dance. I sat away from the crowd, on a hard birchwood chair, and thought of our traditions and our roots. Our ancestors had sat in *tatami* rooms watching Japanese dancers, which were nothing like American dances. Mama said that people didn't dance like couples in her prefecture of Nagano, up in the northern mountains of Japan. There was dancing, but it was not with any romantic intentions. Farmers celebrated with folk dances at special festivals. She said she'd had professional dance lessons twice where the music had been played by a *shakuhachi*, which was a bamboo flute, and a horizontal stringed instrument known as a *koto*. Although she liked the music, unfortunately, she realized she was too clumsy to continue. Her teacher had even suggested she stop taking lessons, saying something about not every fish being able to swim—a comparison Mama never forgot.

Papa used to swing her around the living room as the Glenn Miller orchestra played "In the Mood." He would tell her that she was a good dancer, poised, and skilled. She'd giggle whenever he'd say that. "Oh, you wouldn't know a good dancer from a fish," she used to say. Actually, that was kind of funny because our father did know about fish. But dancing? Mama was right. Since he couldn't follow any rhythm— although he tried—he probably knew nothing about what being good at dancing meant.

❀

Our English teacher introduced us to Emerson and Dickinson right before lunch. I listened for a few seconds, but then my mind wandered. I had more important things to do. I studied each kid and wondered if he or she fit the profile of what Tom saw two nights ago. Slim. That would rule out Lenny Tanaka. Short. Well, most of us here fitted that description. I was only five-nine, although if wishes came true, I would be over six feet. Tom said the thief was a boy, so I didn't focus on any of the girls in the room.

"Nathan?"

Suddenly, I was brought back to reality. Mrs. Kanagawa was looking at me, a ruler in her left hand, a stern expression covering her usually placid face.

The rest of the class had their eyes fixed on me as well.

I bit back embarrassment. "Uh . . ."

"Pay attention, Nathan. It will serve you well."

"Yes. Yes, ma'am."

Snickers followed, and soon it seemed that everyone was laughing at me.

Mrs. Kanagawa turned to Lenny. "What do you think that Emerson meant by his poem?" she asked.

"I think Emerson was trying to say that he thought it happier to be dead, and that's what he meant when he wrote, 'to die for beauty, than live for bread.'"

"Very good."

I sighed. I could have answered that question. Had I heard it.

When the school day ended, I ambled toward our barracks, following others who were headed home. I should have listened to Aunt Kazuko and worn a heavier coat. The wind whipped through my jacket. The peak of Heart Mountain was sprinkled with snow.

Seated in their watch stations, the guards were covered in caps and coats, even gloves. Their steely rifles glistened underneath a winter sun.

"We keep you safe," one said to me when I was getting water for our bucket after first arriving at the camp.

Safe?

Charles said that his father told him there was no more safety for the Japanese in this country.

As I neared our barracks, I heard voices escalating. Huddled in a cluster was a handful of teen-aged boys. Half of them had burlap bands around their heads.

I sensed what was about to happen and, sure enough, someone swung his fist, and then it was like in the movies. Right before us was a real live gang fight between the San Jose kids and the L.A. kids.

Punches were thrown, and I had to run to the side of the path. But Tom was not as quick. He was caught between the gangs, and before I could rush in to pull him out of the crossfire, he fell.

"Tom!" I screamed.

Charles also saw Tom fall and rushed to us.

"Are you hurt?" Charles asked.

I knelt beside my brother. There was no blood that I could see.

Tom let out a faint moan. "Help me up."

Together, Charles and I helped Tom to his feet. It was then that I saw the dark bruise on my brother's forehead. I wanted to scoop him into my arms and carry him. I would have done just that, but Tom insisted that he could walk.

"I'm good, I'm good," he repeated as I put my arm around his waist.

The three of us made our way toward our home and when we got there, Charles opened the door.

I hoped Aunt Kazuko wouldn't bark at us when she saw Tom's bruised forehead. But of course, she was known for speaking her mind, and so, of course, she did.

❈

Inside our barracks, we laid Tom on his cot as Aunt Kazuko cried, "What on this earth happened?"

When we told her, she muttered about boys being too eager to show off their muscles. "These gangs are of the Devil." She removed a pillow from Mama's bed to prop Tom's leg. "Those boys need spankings."

Tom kicked off his left shoe and then I untied his right one and unlatched his brace. I helped him slip his leg out from it and then positioned the pillow under the back of his kneecap.

"Ouch," said Tom.

"What hurts?" I asked.

"My mouth feels bloody."

Aunt Kazuko poured him a glass of water and handed it to him. He drank all of it, not even pausing to breathe.

"That better?" I asked. I pulled up his pant leg and studied his leg. A purple mound had formed on his shin.

When the ruckus outside calmed down, Ken entered. "Is he all right?"

"A bit late, aren't you?" I wanted to say so much more, but stopped there.

"Hey, don't get huffy." Ken tried to soothe me like he often did, but this time, I didn't give in. I kept the frown plastered on my face as I refilled Tom's glass of water.

Ken attempted to tease Tom, and once Tom laughed, Ken must have felt he'd accomplished his mission. He left; the door banged behind him.

I was ready to yell out at him, but noticed Tom's smile in the darkening room. "You take good care of us, Nathan."

The light bulb produced a sizzling noise.

"Did you hear me?"

"Yes." I moved next to him so that he could lean against me; he rested his head on my shoulder.

"Remember that day when we went swimming?"

"In that pond?"

"Yeah. Ken found it. Remember how he came home to tell us about it?"

It was funny that Tom would choose to recall that day at this moment. Ken had been excited to tell Tom and me about a place he was sure no one else knew about. Reluctantly, Mama had given us permission to go.

We'd all put on old T-shirts and shorts and made the trek to it. We'd complained that it was too far to walk, and what about Tom and his leg? But Ken just urged us to keep walking.

"This had better be worth it," I'd said. I recalled how many times Ken got us anticipating something spectacular only to be let down. Once he'd told us the circus was coming to town. But it hadn't been a real circus at all, but rather two old men with an unsteady horse, an overweight woman in a clown costume who claimed she could read palms, and a magician that wore a wool beret. The performance had been held on a sidewalk on Main Street with a sparse crowd that left after twenty minutes when the magician's tricks were exposed as phony.

I'd been disappointed; Tom, a mere five-year-old, had cried. Some of his tears probably had to do with fatigue; he'd been up nearly all night the night before, too excited to sleep, because as Ken had said, "The circus is coming to town, and you're gonna have fun."

The swimming hole had actually been fun. All three of us had splashed in the water and later had stretched out on the tops of three old logs as the sun baked our backs. Ken had packed ham and cheese sandwiches for us and a thermos of chicken soup.

I wondered if we would ever see that side of Ken again, the side that spent time with his siblings, the big brother who cared about us and wanted to be part of our lives.

As I continued to question my older brother's current lifestyle and motives, Tom patted my arm and closed his eyes. "I think I can sleep now."

"Don't you want to lie down?" Before he could respond, I helped him slide into a horizontal position, careful to adjust the pillow so that it continued to fit under his leg. I thought about the day we found out that Tom's leg was permanently paralyzed and recalled Papa's words, "He'll learn to walk with a limp. He'll even play baseball." Papa was a baseball enthusiast. Little did he know that his son would have little interest in baseball; dreaming and writing would be his choices.

Aunt Kazuko warmed a bottle for Emi, and we listened to my sister guzzle the milk from it. My aunt broke the near silence when she confessed, "I have been hungry all day. It should be almost time for dinner."

Tom opened his eyes. "Oh, when you go to dinner, can you bring me back something to eat?"

"Sure," I said.

"Something like a steak and a huge slice of chocolate pie, okay?"

I was amazed that even in pain, he was able to tease. "Want your steak well done or rare?" I asked.

"You know I like steaks well-done. With a side of mashed potatoes."

It seemed that, while the rest of us took to complaining, Tom faced each day as though he had no worries. He had never let his lifeless leg become a threat to his happiness.

"Does it hurt?" I once asked him.

"Nah," he'd said. "It's got no feeling. But sometimes in my dreams, when I'm climbing a tree or riding a bicycle, I fall and then it hurts. Only in my dreams does it feel any pain."

Aunt Kazuko told me to go on to dinner. "I stay here," she said. "I can go to dining hall when you get back."

Dinner was a solemn event that night as members of the San Jose gang sat together in the far corner, talking in low, but angry whispers. I looked for Lucy, but didn't see her.

Perhaps tonight she'd sing something to bring some peace to my troubled mind.

I waited to hear her voice float over the dusty terrain, but when it got to be after nine, I was too restless to stay put in the billet with Tom, Emi, and Aunt Kazuko. Tom said the moon was full, so I went outside to see it, and sure enough, it was like a ball of fire above Heart Mountain. Tom thought it looked like a spaceship, and he was certain Martians had landed. I'd wished him luck with finding them and followed some activity near the rec hall, hoping I could find Lucy.

As I drew closer to the rec hall, I saw that the activity in the middle of the road was a fight between a Los Angeles boy and a San Jose boy. Wasn't the fight that happened earlier enough for one day? I didn't want to get caught up in it, so watched from the sidelines. The L.A. boy was taller, but the San Jose boy was better with his fists.

I wondered where Mekley was. He would have put an end to the fight.

The cheers from the growing crowd of high school kids sounded like we were at a football game back in California. I spotted Lucy, and when she looked at me, I smiled.

The soldier that came by to reprimand the boys was short with a bored expression. "Knock it off," he said. "Go back to your barracks."

The crowd dispersed; the boys from L.A. threatened to get us next time. Once they had disappeared, a group of girls quickly made their way toward Ken. I stood in the shadows. No one rushed over to me.

"Ken, look at the moon," said Suzanne, a girl with a squeaky voice. "It looks like it's glowing."

Ken said he thought it looked wild, full of life.

The girls giggled. No one smiled at me or asked what I thought of the way the moon shone over the top of Heart Mountain.

"Wild like you?" asked one. "You are pretty wild."

I searched for Lucy, but she, like much of the crowd, had left. She was usually with Ken; perhaps tonight she was finally tired of him and his Clark Gable ways.

"Ken, are you going to the dance on Friday?" Suzanne asked.

"Only if you'll be there."

I couldn't take it anymore. "Ken," I called out to him and stepped from the shadows. "I need to talk with you."

"What's up?"

"What about the watch?"

"I told you not to worry." He spat the words out as though they were bullets.

What was wrong with Ken? Why did he always have to be in control? When would he realize that the whole earth didn't revolve around him?

Just because the girls liked him didn't mean he was perfect. Yet I could tell by the way he smiled at a group of them or ran his hand through his hair, he thought that he was indeed created to charm, to enlighten, and to make them smile.

He went on to talk about the gang activity, how his group would put the gang from L.A. in their place.

Who cares about the gangs here? It wasn't like that by fighting, anything was going to be accomplished. We were all the same here. No one was better than anyone else. Behind those jagged fences, we were all considered *dirty*.

Ken held the gathered group's attention as he talked of how there would be a meeting to discuss plans tomorrow evening after dinner. "We'll set those L.A. wimps straight," he said. "We'll get our revenge."

He was crazy. The more he talked, the more irritated I grew. Finally, I couldn't take it anymore. No one noticed when I walked off toward our barracks. No one asked where I was going or called me to come back.

I stormed into our barracks, purposely letting the door slam against its frame.

"What is wrong with you?" my aunt immediately wanted to know.

"He thinks the whole world worships him," I cried.

"The whole world?"

"Yes!"

She put Emi in her crib and came over to where I slouched down on the floor, my back against the wall. Standing over me, she said, "First of all, whisper. Tom is asleep already." She motioned to his cot. "Next, you need to stop complaining about Ken. The watch is gone. He told you he doesn't know where it is. You have to let it go."

Let it go? She might be able to do that. She hadn't had both Papa and Mama tell her how valuable it was and the story around it. How could she think that losing it didn't matter? The watch was history, the Mori history that proved we were courageous, valued, and strong. Ken was the eldest, how come he didn't seem to care that this heirloom was gone? Someone had taken it, and he was doing nothing about it!

I bet we weren't even related. I bet Ken was found under a tree or in a strawberry patch. Perhaps Papa had pulled him in from the ocean on a fishing excursion. He was not a real Mori; he was adopted by Papa and Mama.

Yet it was I who felt alone—the person nobody wanted to be around.

Chapter Fourteen

On Saturday morning, I was the last one to get on the bus. The driver frowned at me in between taking puffs on his cigar, and said, "Well, it's about time, boy."

I offered a muffled apology and went to sit by Charles.

Charles took one look at me and said, "Rough night?"

I opened my mouth, but no words came out, so I merely nodded.

The ride to the Towson Farm seemed to take longer than usual. My mind kept debating about what I should do about the stolen watch. I thought of telling Charles what had happened, but decided against it.

We got to help out with the sheep shearing that day. After the mounds of wool were shorn from their animal bodies, we collected it, shoveling the white and grey fluff into the bed of a truck. My back ached, and my fingers were sore from the way the handle of the shovel pinched my flesh.

When we were given a break for lunch, I drank water from an outdoor spigot before stepping into the kitchen. I wiped my face with Papa's handkerchief, and then shoved it back into the back pocket of my dungarees.

Mrs. Towson served us a vegetable stew for lunch with a loaf of crusty bread and fresh butter made from the milk of one of their cows. Her son Henry sat at the nearby table, coloring on a piece of paper.

I thought about what Charles said about the bedrooms in the back of the house and how Henry's artwork hung on the walls. Curiosity nudged at me, and I cleared my bowl and then went to use the bathroom. I had been to the bathroom only once before. Farmhands were supposed to use the outhouse behind the barn. As I made my way from the bathroom back to the kitchen, I let my desire to see the rest of the house take me further down the hallway. The hallway was long; the walls held framed family photographs. There were stern looking men standing beside a tractor and women holding babies. A bedroom caught my attention. The door was partially opened. *I'll just slip in the room to see what it looks like,* I thought, as inquisitiveness got the best of me.

Once in the room, I felt like I'd stepped into a storybook. This room was inviting, warm; the curtains dotted with yellow flowers; the matching bedspread draped evenly over the double bed. I ached to be in our house in San Jose with real furniture and curtains and a warm security that I had not experienced since we'd left. Sure enough, on one of the walls was a framed picture drawn with crayons that looked like it could be one of Henry's.

"Nathan?" Charles called out to me, and right then, I knew I was where I didn't belong.

On the floor by a chair adorned in a cream and marigold quilt sat a fat duffle bag. Not just any bag, but a military bag with white lettering on it.

"Nathan, where'd you go?"

Turning to leave the room, I saw the dresser. It was then that my heart skipped at least five beats. On the dresser, right on top of a lacy doily beside a brass lamp with a blue lampshade, laid our gold watch.

This watch, this heirloom didn't belong here.

"Nathan? Where'd you go?" Charles called from the hallway. His voice was getting closer and time was running out.

I knew what I had to do, and without another moment's hesitation, I did it.

The rest of the afternoon, Charles and I cleaned sheep pens as I tried to act myself and not let on what I had seen in that bedroom. It is hard to pretend all is fine when it's not. Charles asked me once if I was all right, and I covered by saying that I was just tired from little sleep the night before. When the bus returned us to the camp, I knew I needed to shower, or Aunt Kazuko wouldn't let me into our barracks for long. She wasn't inside, nor were Tom and Emi, but a note on the table informed me that they were having tea with Mrs. Kubo.

I gathered my towel and clean clothes off the clothesline, picked up a bar of soap from off the shelf where we kept toiletries, and headed to the communal washroom.

In the washroom, I was grateful to be alone. Carefully, I peeled off my smelly clothes, laying my dungarees gently on a stool outside the shower. I felt one of the pockets for the watch. The watch had been taken once. I couldn't let it out of my sight and go missing again, but I couldn't take it into the shower with me. As the water and soap washed the dirt and stench from my body, I closed my eyes and listened over the sound of the water. I heard voices outside, but no one entered the washroom.

When my shower ended, I toweled off, and got dressed. Carefully, placing the watch in my pocket, I picked up my soiled clothes, and then rushed to our unit. Just as I got inside, Ken arrived.

I debated whether or not to tell him about my day. He was kin; he should know.

"Ken," I said as I dried my hair with a towel that held a faint aroma of sour milk, "I found it."

From one of the pegs on the wall, he picked up an army green jacket Aunt Kazuko had bought for him at the co-op. "Good for you."

It was as though he hadn't really heard me.

"I found our watch." This time I said it louder. "I found it."

He said nothing, just headed outside.

"What is wrong with you?" I called after him, and then I saw her. Lucy, dressed in a pink sweater that brought out the muted rose of her lips, was standing in front of our barracks. My anger softened, and I smiled at her.

"Hi, Nathan," she said.

"Hi. How are you?" It was a silly question. Of all the suave things I could have said, I went for the least memorable.

As she smiled, I got caught up in her beauty—the curve of her cheeks, the tilt of her nose, the way her long hair hung over her shoulders. She had not given into the trendy hair styles of the day, short and bobbed or curled. She wasn't like that, and I admired that, and so much more about her.

Ken helped Lucy into the jacket, buttoning all the buttons as she looked at him with adoration. "Now you'll be warm," he said, and looking up at me, waved. "See you later, Nathan," and with an arm around Lucy's shoulders, he guided her down the road.

"Hey!" I called out. "I found our watch!"

But either the two hadn't heard me or were just being too stubborn to turn around. They continued walking, even laughing.

I might as well have just slipped under the barbed wire fence and let one of the guards shoot me. At least then I would have gotten some attention. The way I saw it, nobody seemed to care.

I expected to see Mekley smirking at me. He often offered that expression whenever I felt discouragement kick in. A Jeep roamed along the road, but the driver wasn't Mekley. I knew that because he had no toothpick hanging out of his mouth.

Chapter Fifteen

"You must not be mad at Ken," Lucy said to me at dinner the next evening. She sipped from a white mug of water.

"About what?" I wanted to ask. About the fact he is never around to help out? About the fact that Papa left him in charge of the family, and he didn't know how to take charge?

She smoothed the cowlick over my forehead and then let her hand rest against my sweater. "He is a great guy."

Anger boiled. I could feel it rising, and I knew I had to get out of there. I left my bowl, still full of rice. It was better than flinging it across the room. I ignored the murmurs that buzzed as I stormed past tables of people. I made sure the door banged hard when I exited the mess hall.

Ken was a jerk. How could she call him a great guy? I cursed my luck for not being born handsome, witty, clever, and with sparkles in my eyes.

Aunt Kazuko had Emi in the highchair, one that Mr. Kubo had built. "She has eyes like your Mama's. Have you noticed?" My aunt tickled Emi until she let out a robust laugh and then my aunt repeated the action. "See those eyes? Look at them, Nathan."

I didn't want to look, but my aunt was persistent, so I glanced at my sister. I searched her face as she guzzled from the bottle. Mama's eyes? How could you really tell in a baby?

"Eyes," said Emi. She lowered the bottle onto the highchair's tray and, with a pudgy finger, pointed to her left eye. "Eyes. Eyes."

"She's a smart one." My aunt was obviously amused. "Not even a full nine months old and she can say 'eyes'!"

I didn't know whether to be happy or sad. Charles had told me that most babies' first words were Mama or Papa. Of course, why would Emi say those? She had no Mama or Papa here in camp.

"She speaks like an American," said my aunt with pride.

"She is American! We are all Americans." I recalled the sign we had taped to our fish market that spelled out those very words. It had not mattered that Papa had spent ten minutes writing it, perfecting each letter. The FBI still took him away, accusing him of being a disloyal Jap.

"Well, some people think we aren't worth it," my aunt said matter-of-factly.

"We are worth it. You are worth it. We are all worthy. We are not second-class citizens!"

"No need to tell me that," she said as she folded Emi's shirts. "I know we are all God's children."

Outside, I sat on Tom's rock and watched the lights come on across the camp. "Papa," I said, "where are you? I miss you, Mama, but I'm glad you're out of this mess here."

I thought of Mama, her hair curled, her face filled with a smile and heard her say, "You are my favorite son named Nathan." Yes, it was good that she wasn't here having to combat all the sadness in this camp. It was good she'd left us.

A tear slipped down my cheek. I batted at it, wanting to remove it as though it was some sort of disease like pneumonia, like polio. But my lungs and legs were not weak due to illness, but to something far worse. I felt fear spread over me. Fear that I would no longer be able to live. I really didn't want to live. Not here, not like this.

My will to die must have sent a message over the camp because moments later, I looked down the road between the barracks to see Lucy. Lucy, dressed in a gold and dark pink kimono, a silk hibiscus positioned behind her right ear. The flower was the color of a sunset over San Jose.

"It's almost time for the talent show," she said as she approached me. "What are you going to do?"

Talent show, I inwardly groaned. I really had very few talents, and none of them was worthy of being staged in a show. "Are you singing?" I asked although it was a stupid question. Of course, she was going to sing, she was Lucy Yokota and singing was what she did best, well, next to making my heart palpitate. "I guess I'll head over to the rec hall," I said, standing.

She fell into step with me. It felt so right having her next to me.

"So Nathan, what talent are you going to share with us?"

"I don't know."

"You should play the piano."

"There isn't one."

"Someone donated one to the church yesterday."

"It's been so long since I've played."

"It's like riding a bike, right? You never forget how."

"I suppose." Again being witty or charming eluded me. I took a deep breath. *Get it together, Mori,* I said to myself. *Say something intelligent. Make an impression.* But my mind was blank, just like a newly erased chalkboard.

The rec hall began to fill; in the chairs were many I recognized, even Mrs. Busybody was there, telling a group of ladies that this camp was not fit for a dog. "That's why there are no dogs here," she said. "Because this place isn't fit for one."

I found a seat far from her, near Charles. Tom later slipped in the vacant chair beside me, carefully maneuvering his braced leg so that it didn't bump against the chair in front of him.

One of the newly-married men was the master of ceremonies. His wedding ceremony had occurred shortly after the New Year, and Aunt Kazuko had attended while I stayed in the barracks with Emi and Tom. She spoke so highly of the service and dabbed at her eyes hours after she returned back to our billet. "It was so grand," she'd repeated. "So lovely, like painting. Yes, I cried. An old woman should have a good cry at least once a week."

The emcee welcomed us all, and then announced that the first talent was a *shamisen* piece, to be followed by a flute duet. After those performances and much applause, a band of five young men with mandolins and guitars stepped onto the stage and sang to Hawaiian surf music.

Lucy's two songs came after that. She sang about freedom and love and God, and all of the words were so beautiful that a few women were wiping their eyes with handkerchiefs before she finished. As I looked around, sure enough, there was Aunt Kazuko with my sister on her lap, blotting her cheeks with one of Emi's blankets.

"You sang really well," I said to Lucy, as we followed a group back to our block.

"Thank you."

"You were the best. You could be a professional."

"I don't know about that."

"Here she is, the talented Lucy Yokota." I tried to sound like the master of ceremonies, but my voice was not as deep as his.

"I always thought I could be called Meredith Rose."

"Meredith Rose?"

"Don't you think that has a nice ring to it?"

"I suppose." I motioned toward the silk flower in her hair. "How about Hibiscus Silk?"

"That sounds like the name of a woman with a questionable reputation."

"Oh. Really?"

"Yeah. I think it would have to be Meredith Rose."

With an eye toward Heart Mountain's distant peak, I said, "What about Heart? Rose Heart? Or how about Lucy Heart?" Perhaps those were all stupid suggestions. Quickly, I said, "Whatever your name is, you'll be great."

Her eyes sparkled as she smiled. "You are such a kind person, Nathan."

"I try," I teased.

I realized that the evening had been a good one after all. Although the walk to the talent show had had me kicking myself for not sounding intelligent, by the end of the show, I had overcome my fear and had been able to even tease. Perhaps there was hope for me. Perhaps I wasn't such an idiot after all.

"Her voice is perfect," I said to Ken later that night.

Our aunt put Emi into a pair of pajamas with tiny white bunny rabbits while Tom removed his brace.

"She's okay," Ken said. "I mean she sings pretty good."

"Pretty good?" What did he know? He hadn't even come to the show. "Where were you? You missed the talent show."

He grabbed a cardigan off his bed, put it on, and buttoned it. "I have to go."

"You're never here."

He shot me an angry glare. "Just keep your thoughts to yourself, Nathan. And anyway, Lucy isn't right for you. She'll never be interested in your type."

The urge to smack him overcame me, and I caved. With a punch to his shoulder, he teetered. I'd caught him off-guard.

He grabbed my wrist, bulldozed into my stomach, and knocked me to the ground.

Emi screamed from her crib. Tom moved quickly so he wouldn't be in the way, and our aunt shouted, "That's enough. Stop it now!"

We rolled onto the floor like two angry animals, clawing at each other. My foot hit a bottle that had somehow fallen to the floor. It shot under Ken's cot, and shattered.

Aunt Kazuko had to pry us apart. When she stepped between us, so that her feet were at our heads, we both stopped. Dizzy, I clung to my bed before standing.

Ken stormed outside.

"You boys, stop nonsense!" Aunt Kazuko spoke with an authority that made me cringe. With a finger pointed at me, she said, "You have to realize that we need each other right now. We need each other much too much to be at each other's throats."

Tom had Emi in his arms, patting her back to quiet her sobs.

Aunt Kazuko hadn't shouted, "Shame on you," but it was as though she had, because in that moment shame covered me from throbbing head to throbbing toe.

I crawled onto my cot. It had been such a nice night talking and walking with Lucy. Why had I let my emotions get the best of me?

You're such a kind person.

At least Lucy hadn't seen the fight. Perhaps I could still be a kind person in her mind. At least that was what I hoped as I swept the broken glass off the floor and into the waste can.

Chapter Sixteen

I would still be a kind person. I had it all planned out. I'd ask Lucy to dance with me at the next dance. I'd practice being more confident and less fearful. She would have to like me. She wouldn't be able to resist. I was two years younger than she and Ken, but that wouldn't matter. She would see how much I cared for her, and that would win her over.

The next morning, I was ready to go with my plan to show Lucy just how suave I could be.

But the knock on the door that morning was not in my plans. The knock on our door was soft at first, and then grew louder.

Aunt Kazuko stepped into her slippers and went for the door, Emi in her arms. As dampness from a wet spring morning blew in, there stood Mr. Ikeda and Mr. Ohashi, two of the block leaders. Like me, both had been born in California; we were *Nissei* (second generation Japanese-Americans).

"Is Nathan Mori here?" asked Mr. Ikeda. He had a scraggly beard and a pair of thick spectacles with black rims. "We need to speak with him."

I got that awful feeling in the bottom of my stomach that something bad was getting ready to happen.

When I looked into Mr. Ikeda's face, I wished that I could sink into the floor.

"We need to question you about the watch."

"Watch?" I tried to play dumb, tried to take on the persona of Henry.

"You know about this." Mr. Ohashi gave me a stern look, worse than any look my aunt had ever come up with.

"Come with us," said Mr. Ikeda. He motioned for me to follow him out of our unit.

"Where? What are you doing? He's only fifteen," Aunt Kazuko sputtered.

"It has already been decided. Come on, Nathan."

My aunt drew my sister closer to her chest. Her next words were all in Japanese. I picked out the gist of their meaning: What has been decided? What are you talking about?

In a building on the other side of the camp, court sessions were held. Seven judges had been appointed by the project leader. I recalled hearing bits and pieces about the need for civil cases within the camp, but up until this moment, it had not been anything that had interested me. Now things had changed. Suddenly, I wondered what the procedures were.

When I got inside the stark barracks, the first thing I saw was the American Flag hanging on the far wall. I wondered if they wanted me to pledge to it. Was this going to be a test to see whether or not I was patriotic? If I proved to be, would they let me go?

But of course, the reason for being brought here had nothing to do with patriotism. From the first statement on, I knew that this session was to interrogate me about the watch. If only it had been to show allegiance to a flag.

Mr. Ikeda pulled a single wooden chair into the center of the room and asked me to sit down.

Obediently, I obliged. I wondered if the seven judges were going to appear, and if this was going to turn into a court case.

"There's been an accusation," he said. He stood in front of me while Mr. Ohashi stood to my left. "You have been accused of stealing a pocket watch from the Towson Farm."

"Who said that?"

"We were told."

"By whom?"

The two men exchanged glances.

Finally Mr. Ikeda spoke. "A soldier staying there for a weekend of R and R said it was missing. He brought it to the attention of Mr. and Mrs. Towson. They called the police, and the Cody police came to their house. After questioning, they came to camp with your name and the name of a few others."

"All were people from camp who work on the farm," Mr. Ohashi clarified.

"You stole the watch, didn't you?" Mr. Ikeda glared at me.

I thought of Papa and how he'd been accused of disloyalty to our country. The day he'd been questioned at our home, he'd kept his head steady, his eyes focused, but not on anyone's face. I wanted to be brave like my father.

"Didn't you?"

I refused to answer.

"Do you want to have a court case or just hand over the watch?" Mr. Ikeda asked.

"Why don't you just give the watch to us?" Mr. Ohashi said. "That would be the easiest way to go."

"No, I'll take my chances," I said.

"You want a court case?"

I steadied my voice, determined to rid it of all fear. I looked Mr. Ohashi in the eyes. "Yes. Yes, I want a court case."

I didn't sleep any that night, just lay in bed listening to the others snore and wondering where Ken was.

The next morning, right about the time the sun was displaying its late spring light onto Heart Mountain, there was a rap at our door. My heart froze. I wanted to disappear, but it was too late, my aunt was telling the visitor that I was here.

Quickly, I pulled on my clothes.

Aunt Kazuko whispered to me, "Tell the truth, Nathan. It's Mr. Kubo, and he is on your side."

Mr. Kubo said, "Good morning, Nathan."

"Good Morning." I tried to sound both confident and pleasant. "How are you?"

"I need you to hand over the watch."

"What watch?"

"The one you took from the Towson Farm."

I wasn't going to hand over our family watch.

"Nathan, it would be in your best interest if you would hand over the watch."

"No, I can't."

"Listen, we have to take care of this matter." There was urgency to his tone and when he repeated himself, my aunt came to the door.

She reminded them that I was just a boy of fifteen. "He is a child. Children make mistakes."

But that didn't stop him from saying that he had been told he was to take me to a building that would be my confinement.

"Confinement?" Aunt Kazuko cried, as my sister began to whine.

"Why? You mean jail?"

I was told to follow Mr. Kubo to the other side of the camp. Other evacuees greeted me on their way to the mess halls for breakfast. To them it probably seemed like a normal day in camp. But with each step, I knew that I was in trouble.

Mr. Kubo stopped at a building and opened the door. He ushered me inside a dark unit.

"This is your cell, Nathan. You are to stay here until they decide what to do." He switched on the light bulb. Even its light barely lit the room. "A guard will be stationed outside your door. When you need to go to the latrine or need more coal for the stove, knock on the door two times."

Although I had questions, there was no time to ask them. Mr. Kubo was gone; the door was closed and bolted from the outside.

I was alone.

The room was stark, dank, and held a cot and a pot-bellied stove with a box that was filled with coal. There was no shovel or scoop in which to add the coal to the stove. A metal container sat on the wooden floor in the corner, like a guest that wasn't sure whether or not she should be at the party. It didn't take me long to realize that the container was my chamber pot.

I waited for the tears to come. I felt them in the back of my eyes. But my eyes were dry. I sat down on the cot, wrapped one of the wool army blankets around me and tried to think. Thinking clearly can be hard to do when you've just been shoved into a jail cell.

Hours passed; I wasn't sure if two or three had slipped by. I heard a noise at the door, and a soldier opened it and pressed a bowl with rice and strips of pork into my hands. From his shirt pocket he pulled out a lone fork.

The meal was oily and lacked flavor; the rice was cold, but I was hungry and ate. I finished every last grain of rice.

Later in the afternoon, Aunt Kazuko was outside my cell, telling the soldier at the door that she must see me. "He's my nephew," she said. "I need to make sure he is all right. He is only fifteen. He's a good boy."

I doubted she'd be let in, but the door opened, and the soldier told her to knock on the inside of the door two times once she was finished with the visit.

My aunt plopped herself onto the chair. "I walk forever to get here," she said. "First they tell me you are over by block number seventy-six, but when I get there, that is not where you are. So I asked at the hospital, and they tell me to come to block eighty-five, then they tell me unit A, then no, it is unit C and oh, I was so frustrated."

"Thanks for coming to see me," I said.

"You must tell me where the watch is."

I bit my lip and wondered why she was certain that I knew where the watch was.

"Nathan, please. You must confess what you have done so that you can come back to our barracks."

I kicked myself for failing. I had grabbed the watch on impulse the instant I had seen it on the dresser in the guest room at the farm four days ago. I knew it was ours, and so I took it. At that moment I hadn't thought that it would come to this moment. My plan had been to get the watch; for whatever reason, I hadn't played the What If game. Had I played it, I would have gone further in my thinking, asking myself pertinent questions: *What if the soldier who is a guest tells the Towsons he's been robbed? What if the Towsons hand over all the farm employees' names for questioning? What are you going to do then, Nathan?*

Back at camp, I had hidden the watch, not in its old hiding place of Mama's suitcase, but inside a box that once held a doll for Emi that my aunt had ordered from a Sears and Roebuck catalog. The box looked like a kid's toy was inside. I wrapped the watch inside the silk cloth for protection, sealed it inside the box and then stuck it under Emi's crib.

"You need to be truthful," said my aunt.

"I am to have a court case," I said. "I'll testify then."

Aunt Kazuko looked doubtful.

"Don't worry," I said. "It will be all right." The truth had to come out. Wasn't truth supposed to prevail?

After she left, I pushed the chair near the window and watched people walking along the roads between the barracks. When it got dark, I pulled the curtain across the window and wished for someone to talk with.

Mr. Kubo was let into the jail that evening. He brought a plate of rice and vegetables, sprinkled with a bit of something that looked like sliced Spam. "Tonight's dinner," he said.

Eagerly, I took both the plate and fork from him and ate.

"You know, Nathan, you just need to admit what you have done. You need to let everyone know that you are remorseful for having stolen the watch and that you are sorry."

"It is our watch. It was my grandfather's brought over from Japan," I said between bites. The mystery meat was, in fact, Spam. "It's been in our family for three generations. There isn't another watch like it. Well, not in the United States. It was crafted by a man in Hiroshima."

"It is a beautiful watch and clearly one from Japan. I recognize the fine craftsmanship. It's probably worth at least three-hundred dollars."

"You've seen it?"

"Yes. Earlier today, we asked to search your unit. But before Mr. Ohashi and I did, your aunt handed us the watch."

"No, she didn't." This was a ploy! There was no way anyone knew where my hiding place was. "When do I get to testify in court?" I asked.

"We aren't going to do that."

"What?"

"You see, we have to do it this way. The people of Wyoming are not happy about what happened. Think about this for a moment. A Japanese boy steals from his workplace and that makes the daily news. The people in Powell and Cody already have bad feelings toward the Japanese-Americans because of Pearl Harbor. Many of them have sons fighting in Europe and Japan. It's very sticky."

"When do I get my session in court?"

"Justice has to be served, and I'm afraid this," he said, moving a hand around to indicate the cell, "is the answer to the call for justice."

I didn't want to hear any more. I thanked him for coming to visit me and hoped he would feel free to leave me. I had nothing else to say.

❀

I was not summoned to present myself before the panel of leaders in a court-type hearing.

That was a shame, because had I been given my day in court, I would have done a great job. Papa would have been proud of me; Mama would have given me her brightest smile. When the judge asked, "Nathan Mori, did you steal a pocket watch from the Towson Farm?" I would have stated that I had but only because someone had stolen it from me, from our family. "I stole it back. It is ours." That's what I would have said. I would have been let go, free, applauded. Everyone would have agreed that it is an honorable act to fight for that which belongs to you. Wasn't that why our country was at war?

As the sunlight seeped through the curtain, and the soldier opened the door to let me out to use the latrine, I knew I was right. I was not at fault for retrieving what had been taken from me.

Chapter Seventeen

A s the sky filled with cumulus clouds the next morning, my aunt brought Emi to see me. She held a small bag with my toothbrush, a tube of new toothpaste she must have purchased at the Ohashi store, because it was a brand the co-op didn't stock, a bath towel, and a bar of generic soap. In another bag she had packed two of my shirts, a belt, and a pair of cotton briefs. She also brought Mama's Bible. "You read and feel better," she told me.

I scooped Emi into my arms and positioned her on my lap. She fussed. "Did you bring a bottle for her?"

"I fed her before I come here. She's not hungry, just sleepy."

I rested my sister against my chest and patted her back. She let out a few weak cries, and then quieted.

"She misses you," said my aunt. "Tom misses you."

"Have you seen Ken?"

"He is working."

"What do you mean? He's never worked at any of the jobs he's asked for. He only hangs out with that stupid Samurai gang."

She raised her hand, indicating that she didn't want to talk about Ken.

But I was not about to let her have an easy visit. Something had been bothering me all night. Making sure I had her full attention, I said, "Mr. Kubo told me that he found where I hid the watch."

She put her hand to her mouth. I knew that gesture of hers well. It was her innocent little girl move. I didn't buy it.

"What did you do?" I demanded.

"Nathan, the men were going to search our apartment. I didn't want that, and they really didn't want to have to do that. It was much better to just give them the watch."

"But how did you find it?"

She gave me a slight smile. "A doll box under your sister's crib? A box taped up with almost whole roll of tape? How could I not know that was it? I wasn't born yesterday, you know. I am almost fifty. I have lived a long time." Last year my aunt was almost fifty. This year she was almost fifty. In reality, she was only going on forty-six.

Peering into my eyes, she spoke firmly, "It's not right that the watch was taken from us by a thief. I understand you want it back and why you steal. But look at where we are!" She lifted both arms into the air. "We have no justice on our side! You must apologize for stealing it from the farm. Write a letter so everybody will see how sorry you are. Do it tonight, all right?"

When I said nothing, she asked if I had heard her.

I shook my head, dismissing both her question and her advice.

She shook her head, too, and then took Emi from me and left.

Later, as the wind scattered rain across the camp, Tom came by with a story he'd written.

It was nine pages long, and he said he wrote it just for me so that I would have something to read.

I appreciated the visits but wondered why Ken hadn't come to see me. Something told me that Ken had something to do with Mekley having obtained the watch. The more I thought about it, the more I realized that he had most likely given it to Mekley. Probably to pay off some debt he owed. Yet, it didn't make sense to me. He was the *chonan* and what *chonan* worth his birthright would hand over an heirloom without consulting the rest of the family? What right did he have?

In the days that followed, I sat by the window and watched people who couldn't see me. It was like they were part of a movie, performing for my entertainment. Children tossed a baseball, others held hands and skipped. Adults ambled to the mess halls and carried buckets of water from the washroom to their barracks. Our *camp house* was not near this jail, so the people I saw were not ones I knew. Yet their camp life mirrored ours; the truth was, we all looked the same.

As I sat, I remembered a sermon about Paul and Silas being thrown into jail. Then there was the story of Daniel in the lion's den that I had been taught in Sunday school in San Jose. But perhaps the biblical character that I could most identify with now was Joseph. He had been sold into slavery by his own brothers. How he must have cried out to God, wondering why he had been put into such a dismal situation.

Speaking of prayer and God, where was He? "Why does He allow these things to happen?" I asked in the solitude of my confinement. Wasn't it enough that my family and friends, neighbors, and schoolmates had been ordered to leave homes and businesses to go to this camp? Wasn't it enough that they had broken our family up by sending Papa far from us, and allowing Mama to die? I thought about pneumonia and birthing a baby and wondered which one had caused Mama the most pain.

"You stole, son." The words from Mr. Kubo rang in my ears over and over. *Me, a thief? Me?* But the watch was ours. How did that make me a thief when I was only taking back what was mine?

If Papa were here, all would be set straight. He'd be my advocate, making what was wrong right again. He had a way with words and knew the hearts of people. I'd watched him at his fish market with the customers. He knew how to sell, but he always knew just how much his customers were willing to pay for a mackerel or a flounder.

Closing my eyes, I recalled how he worked at his shop donned in his black apron and thick black rain boots. I remembered how excited he'd be when a truckload of fresh fish, caught by one of our neighbors, would pull up to the store. As a young boy, the slippery fish were usually too large for me to hold. But Papa showed me how to grab a fish with my bare hands and place it into a bucket with other fish. At first, I recalled being scared that the fish might slip from my hands onto the floor. At first that was exactly what happened. But Papa didn't scold me, in fact, he'd laughed. "Oh, look at that fish swim away!" Of course, the fish merely lay on the floor of the store, its lifeless eyes grey. Since he'd been caught, he'd relinquished his swimming days. Papa picked up the fish, pretending that it was fighting with him. With much drama, he'd wrestled the fish into the bucket. "Stay there!" he'd commanded while I giggled. He'd raised his hand as though that gesture would keep the fish in its place. "Look," he then said to me in mock surprise, "the fish is obeying me!"

Mr. Kubo came to see me after a day of loading coal. He had not showered, and his hands and face were blackened from the soot. He apologized for being in his work clothes.

I didn't mind, I was just glad to see him. After yesterday, I thought he'd never come back.

"I know you feel you had a right to take back the watch," he said.

"It is ours, you know that, right?"

"Yes, but the word has spread to Cody and Powell, and rumors have twisted the truth." He showed me a page from our camp's newspaper, the Heart Mountain Sentinel. The paper was creased because he'd had it in his trousers' pocket all day. "There's an article in here that is responding to one in the local Cody paper. It comments on how the locals are calling us Jap thieves."

"We aren't!"

"I thought you should know that Charles and the two other men are no longer able to work at the farm. The Towsons felt it best not to have anyone from camp working there until this matter has been taken care of."

"Why?" But I knew why. We were now not only dirty Japs, but thieves, and no one wanted to be associated with crime. "Someone stole the watch from us!" I shouted.

"That part people don't want to believe."

"But that part is the truth!"

"Nathan, you must realize that you are in a very precarious position. You are Japanese."

"I am American!"

"Not to the people outside of this camp. You are the dirty Jap."

"But it's that court—those men—that . . ." I sputtered, unable to recall what the council of men was known as. I knew these men had either been appointed or elected to ensure civil justice to our camp.

Seeing that I was struggling, Mr. Kubo said, "You have to be patient."

What was he talking about? Patient? Why? I had to know something, so I asked, "How did Mekley get our watch?"

He just shook his head and said that he had to go.

How did Mekley get our watch? No one would touch that subject. It seemed everyone knew how, but no one would tell me.

"I'm no threat to anybody," I said to Mr. Kubo. It was crazy to lock me up when I was already locked up behind barbed wire in this camp.

I was ready for him to argue with me. I wasn't expecting him to say what he did. "I know," he said calmly. "I know you are innocent. Nathan. Just hang in there. We are praying for you."

After he left, I paced the twenty by twenty unit until my legs ached. Then I opened Mama's Bible and read. "Thou wilt keep him in perfect peace whose mind is stayed on thee." She had underlined this verse in pencil. These very words must have been a comfort to her during her last months on earth. I said them over and over until I fell asleep.

Chapter Eighteen

If only I had a radio so that I had some voices to listen to, or a good book to read to take my mind off my isolation. But no one had a radio to spare and, so far, my request for a novel was not granted.

After eating the breakfast that my aunt brought me, I remembered Tom's story he'd written. As I lay on my cot, I began to read it. It was a space and alien story, of course; I had expected no less of my baby brother. But it was so much more, and the last paragraph had me fighting back tears. I chose to read it aloud for two reasons. One was so that I could hear an audible voice, and the other was because I felt this portion of the story needed to be savored.

The mother said she had to go. The spaceship had come to take her away. It was not a regular spaceship but one decorated with angels' wings, and it was as golden as the sun. The mother hugged her children and said, "Don't cry, my little ones. I will see you again one day. Don't cry. When you look up at the moon, always remember that I am beyond the moon and the stars in a place where life is happy and peaceful. There is singing there every day." So the children did not cry. But every night they watched the heavens and knew that their mother was safe and happy. The End.

After six days of being locked up, Lucy came to see me. Underneath her unbuttoned coat, I could see she was wearing a dress with yellow flowers. I asked what kind of flowers they were.

"Sunflowers."

"I thought sunflowers were bigger."

"In San Jose, they are. Maybe these are Wyoming flowers, and they grow smaller because they get less sunlight."

She made me laugh. How good it felt to laugh.

But after a moment, her face grew somber, like when a cloud passed over Heart Mountain and blocked the sun. Suddenly, I felt cold, as though a draft had entered the room.

"I need to tell you something." She sat on the chair.

Shivering, I asked, "What is it?"

Silence filled the room as I waited. Perhaps she would say that she loved me. That she wanted nothing to do with Ken, that she loved me and only me. She would ask if we could dance together and be impressed by all the practicing I had done in the cell.

She looked me over and then said, "I don't want you to be mad at Ken."

"Why? Did he take the watch? Give it to Mekley?" I had wracked my brain to try to come up with some reason the watch was gone and in Mekley's possession. Had Ken given it to him, and if so, why?

She shook her head, fumbled with a few words and then looked lost.

"What did Ken do?"

Standing, she covered her eyes and then knocked on the door, knocked to be let out.

"You know what really happened, don't you?" I shouted.

"I don't."

The guard opened the door and she was gone.

I slammed my fist against the wall. I wished she hadn't bothered to visit me. From now on, I'd let it be known that I wanted nothing to do with the others in the camp.

But by the next morning, I regretted my words. I asked to be let out to use the latrine, and later asked to take a shower. The water was lukewarm, like the food I was being fed, but that didn't matter. I felt much more human and presentable after my shower. I combed my hair with my fingers and put on a fresh shirt.

"Somebody must pay," Aunt Kazuko said when she stopped by. Emi was napping, and Lucy had offered to watch her. "If you are innocent, then Ken is guilty. Don't you see?"

I didn't want to see.

"They said you must stay here for another two weeks."

"Two more weeks!?"

"At least . . ."

I wanted to curse, to yell, to scream. To use all those words that Mama and Papa had said I must never utter.

Instead, I told my aunt to go back to our barracks and take care of Emi. Emi was innocent, too. And she deserved a chance at life.

"You could say you are sorry."

"Sorry?" The word sounds like a number of Japanese words I was unfamiliar with. "What should I be sorry for?"

She snorted. "Apologize any way you can. Apology means you will go free."

I wondered if she realized what she was asking me to do. "The watch belongs to us. Somebody stole it from us, from our barracks. What exactly am I supposed to apologize for?"

She just looked at me and shook her head. "You are too much like your father. And you know where he is."

Certainly she didn't believe that her brother-in-law was a spy as the FBI accused him of being? How could she?

Charles came to see me, and I thought he'd be angry since he had lost his job because of me. But he smiled and said, while he felt sorry for me, he wasn't mad.

"I know Mekley took the watch or got it somehow. I know you only wanted to take it back because it is yours."

Charles' visit boosted my spirits, even though he did bring me homework from my classes. If he believed me, then perhaps others would.

Since no one had bothered to bring me anything of interest to do during my lock up, I began to daydream. Along with thinking about Lucy and wishing I could hear her songs in the night, I thought of the war ending. Certainly, it would. And when it did, we would go back to San Jose, meet up with Papa, and open another fish market. I thought of how much work it had been to help out in the shop with Papa and yet, how rewarding it had been. I wished that I had a notebook that I could write my plans in. Next time someone came to see me, I'd ask for one.

Along with my homework, Charles had brought me two pencils. I was using one of them to write an essay for English when Mr. Kubo came by.

"How much longer do I have to be here?" I asked, as he sat on a chair facing me.

He sighed and then let a stream of air escape from his lips. "The council said we have to show the community that we can't tolerate this kind of behavior. We also have to show the local towns that we believe in reprimanding those who do wrong."

"I think I've served enough time. Can't you do something?"

"I have been an advocate for you, Nathan. I've known you since you were born. Of course, I understand how this all happened. But I think you are stuck here for a few more days."

"A few more days?" My throat felt congested; I coughed. Thinking of Mama's last breath, I thought of lungs filled with congestion, lungs swimming in an ocean of fluid, short raspy breaths and then lungs no longer able to fight, lungs at rest. As I took a deep breath, I became aware of the very act of breathing that I so often neglected to view as a gift.

"Perhaps only a day or more." Mr. Kubo offered me a weak smile.

This wasn't fair. My anger turned from Mama's death to anger at Mekley. Mekley deserved to be in a cell, not me.

"Sometimes we just have to forgive. We can't keep bitterness as our companion for long or we then turn into the very beasts that have taken from us."

I wanted to complain some more, but he stood from the chair and said he had to go. "Oh," he said as he raised his hand to knock on the door to be let out. "The watch . . ."

"Yes?"

I thought he was going to face me and continue talking, but instead he kept his face to the door. As the attending guard opened it from the outside and a cloud of dust blew, Mr. Kubo said, "It was returned to Mekley."

"What?"

"I am afraid that members of the council went to your block leader and asked that the watch be taken from your barracks and handed back to the soldier." He stepped down from my confined room and without looking back, walked away.

I felt my stomach sour. I raised my hand to punch the wall. But, instead, I just sat on the chair as defeat consumed me.

The guard closed the door, and I suppose he locked it. I was too frustrated to hear anything but my own anger.

I lay on my bed and stared at the ceiling, and then I thought, I will just have to do the best I can.

I wasn't sure what that meant or how that looked.

I dreamed of Mama that night. I dreamed of her reading to me a book she and I both loved. A book about a courageous lion who saved all the animals in the jungle. Then I recalled the story of Shadrack, Meshak, and Abednego in the fiery furnace. God protected them, He even came to stand among them.

I scanned the stark walls and shivered in the cold. Would God protect me here in my furnace, which was more like an ice box?

Forgiveness was not as easy as it sounded. My heart was like a huge boulder, like a jagged rock on the coast of California, hammered by waves, refusing to budge.

"Patience," Mr. Kubo had said. Perhaps that applied to forgiveness as well.

Chapter Nineteen

They let me out of jail on the first day of summer. I had been a prisoner for nine long days and eight nights.

As the door to the jail shut behind me, I stood on the stoop with a tomato crate that contained my belongings. Over the days, the items brought to me—the books, the clothes, a notebook, pencils, the stories from Tom—had increased and could not fit into the bag my aunt had first brought. Mr. Kubo realized that, and had provided the crate.

I blinked as the June sun caressed my skin. When you've been set free, the sun feels like it's a gift to you, as though it's celebrating with you in your freedom. Even though the dust blew in my face and made me sneeze, I walked with my chin up toward our barracks. When I looked over my shoulder, the guard who had told me to go was no longer there. No more being guarded in a cell! The thought was invigorating. Laughing, I waltzed into the washroom, set the crate on the floor, and splashed water onto my face.

Continuing to our barracks, several eight by eleven posters taped to the street posts greeted me. One listed the movie schedule for the week. Orson Wells' *Citizen Kane* was showing at the camp theater. Another poster announced that there was a dance that night. I didn't feel up to dancing to Glenn Miller, Count Basie and Bing Crosby or seeing Ken snuggle with Lucy and all the other girls. I was ready for something to celebrate being out of the jail cell, but not a dance. Besides, I had written off girls. I would get close to no one. No one could be trusted. I vowed to live differently now. First I'd find another job. In seven weeks I'd be sixteen and, along with that, my work experience on the farm should make me a good candidate. While no one in Cody or Powell would want to hire me, surely there was work for an experienced worker inside this camp.

I stopped by the rugged fence and breathed in the fresh air. Heart Mountain was clear, just a few wispy clouds draped over her. Had she been a woman, those clouds would have been at her neck, resembling a scarf. She would have smiled at me, shaded her eyes from the sun, and in a soprano voice called out to me, "Nathan, welcome back."

The mountain, a woman? And a talking one at that? *Really, Nathan, your stint in solitary confinement has made you loopy.* Even so, I laughed again. The sound of laughter out in the open sounded much different than it sounded inside closed quarters. Yet the dismal barracks and barbed wire reminded me that I was not really free. This camp still had me as its prisoner.

My steps were not as energetic as I continued toward my block.

"I see that they let you out at last." The voice came from Mrs. Busybody. She held a pitcher and poured water from it onto a cluster of yellow flowers that were secluded in a bed near her front door. "Do you know that families have left us to go off to live with their relatives in Chicago?"

I was about to respond, but the woman was quick to continue talking. "Just think of the joy it would be to get out of this place once and for all! Do you have any relatives in other parts of the country?"

"No," I said. "We are all still in California."

"You mean you *were* all in California. You won't get to live there again."

Never live in San Jose again? Surely, she was mistaken. I gave her a slight nod and made my way down the road as a truck rumbled by, dispensing dust over us.

"You need to think about some place to live once this war ends, you know," she called out after me. "We can't live here in this horrible place forever. One day they will pay for this! One day they will be punished for this atrocity!"

❦

Inside our unit, Aunt Kazuko stood by Emi's crib, a cookie to her lips. "Well, look who is here!" she said, placing the rest of the cookie into her apron pocket. "It's about time! I have been suffering here doing everything."

Emi gurgled when she saw me and reached her chubby arms toward me.

I dropped the crate onto my cot and bent down over her crib to scoop her up. "Did you miss me?"

She stuck a sticky finger in my neck. She smelled of talcum powder and milk and softness—if softness could ever be bottled.

"Put her on the quilt," said my aunt, motioning toward the floor where a patchwork quilt we'd gotten from someone was spread out. "Look what she can do."

No sooner had I sat her down than she scooted over the quilt on her bottom and then clapped her hands. Then she reached out, held onto my arm and, using it to brace herself, pulled up. Her hands were in my hair, pressing down as she steadied herself on her chunky legs. Suddenly, she let go. She was standing in front of me. All by herself.

"Look at her," my aunt said, and laughed. "Just look at her. No worries." She took Emi's hand and coaxed her to take a step. Emi took two steps and then plopped down on her bottom.

The door swung open and Ken entered. "Little bro!" he cried and, as I stood, he embraced me in a bear hug. "You made it back!" From his back pocket he pulled out a bottle of Coca Cola. "Here, drink up!"

I wondered if this was his way of offering the olive branch. I gripped the bottle; it was cold. Where did he get the Coke? A soldier probably bought it for him. Thinking of soldiers made me think of what I had just been through over the past weeks. I shoved the bottle back into his hand. "You can drink it." Turning from them all, I rushed out of our unit.

He called out to me. "I'll be gone soon!"

What did he mean?

"Me and some of the others from San Jose, we're going to fight."

I stopped on the road to hear him add, "We've enlisted. We leave next week for Fort Douglas in Utah."

"Utah?"

A small voice came from behind me. "Wanna see my pet, Nathan?"

In my anger, I'd not seen Tom seated on his rock.

He had a wooden crate, one used to haul vegetables in, and when I stepped toward it, a brown horned toad jumped over the edge.

Tom laughed. "He likes you."

Next to Mekley, the toad was about the ugliest creature I had ever seen. "He's your pet?"

"Yeah. He's Bogart."

"Bogart?" For a kid who liked space stories, I didn't think he would be one to name a toad after an actor.

"Yep. Isn't he cute?"

I shrugged.

"He's fast, too. He jumps around. I even watched him catch a fly. Do you want to pet him? He doesn't bite."

"No, not now." I moved away from Tom and Bogart. Emotions raced through me. I was home, well, back with my family. I was all ready to be different, to live better, to be the best I could. In the cell, I thought it would be easy. But I hadn't expected to be faced with Ken's decision to leave us. Aimlessly, I walked. How could Ken really leave us to fight? How come no one had told me when they'd come to visit me in jail? What else had I missed while locked away?

Look at her, no worries. As I walked across the camp, my aunt's words about Emi came to mind.

And no bitterness in her heart either, I thought. She was still so unspoiled by what the human heart could be—angry, despising, jealous, and worse. Her heart was tender, sweet. Pure, like snow before being trampled on by heavy boots.

I watched people enter the mess hall for dinner. I was going to be able to dine with people instead of having to eat alone, and yet, I didn't care. I wasn't hungry.

❦

Mr. Kubo said he'd found a position for me. I could work in the mess hall preparing our meals.

"Help is needed in the mess hall where our block eats," he said. "You can chop vegetables and wash dishes."

Those in the camp who had had orchards and farms before being evacuated were masters at making the dry wasteland into productive fields. By summer we had our own cucumbers, tomatoes, and squash. On the walk to the mess hall, I often stopped to watch the men and women picking the ripe crops and loading them into truck beds.

Preparing meals kept me indoors, but it also gave me time to think. In my confinement I'd spent hours thinking of what it could be like to be rid of Heart Mountain and return to San Jose to open a shop. Now, as I chopped onions and potatoes, I continued my daydreams. I wanted to make money. My fish shop could be the best in San Jose. I'd find some trusty fishermen and buy fresh fish from them. Papa would help me and, together, father and son, we'd be a team. These thoughts kept me going and kept my mind off of the watch situation, my anger toward Mekley and Ken, and almost kept me from thoughts of Lucy. Almost.

One evening, after cleaning up the kitchen with the other mess hall workers, I headed back to our barracks. The moon was a sliver over Heart Mountain, and the air was as crisp as a newly picked cucumber.

Under the beam of a street light, I saw a figure. As I drew closer to it, I knew exactly who this person was. My stomach knotted; my pulse quickened. I braced myself for the worst.

"Mori!" Mekley, dressed in his uniform, leaned against the side of a warehouse. "How are you, Mori? Glad to be back with us? We missed you." The grin that stretched across his face resembled a look I'd seen from Tom's toad. "Ask me the time, Mori!" With a large gesture, he put his hand into his pocket and pulled out a watch.

I recognized it immediately. I lunged toward him, desperate to take what belonged to me.

He batted at my hand. "Not yours!" As he laughed, I smelled the familiar aroma I associated with this soldier—beer. Dangling the watch by its chain, he said, "Ask me the time, Mori! Go on, ask me."

I stormed past him. Forgiveness? Why? Never! I was no different from Mrs. Busybody, complaining about injustice and unable to do anything about it.

❦

Ken, along with six of his gang from San Jose, did leave us for Fort Douglas. They were talking loudly about how eager they were to serve their county in the army. At first, some of them had protested. Why had they been classified as aliens with a 4C Enemy Alien on their draft cards just a year ago after Pearl Harbor, and were now being recruited to protect our country? Ken protested just because he liked a good fight. But, really, he didn't care about the principle of the matter; he was ready to get out of Heart Mountain and see some action.

Lucy didn't hide her tears.

I refused to cry.

As the weeks passed, Lucy talked of Ken often, wondering aloud what he was doing and when she'd hear from him.

She also talked about her aunt and uncle in Manhattan. I'd never heard her mention these people before, but she was adamant that they wanted her to live with them and that they were wonderful. Her uncle knew a record producer, and he had asked her for a demo tape. She was nervous, but wanted to record herself singing. She thought she'd go to the rec hall some night when the camp was quiet and sing into a tape recorder. "My dad said that the admin office would let me borrow a tape recorder."

When she knocked on our door two days later, she had a letter in her hand. Of course I knew by her smile who it was from. "He's in training at Camp Shelby," she said. She knew my geography stunk, so for my benefit added, "That's in Mississippi."

She laughed as she read a line to me. "He says don't sit under the apple tree with anyone else but me."

Glenn Miller, yeah, leave it up to my brother to borrow a line from a songwriter.

I asked if the letter was censored or opened before she'd picked it up at our camp post office. All of mine from Papa had been opened.

She said, "No, not censored, but sealed. With a kiss."

I felt like throwing up.

The next day, she knocked on our door to ask if I'd listen to a recording of her singing. I went with her to her living quarters where a reel to reel tape player sat on a table. She punched a knob and, after a little static, I heard her recorded voice singing a song about freedom and love and hearts of sadness.

"Do you like it?"

"Did you write it?"

She lowered her head and nodded.

"What's it called?"

"'My Soldier and Me.'"

I supposed she had been thinking about Ken as she wrote it. "Yeah, it's good."

"Really? Do you think I could make a record?"

"Yes."

"Thanks." She smiled and, with a graceful gesture, smoothed back her long hair. "That means a lot coming from you, Nathan."

"Why should it mean a lot coming from me?"

"Ken told me that you not only play the piano but have won several competitions. You never told me that."

"There's a lot you don't know about me," I wanted to say. If you'd quit focusing on your soldier and you, you would be surprised what a swell guy I am. But I would never say that. That would then mean that I had become my older brother.

She continued to talk about her aunt and uncle and what she'd heard about New York.

"How do your parents feel about your leaving them?" I asked.

"They're fine with it. I mean, I am eighteen. I think I'm old enough to make my own decisions, don't you?"

There was a dance that night. The music seemed louder than usual, the air electrified with romance, as boys and girls danced closely to the slow songs. I looked over all the girls and wondered why I only wished to dance with one.

At the start of a slow song—Dinah Shore's "He Wears a Pair of Silver Wings"—I carried through with my plan. I walked over to where she was seated. Ken was hundreds of miles away, so I knew that there would be no competition.

"May I have this dance?" I asked. It was a little formal, but at least it was polite.

Lucy smiled up at me and then stood from her chair.

We stood like that for a few seconds until I realized that I needed to get the two of us out onto the dance floor. I stepped back a couple of steps, not taking my eyes off of her. I was aware that my chest was moving, taken over by a force far greater than anything I had ever felt before. I hoped Lucy couldn't hear my pounding heart.

Still smiling, she followed me. Gently, she rested one hand on my back and reached for my other hand. The top of her head was just a few inches under my eyes. I slipped my arm around her waist and tried not to grip her hand too tightly.

As we slowly swayed to the music, my first thought was how nice this was. I was dancing with Lucy Yokota at last! I tried to breathe normally, tried to move as I had practiced in my jail cell, tried to concentrate on my feet and not tripping. I was dancing with Lucy. Yet as the music continued, it seemed to deliver the truth. And the truth was there, unavoidable. I knew. She was not mine. I could feel her thoughts, falling against my chest, all of them like tiny daggers tormenting me because none of them were about me; they were all about my brother.

The day my mother died was the worst day of my life.

The next worst day was when Lucy left camp. She did not say good-bye.

Days before she left, I was peeling potatoes in the mess hall.

The project director asked if I knew of any good recipes for cucumber chutney. "We have so many cucumbers," he said. "The men and women working in the fields must be using some good fertilizer on those vines. We have more cucumbers than any local farm around here."

I couldn't come up with a recipe. I wasn't sure I even knew what chutney was.

There was a rattle at the back door. I looked up from the mound of potatoes to see Lucy.

I asked the director if I could step outside for a moment. "It won't be long."

He gave me permission and I asked Lucy to follow me behind the mess hall so that we could talk in private.

But she was too eager to follow. "I'm leaving," she said. "I got my papers to leave tomorrow."

"You're doing what?"

"I'm going to Manhattan."

"So soon?"

"I told you that it was going to happen, Nobu."

I felt betrayed, angry, and a dozen other emotions that I could not name. "Don't speak to me again. Ever."

"What?"

"Just go. But don't come back crying. Or defeated. It's a tough world out there." I didn't know why I said that or where I'd heard the expression, but I thought it sounded good.

She bit her lip, then took a little breath. "If that's how you want it to be, Nathan." And without another word, she turned and walked toward the rows of barracks, Heart Mountain before her.

I watched her go.

She didn't look back.

The next day she was gone.

Ken had left to go fight for our country. Papa had been taken from us as had Mama. Aunt Kazuko said we could go elsewhere if we had an elsewhere to go. "We stay here at Heart Mountain," she said as she nibbled on a raisin cookie. "We stay because we have no one to take us in, and I know I can't sing to make a career."

It wasn't supposed to be this way. With Ken gone, Lucy was supposed to be interested in me. She was supposed to want to sit under the moon with me beside her.

That night, as the moon refused to slip out from behind the clouds, Tom and I went to the washroom to brush our teeth and fill a bucket with water.

As he squeezed toothpaste onto the bristles of his toothbrush, Tom said, "I am glad you are still here, Nathan."

What did he think? A spaceship would come whisk me away with the evening wind?

I should be so lucky.

Chapter Twenty

On nights when I wasn't scheduled to work in the mess hall, I got to sit with the others on our block and eat with my family and friends. Otherwise, I usually had to wait till after everyone was served to eat my dinner.

This particular night was still warm; breezes blew into the mess hall windows while we ate. Emi sat next to my aunt in a regular chair. Tom and I sat across from them. Charles, his parents, and his two sisters—twins with identical haircuts and rosy cheeks like Charles'—joined us. Aunt Kazuko was saying how nice it was that Emi could sit at the table, albeit on a thick dictionary, by herself. This freed up my aunt from having to hold her in her lap during mealtimes.

It was a September night, but not just an ordinary one. It was an anniversary; it had been a year since we'd arrived in camp. I was thinking about the long train ride we had taken from Santa Anita to Wyoming and how Mama had felt sick for the majority of the ride. We had tried to make her comfortable and even rubbed her swollen feet. I had wished that she wasn't pregnant, that she could be like the rest of us, not encumbered by her shortness of breath and bouts of weakness. If only I had gotten her more water when she complained of thirst, I thought. If only I had given her a pillow or ginger root or—

"Mekley's gone," a boy from a nearby table said through a mouthful of carrots.

I dismissed my thoughts and paid attention.

"He's not here anymore," said another boy at the adjacent table where he sat with his parents and siblings. "He's gone. Make sure that Nathan knows."

Charles poked me. "Did you hear? Mekley's gone."

No wonder I hadn't seen him in a while. "Maybe he got fired?" I said. And, oh, I was so guilty of hoping that this was the case.

"Can the army fire you?" asked Tom.

I didn't want to gloat. But maybe the truth had caught up to him.

113

Perhaps the army realized he was a thief and had discharged him. I ate my carrots, chicken, and rice with a sense that justice had been done.

"What happened to Mekley?" I leaned over the table and looked at Charles.

Charles seemed to know everything. Perhaps it was because he wore glasses. "Mekley was transferred overseas," he said.

"Really? Are you sure?"

"Yep, he's now fighting the real Japs. You should be happy."

Overcome with horror I said, "Don't use that word."

"Happy?" Charles looked confused.

"No, that other one."

"What word?"

"You know." I couldn't repeat it. Saying it was as bad as breaking one of the Ten Commandments and taking the Lord's name in vain. "Just don't. They are Japanese."

"But they are Japs. They're our enemies."

Anger boiled through my veins. "No, they are where we are from."

"I'm not from Japan. I've never even been there."

"Our ancestors, Charles. Some of us still have family over there."

"But we aren't *them*."

I let it go. My aunt once told me that I needed to let some things go. Mr. Kubo told me that bitterness is one of the worst emotions. I ate the rest of my dinner in silence.

As I sat on the steps in front of our barracks that night under a crescent moon, the toad in the crate next to my feet, I was glad that Mekley was gone. He was the only one that I was glad to be rid of. I would never have to see his smirking face again.

On weekends, the men sat around playing chess and listening to the radio. They smoked cigarettes sent to them from friends. They talked and argued. But mostly, they hoped that this wretched war would end.

I did, too. We were nearing our third year at Heart Mountain and I was beginning to believe that this was going to be our permanent home.

"The war is going to end soon," said Mr. Kubo as he read our Heart Mountain newspaper, the *Sentinel*. "The editorial here by Fukuyama-san says he feels it will be only a matter of months."

"How does he know?" I asked, trying to avoid eye contact with the paper. Nearly two years ago, Mr. Fukuyama had written a nonflattering piece about me and the watch, and since then the camp paper gave me indigestion.

"He's a history buff," said Mr. Kubo. "Have you seen his library of books? Since he's been here, he's written a manuscript on the Battle at Gettysburg and a biography on Robert E. Lee."

I didn't care about Mr. Fukuyama's accomplishments. "Will we be allowed to return to California?" I asked.

He paused, looked up from the paper and gave me a pensive look. "I think so."

"Will you return?"

"I might go east."

And then it happened. Three months later, it was announced that the United States had bombed Hiroshima. That threw me into a panic, and I didn't want to eat for a few days. I feared for my aunts, uncles and cousins—all on Papa's side. A few had come over to California with him and his parents in 1919, and I knew that his three sisters had later returned to Hiroshima to get married. Had Papa heard the news? Who was comforting him as he worried about his kin?

"Wow, an atomic bomb. Wonder how they got it inside the plane?" Tom pondered aloud as he sat on his rock.

"It destroyed the city," I said. "Innocent people died, people like you and me."

But Tom didn't let the weight of my words make him remorseful. With a smile, he grabbed his pen and started to scribble in his notebook. Now, at age thirteen, his stories were far superior to those he had written when we first arrived in Wyoming, but they were still about aliens.

Three days later, Nagasaki was bombed and then we heard the inevitable news: Japan had surrendered.

There was a different feel to the camp then. Had our nearby mountain been a soldier, he would have saluted. A few puffs of clouds accumulated over the mountain's flat peak, clouds that, when you used your imagination, looked like they could be victory confetti.

I left Tom to his creations and walked down our block of barracks to where men were engaged in chess.

"The war is over, but we will never be the same," said Mr. Kubo as he moved a knight across the chess board. He and Lucy's father were in the midst of a game, tea cups at their elbows.

"We have lost so much," said Mr. Yokota, gripping the edge of the table so that his tea cup rattled. In a voice that sounded more like it belonged to a child than to a grown man, he said, "We have lost too much."

The next big announcement was that we were free to leave camp. All of us. We could head back to California, pick up the pieces, make a living, and a life.

"Where are you going?" I asked Mr. Kubo when I found him seated outside his unit's door on the porch he had made. Today he was seated in one of the two chairs he'd carved, one was for his wife, and one was for him.

"We plan to go out east."

"East?"

"Yes." He lit his pipe. "I have a friend in Durham, North Carolina."

"Is that near New York?"

He laughed. "South. Way south."

Perhaps my geography still wasn't the best. My teachers had let me know over the years that I needed to spend more time with world maps.

"Who is your friend?"

"His name is Shorty Olson. He works at Lucky Strikes."

"He makes cigarettes?" I'd never thought about actual factories that produced those items Papa liked to smoke after his bath on a Saturday night.

"Yes, he does. Once I can convince Mrs. Kubo to head east with me, we are going, Nathan."

"I wish you both the best. I hope your wife will like North Carolina."

"Thank you. How about you?"

I had had lots of time to think about the future when I was in jail. But I reminded myself that I trusted no one now. "Oh, yes, I have some plans." When Mr. Kubo looked at me with an apprehensive expression, I said, "When we get back to San Jose, I think Aunt Kazuko should give English lessons."

I was glad to see Mr. Kubo laugh. I was afraid he might think I was being rude or unkind, but I guess he could see through my teasing and knew my heart. My aunt was one of the best advocates I had. If I weren't careful I just might let on that, deep down, I adored her.

Well, almost.

PART II

San Jose, California

Chapter Twenty-one

Six months after our return, San Jose was balmy, full of sunshine, and well-manicured flower gardens. Yet it was not the same hometown that we'd left three years ago. It was true when they said that war changes people and places. It was true that life never fully gets back to the way it once was.

Papa's old fish market he'd rented was now a Chinese restaurant called Golden Pagoda, and a neon sign with the "G" burned out flashed against the glass in the window—olden Pagoda. Once the interior held bass, mackerel, and other catches from the Bay of San Francisco. Now it belonged to a Chinese woman who had married an Italian. Hadn't we been at war with the Italians, too? Yet it seemed either people forgot, didn't care, or had decided that the Italians here in this country were fine folk after all.

This was not the case for us. If you walked further south down Eleventh Street, the windows in the shops held signs that read: No Japs. No work for Japs! No Japs Wanted! Along with the written words, verbal words of hatred were spoken in many of the streets. It wasn't just the painted slogans on the sides of buildings and boarded up houses—homes once occupied by *Issei*— it was the attitudes and actions of people that made me queasy.

We were not the enemy, and yet we looked like the enemy.

True, this was not the San Jose from years ago when I'd been a boy in school. People looked at me differently now. I overheard conversations while I waited in local banks to see about getting a loan to start our new venture.

"I see the Japs are back."

"I wish those slanted-eyed yellow bellies would leave again."

On my way to the bakery to get a chocolate éclair for Aunt Kazuko and a few cookies for Emi and Tom, I saw a familiar face. "Anna," I called out to a girl who was looking into a clothing shop's glass showcase.

Turning toward me, she smiled.

Yet the closer I got to her, the more confused she looked. Her smile disappeared as quickly as it had appeared.

"How have you been?" I faced her on the sidewalk.

"All right." Nervously, she backed away from me.

"Are you okay? How have you been?" Perhaps she had lost someone in the war. I knew that hundreds of families had been given the horrible news that one of their sons had died in combat. Even I had feared that we would get that telegram from Western Union announcing the worst about Ken.

When Anna's look of silent perplexity continued, I wondered if it was because she'd forgotten who I was. To help her out, I said, "I'm Nathan. Nathan Mori, remember?"

"I have to hurry."

"Can't dilly-dally, huh?" I smiled at my own choice of words. Aunt Kazuko seemed to have an effect on me no matter where I went.

"I have to go."

I stood on the corner of East Taylor and Eleventh, unable to move. I thought of how I'd known Anna all through elementary school and middle school. We had sat together at lunch time. Once she shared half of her ham sandwich and a blueberry tart with me when I had forgotten my lunch and had no money to purchase food at the cafeteria. She'd played the flute in the band and I'd told her that she played well, was talented. I complimented her on being friendly, amazed at how everybody liked her and how nice that must feel.

Moments ago she hadn't answered my questions. She'd just wanted to get away from me. The way she'd looked at me was as though my face were covered in manure.

Anger seeped through my veins as I picked up my pace. I took a left on Taylor and paused at the butcher's shop. I peered into the window to get a look at my face. There was nothing on it—no stain, no crumbs from toast around my mouth. I was an American, American born. In camp, we had pledged allegiance to one flag, and to one flag only.

I thought of Mr. Kubo who said that he was going east. Was life better for Americans who had black hair and dark eyes in the eastern part of the country?

In a dress shop, next to a "Welcome Home Soldiers" sign, was a poster board with the words to the popular song: "Don't sit under the apple tree with anyone else but me till I come marching home."

Now those words were painful to read, taking me back to a girl with a voice I had not heard for over two years. I stood on the side of the street as a few cars whizzed past and I wished for yesterday.

When I returned to our tiny apartment near Columbus Park, I was empty-handed.

"What?" said my aunt as she raised her head from a paperback with a cover of a woman gazing at a man. She took off her reading glasses, and cried, "Where are the chocolate sweets?"

"Sorry," I mumbled.

"You get our hopes up and you crush. You just crush." She hit the book against her chair.

I had no response for her. I just kept silent.

We had lived in a house in Japantown on Seventh Street and now someone else lived in it. Some other family—Caucasian—with a white poodle and two children with bicycles. Each time I walked past that tan-colored home with the palm tree in the front lawn, it was as though my heart had been removed from my body and hung out to drip dry.

Walking near it brought the past back in full swing. In April of 1942 we had been told to pack up our belongings and place them in the middle of the living room. They would be sent to us, depending on where we were assigned to go. Our refrigerator, washing machine, toaster, and blender had to be sold immediately, and we got only half of what they were worth.

"What is this Executive Order 9066?" my aunt had asked, as she scurried around the kitchen, tossing containers of green tea and other personal items into a box. "Why do they say all people of Japanese ancestry must leave the west coast? We have done nothing." We were told to pack one suitcase each. I thought of Papa who months earlier had not been allowed to pack a thing. Had it been that moment when men who claimed to be FBI carted him off that he had entered his dismal state?

Those days of evacuation played across my mind like a movie stuck in a reel of disbelief. Had we really been away this long, first in an assembly center, and then years inside an internment camp? Did anybody care what we had been through? Was anyone going to help us?

I thought of how Mama had played "Rocks of Ages" that night before we had to take the train to the Santa Anita assembly center. She'd asked me to join her and together we sat, trying to play for Tom and Ken, each of us trying to be brave. She said her baby inside her kicked a few times as we played. She told me that meant we had played well.

The next day, neighbors said they'd take care of the piano for us. Other belongings were placed in the middle of our living room floor, and we were told that a truck would pick them up and get them to us. The day we left our home, the piano was still in the living room, and I knew that Mama was trying to get us to believe that she was not worried about it or about what would happen to us. She pasted on her brave face, the same one she had worn ever since Papa had been forced to leave us.

As I looked at her, all I could think of were the words to "Rock of Ages." The lines kept running through my mind over and over as though I was trying to gain strength from their meaning. *Nothing in my hand I bring. Simply to Thy cross I cling. Helpless, look to Thee for grace.*

Helpless! That had been us. And now? We were free, but the helplessness prevailed.

On my walks, I wanted to find a place to rent for a shop. But I also wanted to find our piano. On two occasions I'd gone to our old house and peered inside the windows until the poodle yipped so loudly that I was afraid I'd be arrested for causing a disturbance. When I'd inquired about the neighbors, the ones who were going to care for our piano, I was told that they'd moved to San Francisco.

I continued to walk down East Taylor Street, made a right onto Seventh Street and a left onto Empire Street. It was quite clear that while we'd been nestled away in Wyoming, life had gone on here in San Jose. We were just a nuisance. We were not wanted.

A shop that sold men's clothing got my attention, and I slowed to window shop. A mannequin in a black fedora, just like Papa used to wear, caught my eye. If he were here, I'd buy it for him. Afterward we'd find a coffee shop and sit and talk about the war and laugh at as many jokes as we knew the punch lines for.

Weary, I decided to go home. *Home*, the word sounded strange as I repeated it in my head. It was as though home was not an English word, as though it was a word I no longer knew the meaning of. But for now it was a tiny apartment on the second floor, a place that the landlord said we could rent as long as we didn't do anything *illegal*.

"Are you all *Issei*?" the landlord asked the day we inquired about the apartment. He pronounced the word with a strong emphasis on the last two syllables, dragging them out so that they sounded like *say-eeeee*.

"We were born here," I said. "We're Americans."

Frowning, he looked the four of us over.

I hoped that he couldn't tell that we'd been sleeping on the floor of a Sunday school room at our old church, because upon our return to San Jose, finding a place to rent had been nearly impossible. I hoped he could tell that we were clean, even though our bathing took place in the church's restrooms. I stood tall and gave my best smile.

Pointing at Tom's right leg, the man said, "I see you got one of those."

Tom's trouser legs were short, shorter than they should be, and his brace showed.

I felt my heart sink. The landlord was going to refuse us a place to live, not only because we were Japanese, but because Tom was a polio victim. I wanted to say something—anything to change the outcome of this conversation. But before I could speak, Tom said, "Our former president and I have polio in common, sir."

The man nodded. "Not only you and FDR, but my daughter, also. She's about your age."

"I wish her the best," said Tom with sincerity.

Emi peeked out from behind Aunt Kazuko and took her thumb out of her mouth. "I wish her the very best," she said.

And then without further ado, the man handed me a key. "You pay me every third of the month, all right? Pay me. Not my wife. She'll spend the money on a new dress or hat."

We moved in with our sparse belongings; we had no furniture until later when we were given beds, chairs, a sofa, and other furnishings. We slept on the floor during the first nights, just as we had slept in the church, but something about sleeping on our own floor felt better than sleeping on a floor that did not belong to us.

The apartment was tiny, but it was ours. The front door led into a narrow hallway and off of that were two bedrooms and a bathroom to the right, and the living room and kitchen to the left. Tom and I shared a bedroom and Emi and my aunt squeezed into another.

"When Papa comes back," I said, "Where will he sleep?"

But Aunt Kazuko pulled me aside, away from my siblings. "We don't worry about that now. We just be grateful. We learn the art of grateful."

We wrote to Papa to tell him where we were. Ever since the war ended, we weren't sure where he'd gone, but I addressed the letter to Lake Tule, as it was the only address we had for him. I prayed that someone there would make sure he got it, even if it meant forwarding it to him.

I pictured Papa finding us, running into our arms as he had in all my dreams. "Nobu," he'd say, "You did a good job taking care of everyone while I was away. I'm proud of you." Then he'd laugh in his jovial way, even offer me a cigarette because I was now a man. Together, we'd head out to look for a place to rent for a new fish market.

When I entered our apartment that afternoon after my walk, I sensed that something was different. Sure enough, before I could remove my shoes, I heard Tom call out to me from the living room. "Nathan! You're back!" In a softer voice, yet still equally excited, he said, "Nathan's home!" as though he was talking to someone in the other room. Hobbling into the hallway, he said, "Look who's here!"

I took two steps to where he was leading me, and there in the living room on the couch sat a man with a grey fedora.

My feet couldn't carry me to him fast enough. With tears welling in my eyes, I fell into the arms of Papa, knocking the hat from his head onto the floor. At first, I couldn't say anything, but then I got my voice back. "You're here! You're really here. I can't believe it!"

He nodded and reached for my hand. His grip was weak, but I didn't care; my papa was back with us!

"When did you get here? Where have you been? Did you get our letters?"

Suddenly, I realized he had not said a word. One tear trickled down his cheek.

"Let's have some *ocha* (green tea)," said my aunt. She stood and headed toward the kitchen. "Tom, you can help me."

Reluctant to leave, Tom lingered.

"Tom," Aunt Kazuko called, urgency in her voice.

I knew he'd better hurry before Papa scolded him.

But the living room was silent. There was no scolding.

Papa was staring over our heads out the window. His face was solemn, his mouth taut, the tear was gone. And right then and there, I knew something else was gone as well. He was not the Papa from before the war. He might have looked like the old Papa, but he certainly wasn't acting like him.

Of course, I thought. *It's because Mama is dead.*

When my aunt called out for Tom's help, I jumped up and rushed to the kitchen. Let Tom stay with Papa, I would get the tea ready with my aunt.

Inside the kitchen, my aunt had not even prepared anything for the tea. Disgusted with her for sitting on the stool by the refrigerator, I lifted the empty kettle and ran water into it from the faucet as my aunt wiped her eyes with a handkerchief.

"I'll go get Emi," I said, remembering that when I'd set out today she was next door at the Kondo's.

Emi would bring a smile to Papa's face.

My aunt touched my arm. "No. Nobu, not yet."

"Why not?"

"Can't you see he is confused?"

"What? Why?"

She took a deep breath and exhaled with her head toward the ceiling, the leaky ceiling. "War does that to some."

Yes, I knew this. War made some soldiers mean, like Mekley. War had brought bitterness to the hearts of so many I knew at Heart Mountain. Why would Papa be exempt?

"The camp where he was . . . it was worse."

"Worse." I repeated the word as I tried to think of how a camp could be worse. I thought of my jail cell and how I'd thought that I'd go crazy. Perhaps that was what Papa had experienced.

Aunt Kazuko wiped her eyes again and put the handkerchief into her apron pocket. "Help me," she said. Her voice was soft, soft like when she talked with Emi.

Part of me wanted to collapse in her arms, let my own tears flow; the other part of me knew I could not let myself have that luxury.

Turning from her to the stove, I placed the kettle on a burner and turned the knob under it, watching for a gas flame. "Get the tea canister," I said.

She opened the cupboard and removed the light rose canister, the one we stored green tea in.

Strangeness, like a blanket, pulled over me. I thought that this was the first time she had followed a command I had given. As I reached for saucers and cups from inside the cabinet, I wondered what this meant.

Life was changing.

Again.

Chapter Twenty-two

Papa said that he didn't need a bed. He would sleep on the couch. "No, you can have my bed," I insisted. We had four, a twin bed for each of us, but there was no way I was going to let Papa spend his nights on the couch. It was a lumpy couch with rickety arms. Aunt Kazuko was active again at Second Street, our old church, and some of the members had donated furniture to us.

Papa stared out the living room window and said, "I can sleep here."

"You can have the other bed in the room with Tom," I said. It was my bed, but I figured that if I didn't call it mine, he might agree to sleep in it.

Papa shook his head. He lifted a hand and gave the couch a light tap. "Fine here."

My aunt told me not to fight him; that sometimes you just had to let people do what they needed to do. That evening she scurried about, got a set of sheets, a quilt, and a pillow, and made the couch to look like a bed.

"Thank you, Kazuko," Papa said in such a way that his voice didn't even sound like the voice I remembered. "Thank you."

While the others kissed him good-night, I sat in the living room on a kitchen chair, another piece of donated furniture.

Papa stripped down to his underwear and got under the top sheet. He lay flat on his back, arms at his sides.

"Do you need anything?" I asked.

"No. I am fine."

I watched him fidget for a few minutes. "What was it like at Lake Tule?" I asked.

"Dark."

"Did you get enough to eat?" He looked thin.

"It was food."

"Did you get our letters? Did you hear that Ken enlisted?"

He waited before replying. I thought that perhaps he was gathering his thoughts. But all he said was, "Darkness, so much of it."

"Did you not have lights?"

He lay still, then turned to his side. "Man cannot understand the plight of another."

I gave up after that; perhaps he was too tired to carry on a conversation.

When he coughed, I prayed that he didn't have pneumonia. At last, I heard a snore from his lips; groggy, I left for my own bed.

Once in my room behind the closed door, removed from Papa, I gave myself permission to think. What had happened to him? Perhaps someone else had come and taken over his body.

Tom slept in the bed adjacent to mine, and I envied him for being able to sleep. I thought of all the dreams I'd had of Papa, all the pictures I'd painted in my mind of our reunion. Tonight had been nothing like I had imagined. Where was that lively, strong, and healthy man? I slipped under the covers. I felt I had found him, but only to lose him again.

I was nearly asleep when I heard screams. The piercing sound woke us and within seconds, we were all in the living room.

Papa was shaking, his face contorted with agony. Aunt Kazuko switched on the overhead light. She stood back from him; I expected her to be rushing about to see what was wrong.

Tom spoke first. "What happened? Are you all right? Are you sick?"

Emi repeated, "Are you sick? Are you sick?"

Papa fumbled with his shirt that was in a heap on the floor. He pulled out a pack of cigarettes and a matchbox from the breast pocket. We watched as he lit a cigarette. "I am fine," he said. "Go on back to sleep."

We exchanged worried looks and then followed his instructions.

The next day I expected someone to ask Papa about his screams from what had possibly been a nightmare, but no one spoke of it. Everyone acted like nothing had happened.

After breakfast, Aunt Kazuko put on some lipstick, combed her hair, and went off to work.

For a month, she'd been employed by a *wealthy* family. They paid her five dollars a week to clean their home and do their laundry. She said it wasn't bad work, and sometimes they even gave her chocolate cookies which she managed to eat most of during the cab ride home.

When Aunt Kazuko left, I cleared off the kitchen table and washed the dishes while Tom dried. He headed for school, his book bag lopsided against his back.

Papa sat hunched over on the couch and watched Emi play with her doll. She wrapped the doll in a blanket, pretended to feed it some carrots and then placed it in Papa's hands. He held it for a moment and then returned it to her. As I watched him, I noted how far away he seemed, even though he was in the same room. It was as though he didn't really see us, as though he was looking right through us.

Emi didn't seem to mind that her father had few words for her. She cuddled her doll, smoothed out its matted blond hair, gave it a kiss, and then sang a few lines of "Away in a Manger." It was not Christmas time at all, but I figured she had learned the art of singing Christmas songs off-season from Tom.

Suddenly, she paused from her song, looked up, and said, "Papa."

I watched to see if Papa would give in to emotion, but he only patted her head and then dozed, his head heavy on the pillow.

Chapter Twenty-three

Walking became my respite here just as it had been at camp. Since I was no longer confined to a barbed wire existence, I took advantage of freedom. Walking not only gave me exercise, it also cleared my mind. It provided me with a chance to get my thoughts off my struggles and seek God. I wanted to focus on Him, on who He was, but that was not always easy to do when there was so much else vying for my attention.

"God, where are you?" I cried. I paced down Empire Street. "I trusted you to help us. Now Papa is back and not able to do anything." And since I was complaining, I thought of all the other things that were causing me worry. "God," I said, "What about Ken? What is he doing, and why won't he come home?" The war was over and other people's older brothers had returned to their families. That's what soldiers were supposed to do.

To make matters worse, we were running out of money. All the money I'd saved in camp seemed to disappear faster than it had in Wyoming. Every third day of the month, our landlord knocked on our door to collect the rent. I hated having to pinch together the twenty-two dollars he expected us to pay for a flat that had a leaky ceiling in the kitchen. Aunt Kazuko's money from her job, plus the money we had stashed away from the measly amounts we'd been given when we had to sell our furniture and kitchen appliances back in 1942, barely covered our weekly expenses.

"God, you know our needs." And with that I started to list them. We needed a bigger place to rent. We needed more employment. I'd been looking for a place for a new business. One place on West Saint James had seemed ideal; the Caucasian landlord took one look at me and said he had just signed a lease to rent it to another tenant. But when I walked past the storefront three weeks later, it was not occupied; the For Rent sign still hung in the window. Looking into the sky, I begged, "Help me. Help us."

We were cramped; we were used to being cramped. But I didn't want to have to live as we had at Heart Mountain. I wanted space.

One evening at the end of September, Aunt Kazuko and I spread our money out on the kitchen table. Tom helped us count it while Papa stared out the window, and Emi ate a bowl of grapes.

"We have all of seventy-nine dollars and twenty-nine cents," I said.

"I get paid Friday," said Aunt Kazuko. "I also hear at church that there is a house that the landlord will rent to Japanese." Lately it seemed that my aunt was hearing a lot of things at church. She kept encouraging me to attend more frequently with her, Tom, and Emi, but I said I had things to do. Most of the time, *my things to do* were stretching out my legs and enjoying the quiet of an apartment that was empty except for me while Papa slept and the others sang hymns.

"Do you know how much this house will cost?" I asked.

"It's forty-two dollars each month. That includes everything. Water, gas, electric."

I looked at the money on the table—all those crumpled bills my aunt kept smoothing out as though ironing them with her palm would make them magically morph into more. For a second, I was tempted to take the money to the landlord and beg him to let us rent the house my aunt mentioned. What had I become? I had no idea what this house looked like. It could leak worse than this apartment.

"Have you seen the house?" I asked.

"No, but it has four bedrooms," said my aunt.

"Four," said Tom, a dreamy look to his face. "Four."

"They rent to Japanese," my aunt reassured me, when I wasn't sure whether I should trust her. "As long as there is an American citizen in family. That's what Mrs. Jericho says."

"Mrs. who?"

"Jericho."

"As in Joshua fought the battle of Jericho?"

"You know her?" My aunt looked surprised. "You met her?"

"No, why?"

"I thought you know her. She has son named Joshua."

I laughed, Tom laughed, and Emi said, "I need a cookie." We all sat around the table and ate from a tin of raisin cookies. Papa even entered the kitchen and ate one.

"We could be at this house for Christmas," said my aunt. "We could get a tree with a string of lights."

We were really going to move. And this time, we weren't being forced out of our home with regret. We were all glad to be rid of the apartment.

Thankfully, friends of my aunt let us use an old Ford truck to haul our belongings to the new house. Tom, Papa, and I lifted the four twin beds onto the truck, as well as the lumpy couch, kitchen table, and chairs.

The new house had a large porch with two rocking chairs that made me nostalgic for Mr. Kubo. I recalled how he'd built matching chairs for his makeshift porch at camp, and the thought of him made me miss the strong presence he had been in my life. Inside was drafty with wooden floors that echoed when you walked. But it had space. And four bedrooms! That meant I got my own. My own bedroom! Just putting those three words together was sweeter than a slice of apple pie. Emi and Tom were excited to have their own rooms, and our aunt said having a bedroom to herself was *zeitaku,* which she translated as *a luxury.*

And Papa, Papa planted himself on the couch and said it was fine.

Someone from the church brought over a box filled with three kinds of cereal, a loaf of Wonder bread, bologna, mayonnaise, milk, Granny Smith apples, butter, and a box of chocolate cookies. We feasted on bologna sandwiches, apples, and chocolate cookies the first night in our new home.

We had cutlery and plates, a few glasses, and cups for tea, but we realized that in a larger house it was much more evident that we had less than we thought we had. Our belongings were sparse.

"Once we had lots of dishes, and linens and blankets and even antiques from Japan," my aunt recalled. "But where did all that go? They told us to put our items in boxes and that they would ship them to us." She said no more after that.

The day after we moved, I took a trip down to the pawn shop to look for items we needed.

The owner, Mr. Rizzardi, was an immigrant from Italy and spoke with his hands. Each time I inquired about an item, he told me the price by lifting his hands and wiggling his fingers. It was comical, but I tried to hold my laughter. I didn't want to offend him, and hoped he would cut me a break and give me some poor man discounts.

In the corner, I saw a wooden bed, the headboard carved from red oak. Immediately I thought of how nice the bed would be for Papa. I tried to bargain with Mr. Rizzardi. "Five? I'll give you five."

"Five? You joking with me?" He raised his hands. "No, no. That bed is not going anywhere for less than fifteen."

Papa probably wouldn't sleep in a bed anyway, I thought, even if I told him I'd bought it for him. I moved from the bed and walked around the shop. I saw bookcases, armchairs, and even a red wagon. But what caught my eye was in a corner. Inside a box was a pink teapot. Along with the pot were matching plates, eight of them. I looked one over and checked for cracks or chips. "How much?"

"Twenty cents."

"Ten."

He started to raise his hands and instead, slapped them both against the glass showcase that held jewelry and watches. "You got a deal!"

In my pocket I found a dime and paid for the dishes. Aunt Kazuko would be excited to have a new teapot to make her tea in, and eight plates would be perfect to set our kitchen table with. The whole walk home I felt happy.

When I stepped onto our porch, Aunt Kazuko greeted me. She must have been waiting, seated on a rocking chair. "You never believe this," she said.

"What?"

Leading me into the living room, she giggled.

And there it was, a piece of our past—Mama's piano! The box of dishes almost slipped from my hands. I handed it to my aunt and then just stood there, staring. Certain that I was dreaming, I looked for other signs, something to tell me that I was not. Quickly, I went over to the 1927 Gulbransen fifty-five-inch upright, but before getting to it, I tripped on one of Emi's building blocks and jarred my ankle. The pain helped me know that I was fully awake, and that this piano was actually here before me.

Emi and Tom entered the room, singing in unison that we had a piano. Tom sometimes forgot that he was a teenager around four-year-old Emi. Instead of acting older, he played along with her as though he were a pre-schooler.

Aunt Kazuko said, "Henderson brought it over. He called and said, 'I have your piano.'"

"Who is Henderson?" I touched the walnut top, the matching bench, opened the seat, and felt a lump fill my chest as I saw the music sheets still nestled inside. I pulled one out: "Jesus Loves Me." Mama had taught me how to play that. She hadn't let me outside for the neighborhood baseball game until I'd gotten it perfect.

My aunt repeated my question. "Who is Henderson? Who is Henderson? Our old neighbors. Henderson O'Farley worked at the canning company. Don't you remember nothing?"

Ah, yes, the O'Farley family. Good folk who had come to America to escape some sort of family feud in Ireland.

"They kept our piano for us. When they moved to San Francisco in 1943 to work at Henderson's brother's restaurant, they asked for somebody else to keep piano for us."

"And who did?"

"They stored it here, at the canning company. Can you believe it?"

"No."

"Today Henderson was in town visiting sister and had the piano put on a truck to bring to us. And also, boxes. My things I put in boxes when we had to go to Santa Anita!" She'd already opened one of the boxes and pulled out a few books. Now she shoved a grayish photo album into my hands. "This was what I put in a box when they said to pack up all our things. I put it on the piano bench and Henderson kept it for me. Can you believe it?"

"No," I said, which seemed to be all I was capable of saying today.

"Sure enough, there was my money still inside the photo album. Just like I always told you."

My attention turned from the piano. "Money? How much?"

She glistened like a Christmas tree ornament. "Sixty dollars."

"That's great."

"I know. I am so happy. I thank God over and over and then I must call Mrs. Jericho to tell her that was answer to prayer."

I smiled as my aunt continued to beam at us all. *Mama*, I almost said aloud. *We are reunited with your piano.* I bent over to check the front right leg of the bench and sure enough, there was that large scratch on it. That scratch was what made us able to afford it. Papa said afterward, "It is amazing how one little blemish can make ordinary folk think that an item must be discarded."

"Well," said my aunt. "Don't just stare. It won't bite you. Play."

Could I play? What should I play?

"What can you play for us?" Tom asked, as though reading my mind.

135

Hesitantly, I sat on the bench and opened the lid to display those ivory and black keys. I breathed in nostalgia, a summer breeze, the feeling of being ten and eleven years old, even the aroma of hot dogs grilling on a Sunday afternoon.

"Look at it," said Tom. "It's a real piano."

He and Emi crowded around my elbows, one on each side.

"Let him play. Now shoo," said my aunt. "Come into the kitchen with me to help me with dinner."

They protested, pleaded to stay, but soon knew that listening to their aunt was the best decision. They followed her into the kitchen, leaving me alone in the room.

Now it was just me and the piano.

I lifted my right hand and let my fingers rest against the middle C. Pressing it, the sound that came out was hollow. I hit it again. It was hopeless. It was as though my fingers would not bend to the keys. My joints felt stiff. After a moment, I spread my fingers over the keys and let the weight of them heave against the ivories.

"What is that noise?" Aunt Kazuko rushed into the living room, her hands holding a dish towel.

I looked up. "I think I'll go for a walk," I said.

"You need tea?"

No, no, I don't need tea. I shook my head.

"You need a good woman."

"What?"

"You need love, sharing an ice cream float with two straws, a movie at the theater, a ride in a convertible. Top down."

"You've been reading too many of those paperback romances."

She snorted. "At least I know what to do. You—you just sit and dream. Too much dreaming is no good. You have to start living."

Chapter Twenty-four

I t was easier to dream than it was to face reality.
Reality reminded me that we needed money. When we first arrived back in San Jose, I had my savings from working at the camp. My aunt had been smart to hide money in a photo album. But all of our money was running out. I needed to find work. My dream of owning our fish shop again seemed dismal to me now. I didn't know enough about fish to hold a business based on buying and selling them. Back in jail, I had dreamed about Papa helping me, but that was back before I knew what accusations, confinement, and losing a spouse could do to a man's heart.

On one of my walks I went down East Empire Street to see a shop that was for rent. SHOP FOR LEASE the bold letters read from a thick piece of plywood that was propped up inside against the showcase window. Seeing that there were no derogatory words against my race on that sign or any in the window, I wrote down the phone number that was also printed on the sign.

My pencil and pad of paper were often stuffed into my back pants pocket. An English teacher I once had, repeatedly told our class to always carry pen and paper because one never knew when inspiration might strike. "Be ready," she'd said. "Never expect your memory to recall a great thought. Always rely on writing it down. That way it is saved forever."

Within seconds of copying the number, I realized I was not alone on the sidewalk.

"Evening." A middle-aged man in a hat and cardigan greeted me.

"Good evening."

"It would make a fine place to have a store."

"Do you know how much it is to rent?" I asked, as I peered in the window and saw a bare floor, a counter, tables, and a few empty crates.

He eyed me a few times. Gruffly, he said, "Sixty a month."

Taking in a breath of air, I ran the number over in my mind. The shop was nothing special; how could he get away with asking sixty? The house we were renting was far bigger than this place, and we only paid forty-two dollars each month. "Sixty," I said. "Sixty," I said again, realizing the enormity of the number.

"That would be affirmative."

"Are you the one I would rent from?"

"That would be affirmative, too."

"Can I go inside?"

He looked me over again. "What is your name?"

Quickly, I crammed the pencil and notepad into my pocket. I stood as tall as I could and extended my hand. "Nathan Mori," I said. I tried not to flinch when he shook my hand with the strength of a bodybuilder.

"Lived here long?" he asked. He locked his eyes with mine.

Discomfort came over me. Was I going to have to tell him that I used to live here but had been sent away after Pearl Harbor? That I was born here but not recognized as a citizen with constitutional rights? I swallowed hard. This was not the time to voice political views. I only wanted a shop and a way to provide for my family. Yet, if I gave him an answer he didn't like, would he choose not to let me in? *God, help me,* I prayed. What was the correct reply? My mind buzzed until at last the words came out. "I love San Jose. How about you?"

"You can't beat the weather here, that's for sure," he said. "I'm Jonathan Jones, by the way." And then, he was unlocking the front door, and soon I was inside.

The next day while Tom was at school, my aunt was cleaning the *wealthy* house, and Emi was playing at our neighbor's, I prepared to set out to the Empire Street location again. I was going to talk the man down. Sixty a month was too much. During the "tour" of the inside of the shop yesterday, I knew that the bare shop with a small restroom in the back and an even smaller storage closet was not worth a sixty-dollar-a-month price tag.

Papa was on the front porch when I headed out. Seated in one of the rockers, he had the morning paper spread out before him. He turned a page and focused on the sports section. "The Yankees won last night," he said.

"What was the score?"

Silently, he turned the page, and became absorbed in something far beyond baseball. I got a glimpse of the caption under a photo: "Hiroshima atomic bomb victims."

I wanted him to put the paper away and look at me. "Papa." I hoped he heard me. "Can I talk to you for a moment?"

He removed a pack of cigarettes from his breast pocket and nodded my way.

"Do you think I should try to open a fish market?"

He lit a cigarette and together we watched the smoke curl and drift away from us. Solemnly he said, "Nobu, you have always been able to do the right thing."

I thought of our watch—gone. Not just gone, but stolen. Or given away. Or something. Regardless of how it left our possession, it was not ours anymore. That was the point. A watch that had been gifted to my grandfather—a man who was no longer alive—would not be passed down to the next generations. I would never be able to tell my children the story of the watch, and at the end, show them the shiny gold piece. I was sure that I had done the right thing to demand it back. But should I have fought harder? Should I have taken it to the court in Cheyenne? Would a jury of my peers have seen it my way?

Papa patted the chair next to him.

I didn't want to sit. I had work to do, decisions to make. I'd sit for a few minutes, just to appease him.

He smoked. I listened to the sounds from the streets. Cars, dogs in the distance, an occasional voice calling for someone, the cry of a cat. A door opened, another one slammed. What did God have for us? How were we to sustain this family?

"Papa, do you think God has a plan for us here? If so, why are things so hard?"

I waited, and when I looked over at my father, I knew that he wouldn't be answering me. His eyes were closed; his head leaned against the wall. He was asleep.

I studied him for a moment before entering the house. What went on in his mind? Why couldn't he work like all the other papas? How could he have let the past reduce him to half a man?

Inside, I sat at the piano. I could play something simple. Something Mama never played. Nothing came to me. All I could hear was a voice that belonged to another woman, one much younger, and equally as beautiful.

I had dreamed of being back in San Jose. Back with the warm breezes, the balmy dry climate, the bright blue skies, the swaying palms, and gardens of flowers. But now that I was back, my thoughts kept returning to Heart Mountain. At least there she had been close by. Always. There, even though I lived through fear, uncertainty, confinement, and separation from Papa, I had had her presence. Each day, I knew that I would see her. If I didn't get an opportunity to talk with her, at least I could watch her from a distance, and at night, her voice filled our billet with her songs.

Now I found myself humming the tunes to those songs. When Tom turned the radio on, I listened for her voice. Her parents who lived on the edge of San Jose said she was in Manhattan making a record. I also heard from someone else that she was in Washington State sitting on a pier waiting for Ken to come back to America. I hoped that the latter was not true.

There were nights when I was desperate to hear her voice.

After dinner, Tom did his homework and my aunt read to Emi from a donated picture book. Papa sat at the kitchen table reading the evening newspaper. I once read the *News*, but then, when a letter to the editor showed that there was anxiety about Japanese—whether they be *Issei*, *Nissei* or *Sansei*—and that propaganda was out there against *yellow-skinned* people, I refused to subject myself to the paper again.

I went into the living room and sat at the piano bench. When Papa found his spot on the sofa, I contemplated pawning the piano. This piano would certainly bring some much-needed money for us. Mr. Rizzardi should be able to sell it to someone. As I recalled the day that Mama had found it at a little shop, and Papa had later bought it for her one Christmas, Papa asked me to play.

At first I ignored him. He seldom responded to any of us, so I felt he deserved the same treatment.

"Play Chopin."

I said I had an appointment to go to.

"Don't neglect your talent."

"What talent?"

He just nodded at me, his chin jutted out like it was a ruler pointing me into some sort of direction.

Suddenly, Emi had joined me at the piano bench.

"Teach her some songs," my aunt said, as she entered the living room, pulling in one of the chairs from the kitchen. She sat on it and opened a worn paperback.

Emi put a tiny hand over a few of the keys. "Can you play this?" She looked at me intently.

I sighed. Could I? Mechanically, I hit each key to play the scales, starting with middle C.

She watched closely. I played them again and again until she said, "Can you do anything else but that? It's getting on my nerves."

"Why don't you try?"

I placed her index finger on the C key. "This is C. Before it are A and B and after it are D, E, F and G."

She pressed C, listened to the sound that the note made and pressed it again. "What do the black keys do?"

After that I taught her the major scales. The piano needed tuning, but Emi didn't know that. She carefully took her time to play each key as I did. Once she paused to bat at her bangs which were in her eyes. Her fingers then slid over the keys to play the scales again. And again. After playing them five times, she paused a second time to give me a sidelong glance. "You never told me you could play the piano," she said.

"You know our mother did."

"You mean Mama?"

"Yes, Mama."

"Her name is Mama," my sister said with great emphasis. "Ma-ma."

"I know."

"Well then, don't call her mother."

"Right."

"Guess what, Nathan?"

"What?"

"Mama loves you."

A lump formed in my throat and, although I swallowed hard a couple of times, it wouldn't go away.

"Mama loves you so much."

"I know. She loves you, too."

"She's with God, right?"

I fought the tears that were edging their way toward my eyes. I could feel them creeping in, I was aware of their urgency to take over. They could not, I would not let them. I cleared my throat. "Yes. That's right. She's with God."

"And angels."

"Yes, and angels." Even the ones who carried her to Heaven.

"Wow, she must be happy." And with that, Emi pressed an index finger to the D key and let the sound from it echo throughout the house.

Chapter Twenty-five

Aunt Kazuko told me that friends from Second Street Church wanted a general store. "So you make one," she told me.

I told her that perhaps a fish market would help give Papa that "pep" to get back to who he once was. When I used the word pep, she smiled.

"So you talking like me now?" She gave me a light pat on my back, but her smile faded. "I think you need to just let your papa do what he needs to do. You own the shop you want to run. I think general store is best."

"Why?"

"People at church say they have no place to sell what they grow or make. Also we need this store that sells things."

"What kinds of things?"

"Like matches and towels."

"Matches and towels?"

"Yes, everybody needs a match to light a stove or a cigarette. Everybody needs a towel after a bath."

"Practical items," I mused.

"You can call them that. Now help me choose which dress to wear on Easter."

❀

When I went to the Easter service with my aunt, Tom, and Emi, I suggested that we sit in the back pew. But my aunt marched up to the front row, introducing me to all her new friends. "He is opening a general store," she told them.

Before the first hymn, three men came over to me and introduced themselves.

"If only we had a place to sell our produce, then life would be so much better," one with a wiry moustache told me.

"I make pickles and need a place to sell them," said a man in a dark suit.

Even a woman tapped me on the shoulder to say, "I can vegetables from our garden and also my husband is a cab driver and says people ask if our town has a general store. A place we can sell everything."

I was about to ask if she knew of a place I could rent for a store like that, when I saw a young woman walking down the aisle. She paused to smile at me. Then she sat in a pew to the left of us so that all I could see was the side of her face. She had on a faded yellow hat, one of those with a fake flower sewn to the side. Her dress matched the hat, dotted with yellow rose buds. I thought of another girl in a dress the same color, only the flowers had been sunflowers.

After the service, I was introduced to the girl in the yellow rosebud dress.

"This is Jennifer," her mother said. "Jennifer Tanaka." Her mother had on a hat, too; a swooping peacock feather stemmed from its brim.

Within five minutes I was pulled aside and asked if I would take this Jennifer out on a date.

"A date?" The words caught in my throat. I'd never been on a date.

"Yes," said Jennifer's mother. "I think that would be lovely."

At lunch, my aunt told me not to be so shocked, often people went to church and found their mates.

The upcoming date was not on my mind as much as opening a general store. What would we call it? I knew that every store had to have a name, but our store could not have a Japanese name. We would have to call it something else. I looked in the mirror, one that had been given to us by some church group my aunt belonged to. I was American. Sure, I looked Asian, but I was a loyal American trying to start a new life.

As I sat on my bed and thought, I heard a few sounds coming from the living room. Curious to see what was going on, I left my bedroom.

There, with only the floor lamp to give her light, sat Emi at the piano bench, her legs swaying back and forth. She touched a key lightly, giggled, and repeated the action. No banging on it like other young children did. It was as if she knew how sacred an heirloom it was. Or perhaps she knew that my emotions weren't able to handle any more obstacles. I needed calm. I needed a nice, hot *ofuro*, the traditional Japanese bath that my parents spoke fondly of soaking in after a long day.

Tonight, as other nights, I had to settle for a lukewarm bath in an American tub instead.

Days later on my way home from the grocer, I checked our mailbox, a metal contraption that leaned to the left and looked as though it wanted to topple over. Inside there was a letter. Each time I opened the box to get the mail, I always hoped for that one special letter. It would be addressed to me and contain pages and pages of how much she missed me and cared about me. I knew that this hope was far-fetched, but many of our hopes in life are unrealistic. We'd heard from Ken infrequently. Apparently, he was still in England and had met a British girl he liked, but that was not new news. When had my brother ever not had a girl or two he liked?

Today's mail was postmarked Raleigh, North Carolina. I put the sack of groceries on the porch, sat on a rocking chair, and read a short letter from Mr. Kubo.

Dear Nathan, I hope this finds you well. I have been in touch with a few from camp and was told you and your family have a house now.

We visited our son in Chicago at Christmas. His wife no longer steams milk for coffee but insists on a clothes dryer. Have you heard of these appliances? They are expensive, but so are the tastes of my daughter-in-law.

Now we are back in Durham, N.C., where we work on a tobacco farm. Our house is a two-bedroom rented place. We are doing well and trying to put the war behind us. I hope you and your family are doing well. I hope Ken has returned safely from the war. He was brave to fight for his country.

Come visit us sometime. You will love the way these Southerners speak our language.

All the best to you, Barry Kubo

I never knew his first name was Barry. As a breeze lingered in the air, I let my mind wander back to the days at Heart Mountain. I saw the mountain, that solid presence that changed with the weather. I saw the barracks—staunch and dark. I thought of peeling potatoes in the kitchen, of Tom's pet toad Bogart, of Lucy's songs. Yet today all I could associate with that cold and dusty place was sadness. *Put it behind us.* I'd take this man's advice.

Forget Lucy. Forget life before camp. All I had was now. And tonight I had said I'd go out with Jennifer Tanaka. A date.

After dinner I sat with my aunt in the living room, as she drank a cup of tea and sewed buttons on men's shirts. Papa took his cigarettes outside to smoke, and Tom lay on the couch and read a book. Emi asked me to help her play "Mary Had a Little Lamb" on the upright.

After Emi seemed to get a grip on the rhythm of the melody, I stood.

"Where you going?" asked Emi.

"Out."

"Out?" said Aunt Kazuko.

"Yes." Suddenly I felt queasy. Why had I agreed to this date with Jennifer? The date was doomed, and I hadn't even arrived at her door to pick her up yet.

"Is tonight your date?" She smiled. When I only groaned, she said, "You not happy? Why you say yes then?"

Why had I said yes to Mrs. Tanaka? Perhaps because there was some flicker of hope that I could be interested in someone local, instead of pining for a girl in New York City.

"At hair salon, I told Mrs. Tanaka that you are a good boy. Work hard. Finger to the bone. Sometimes you dilly-dally."

I imagined Mrs. Tanaka then asking if it would be all right to suggest that I take Jennifer out on a date.

The sky was a creamy peach, as the sun set over San Jose. The colors reminded me of the silk hibiscus someone wore in her hair. I wondered what that someone was doing this night. As I walked to the Tanaka's house, I heard my own voice whisper her name.

When I knocked on the front door, Jennifer peered out the window. Shortly after that, her mother opened the door and welcomed me into the tiny living room where it was just she and I. I was hoping I would not have to be grilled by Mrs. Tanaka. As she asked me about the general shop—when would it open and would we carry fresh salmon, I wished Jennifer would appear. My shirt collar felt stiff and irritated the back of my neck.

And then, down the stairs came Jennifer. She walked cautiously in a pair of heeled shoes and only smiled when she safely reached the bottom step.

We walked to the theater to see *The Big Sleep*. I knew that Jennifer was the type of girl who went gooey-eyed over Humphrey Bogart. She had also said on the phone when I called to ask her out that she thought Lauren Bacall was a stunning actress. I had to agree.

Inside the dark theater we sat together; Jennifer's shoulder rubbed against my arm.

Her hand sat on her lap, and I knew that if I had been any other red-blooded boy, I would have grasped that hand and held it all throughout the movie.

"You really miss her, don't you?" Jennifer said, as we walked back toward the five and dime for a soda.

"What? Who?"

"Your brother Tom told me about her. He said that you really liked her. She was at Heart Mountain with you, wasn't she? I was in Gila in Arizona. I don't know why we didn't go to Heart Mountain. Did they really protest being drafted there?"

My mind spun. I had never heard someone talk so much and not wait for any replies. Jennifer was like a non-stop wind-up toy.

"Did you all have dances at your camp? I danced with this one boy who went off to fight. He died in Germany. He got blown up."

"I'm sorry," I said.

"Yeah . . . well . . ." The next thing I knew she was blowing her nose into her pink and yellow embroidered handkerchief.

I stopped on the sidewalk. "Are you all right?"

Jennifer opened her purse and inserted her handkerchief back into it. "We can go now. You can take me home."

All I could see was Mrs. Tanaka's disappointed face. "What will you tell your mom?"

"I'll think of something."

It was then that I felt sorry for the girl in the pink dress with the shiny heeled shoes she'd bought for this occasion. Why couldn't I like her? Why couldn't life turn out to be like a storybook? Bogart and Bacall made it all look so easy.

We walked to her house in silence. She told me that I didn't need to walk her up to her front door. At the gate, she solemnly said, "Thank you."

Part of me was tempted to blurt that she was pretty in a simple way and that she did look good in those new shoes. But why? Why lie? It was best to just remain silent.

At home, my aunt had finished sewing buttons. She was sleeping in a wingback chair, her head back, her mouth open. The shirts laid in a neat pile on the sofa. I thought of how it was her persistence in getting work to help pay our bills that had kept us afloat after our return to San Jose. Here she was, a woman who had been educated in Tokyo, an accountant. And now she was cleaning a house and sewing buttons so that we could pay our rent. I asked God to help me never think badly of her ever again.

In the kitchen, I got a drink of water from the tap.

"How was date?" I heard her ask from the living room.

Entering the living room, I groaned.

"That good, was it? Need some tea?"

"No. No, thank you."

"Your father is asleep in Tom's room. We got him to move in there. So I fix a bed for him with blankets. Tom is asleep, too, and Emi fall asleep at piano bench after she played and played."

"I guess I'll go to bed, too." I stretched for emphasis to show her that I was really tired and didn't need any more conversation.

But she didn't seem to care how tired I was. "You know, Nathan, sometimes we have to let people go."

I had already lost my mother to death, my brother to some after-war business deal, and my father to his own demons. Who was she to lecture me on the need to let people go? I was trying my best to live with loss every day.

"She is only living her dream. What can be wrong with that? We all have dreams and unless we go out into the wild, we never know if we can fly or not."

"She can do whatever she wants," I said.

"I think she wants to seek the glamour of living for a bit. You know, nice parties, elegance. Maybe."

"Maybe." In my weariness, I realized that we were talking about Lucy without mentioning her name. I didn't want to say her name, for whenever I did, a deep pain gnawed at my heart right at the place where I let her dwell. I suppose that my aunt knew that I didn't want to hear her name, and I was grateful to her for that kindness.

Lucy had one side of my heart, and the other side was where sorrow had taken permanent residence—spaces for Mama, Papa, and even Ken.

I tried to recall the days before the war, before the tearing of our family bonds, back when Ken and I played baseball in the street with the other neighbor boys while their sisters looked on from the sidewalks.

Back when life was safe and innocent. Before I knew that I had a heart that could be so easily broken.

Chapter Twenty-six

Once, in camp, I saw a little girl of about three playing in the dust that blew over the terrain. She had a bucket in her hand, and each time the wind roused a cloud of dust, she ran toward the dust with her bucket.

Her grandma stood near her on the road and asked, "What are you doing?"

"I'm catching the dust," the little girl replied. "Do you wanna see?" She stopped running and walked toward her grandmother. Handing her the bucket, she said, "See?"

The grandmother, a wiry woman with a scarf around her head, peered into the bucket and said, "What is it? I don't see anything."

"It's dust. Do you want some?"

"Why? What can you do with dust?"

The girl laughed and ran to catch some more inside her bucket. The wind whistled through her short black hair and ruffled the hem of her skirt. Yet she still laughed and said, "Come here, dust, come to me."

"What can you do with dust?"

"Lots of things."

"What good is a bucket of dust?"

The little girl didn't mind the persistent questions. "*Oba-chan* (grandmommy)," she said, "you can put it on your table and it's art. Or you can dance with it. You can talk to it. You can even sing to it."

At this point the grandmother had had enough. She coughed as the wind from Heart Mountain clouded the air with the thick dust. "Inside," she commanded. "Now."

But the little girl just laughed again. "In a moment. Let me make sure I have enough dust."

"Your bucket is empty!" The grandma covered her mouth and made her way toward their barracks' door.

"No, it's not," said the girl. "My bucket is full. Open your eyes. It's a dust pail."

I saw that little girl one other time in camp, and she was running down a dry road between two barracks with what everybody else called an empty bucket. But to her, the bucket was full.

I often wondered how she managed to make the best of the dust while the rest of us in camp found no beauty in it and only complained how it swept into our barracks and coated our floors with films of ash.

Perhaps the moral to that story was not to let the circumstances of life get the best of you. Perhaps it was being able to make the most of anything, even something as undesirable as dust.

❀

My aunt was in full force talking about how nice it would be to be able to help me run a general store. "I can do the accounting for you," she said. "I can help you when I'm not cleaning or sewing. Why can't you find a place to rent? I see empty places all the time."

Finally, I said, "I'll tell you what. If the place on Empire Street is affordable, you can get your general store."

My aunt smiled. "I better call the prayer team."

I made a cup of coffee in the percolator that had been given to us by the *wealthy* family. They had cleaned out their kitchen and provided our family with a few sharp knives, a pot for cooking, a fancy egg-beater with a red handle, and other assorted items. They'd offered us a coffee table, and my aunt had brought it home in a cab, calling me from where the cab stopped in front of our house to come and help get the piece of furniture inside. We placed it in front of the sofa. My aunt put her photo album on the table, a few of her paperback romance novels, and Mama's Bible.

When Aunt Kazuko went to work after making a few calls to various women who made up her prayer team, I sat on the couch and drank my coffee.

The photo album beckoned me, but not like an old friend, more like a questionable man selling encyclopedias door to door. At first I picked it up and ran my fingers across the hard binding. Then I opened it to the first page to see black and white photos of lots of Japanese people. There were solemn faces of relatives I had only heard about. Underneath each photo Aunt Kazuko had written the names of the people who were pictured.

When I got to the photo of her and Mama standing outside their home in Nagano in about two feet of snow, I stopped to take it all in. Mama must have been about twelve then. My aunt, seven years older. They were both wearing snowshoes, the old rounded wooden ones with twine that I had seen once in a movie about ancient Japan. The caption under the photo read: *Uncle Taro used his new camera to take our picture.* Mama's smile was wide; I traced my finger along the curve of her cheeks, the way they puffed up and produced a dimple in her left one. I closed my eyes and then shut the book.

The trouble with family photos is, that if you look closely, you can see yourself in every face. All of us children resembled Mama. She had passed her smile on to Ken, Tom, Emi, and even me. And not only her smile, but her dimple.

Quickly, I stood, hoping to leave nostalgia behind me on the couch. I dressed and set out, wanting to appear businesslike. I was going to get a place for our general store. I was going to succeed. I was Nathan Mori, and once upon a time, a nobleman had felt our family worthy enough to bequeath a gold pocket watch to.

I laughed. Who used the word bequeath anymore?

I found Jonathan Jones seated in the barbershop. His face was lathered in white foam, a towel under his chin. As the barber gave him a shave, Mr. Jones looked at me and said, "You still want the shop on Empire Street for your market?"

"Yes, sir."

"It's yours."

"I can't afford sixty dollars a month."

"I know. You can pay me thirty-seven dollars. I need thirty-seven dollars by Thursday, and it is yours."

"Thirty-seven."

"That would be affirmative."

I thanked him, and rushed out of the store. All the way home, I uttered, "Thank you, God, thank you, God." I couldn't wait for my aunt to get home and share the news with her.

Hours later, when she arrived home, she confessed, "It took me a long time to get here. First, I had to make sure make your Papa and Emi were all right, so I stop by to see them at the Shimizu house."

"Were they okay?"

"Yes," she said. "Emi was playing with their new puppy. Your papa was sitting inside drinking tea and eating cake."

"What kind of cake?" I went over to my aunt and rubbed a smudge of dark brown off her cheek. "What kind?"

Innocently she muttered, "Maybe chocolate." Stepping into the kitchen, she confessed, "Okay, yes, I had a piece. I had to or Mrs. Shimizu would have been mad at me."

"Wasn't Mr. Shimizu the one who got carted off to Tule Lake by the FBI right before they came for Papa?"

"Yes, the one they accused of sending messages to the Japanese army. They said he was General Tojo's cousin. That is why your papa likes to go to their house. He and Mr. Shimizu talk and remember." She sat on the sofa and sighed. "Mrs. Shimizu says that some days they just play chess and don't talk at all."

"What happened to them at Lake Tule?" I half expected my aunt to tell me that they had been tortured during their years there, but she only shook her head and asked me to put the kettle on for tea.

"Guess what?" I made sure I had her full attention before I continued. "Mr. Jones said we can have the Empire Street shop."

Clearly, she was interested. She sat upright and asked, "For how much? How much does he agree to?"

"For thirty-seven!"

"When does he need it by?"

"Thursday."

"I don't get paid till Friday. But I have money. I saved some under my mattress for rainy day."

When we told the others at dinner, everyone talked at once. I loved the feeling of excitement in the air.

"What shall we call our store?" asked Tom.

"Where is it? Can I walk there?" asked Emi.

"What would be a good name?" Tom asked, as he shoved a forkful of green beans into his mouth.

After dinner, Papa patted my shoulder, smiled, and went outside to smoke.

My aunt was putting on lipstick. "I'll think of name as I go to church. Mrs. Shimizu is picking me up in her car to take me there."

"Did you count your money? How much do we have?"

"Nathan, don't worry so much. We will have enough by Thursday. You will see. Now, about that name."

I wished that everyone wasn't so consumed with a name for the shop. What did a name matter if we couldn't afford to rent it?

On her way out the door, she smiled, adjusted her hat that had a single feather in it, and said, "I will take all this good news to the table."

"What does that mean?" I asked

"Tonight at church. We have a group."

"What kind of group?"

"We eat, we talk, we laugh."

"What kind of group?" Certainly she must be missing some part of it. Weren't church groups supposed to study the Bible or pray?

"We bring something to the table."

"Like what?"

"Tonight I tell story about how you got to lease a place for shop. Last week I talk about Emi playing the piano."

"So it's a sharing group."

"You bring a story or a food or even a pebble."

"A pebble?" Who would bring a pebble to a group?

"If it has meaning for you, you share it. If it is beauty for you, or an answer to a prayer, then you take it to the table. No matter how poor or bad off, you are always welcome to come and you always have something to bring. What you bring helps you and helps others."

Curiosity got the best of me and so the next Sunday I asked Pastor Campbell what this group was about.

"It was started by a few women," he said. "After the war, many have been deprived. Times have been hard. But the idea behind the group is that we all have God, so we're all rich. We are rich in our stories, our very presence is rich. Even the least well-off financially has the ability to bring something of use. We are all of value to God and to each other. The idea is to bring an object or something, no matter how small. It's not the value of what you bring that counts; it's about knowing that you are valuable."

"What's the real name of the group?" I asked, certain that my aunt had just given it her own name.

"To the Table."

I smiled. I wasn't going to argue with him that no one would name a group To the Table.

"You should come some night," he said. "We eat. We share. We laugh a lot, too. Your aunt is a blessing to each of us."

❀

But my time these days was taken with getting the shop ready for business. We scraped together thirty-seven dollars and put it in an envelope for Mr. Jones. My aunt told me to make sure that I read carefully whatever it was I needed to sign to make the lease of the shop on Empire Street legal.

I obtained the license I needed to run a store. Inside the shop, I used an old broom to sweep out the cobwebs and the dust off the wooden floor. There were some old tables Mr. Jones said I could use to display my merchandise. Actually, I had little merchandise that was mine; most of it was from local folks who dropped it off for me to sell. I made sure that they understood they would get a commission. Eventually, I wanted to buy their wares when they dropped them off, but at this point in time, I had no cash to pay them.

By the end of the second day, when the windows sparkled, and the floor looked glossy, I realized that I needed more items in order to have a thriving shop. The jars of pickled beets, cucumber relish, and spiced pears looked lonely on one table.

Where were all the people who had said they wanted a store where their items could be sold? I told Aunt Kazuko she needed to do a better job about getting the word out.

Emi asked me to teach her a new song on the piano, and as I did, a thought came to me. How much could I get for this piano?

The next morning, I entered the pawn shop. Mr. Rizzardi was occupied with two customers so, while he talked with them, I looked over dishes, beds, and jewelry. A number of items I'd seen when I was last here were gone. After the customers left, I continued to browse. I pretended to be engrossed in a wall clock, but I was really trying to get my nerve up to ask about selling our piano. I planned to describe it to Mr. Rizzardi, tell him that it needed tuning but that shouldn't cost much, and try to get him interested. He could buy it and pay someone to move it from our house. And we'd have cash.

Mr. Rizzardi had the radio on and was humming along to a song. He stopped when the song ended and the DJ said, "And that was Lucy Heart, singing 'I'll Never Stop Dreaming.' That song has hit the top of the charts for this week."

My ears felt as though they had been caressed by velvet. Lucy Heart? Had he said Lucy Heart?

"She has a nice voice, doesn't she?" said Mr. Rizzardi, noting my surprised expression.

I nodded. Lucy? Of course, that had been Lucy. I tried to recall if I had been paying attention to any of the words. "What was the name of that song?"

"'I'll Never Stop Dreaming.'"

Was this a sign? Each time I played the piano or heard Emi practice, I knew that the piano was our legacy. Emi wanted to learn to play better. I knew how Mama had even said she had piano playing fingers when she was born. How could I even consider asking Mr. Rizzardi to take a look at our piano? How could I take away a dream my sister had? We'd get money another way. Somehow God would provide. Somehow, some way. Selling

Mama's piano was not the solution. We needed that piece of memory.

"Where is the closest record store?" I asked, as another song started to play. I made my way toward the door.

"Three blocks, on Thirteenth. Tell them Rizzardi sent you. The owner owes me money, but you don't have to remind him of that. He's my brother, and he already knows because I remind him every day."

"Three blocks and then do I turn left or right onto Thirteenth?" I asked. I really didn't need to hear about how his brother owed him money.

"It's on the corner. You can't miss it. It's called Rizzardi's."

"But this place is called Rizzardi's."

"No, this is called Rizzardi's Pawn, that is just Rizzardi's."

I thanked him and left the shop. But the security I allowed myself to feel about God's provision ebbed away when I passed a newsstand to see the words printed on a flier: *Send them all back to Japan*. I'd read about how there were organizations determined to rid the country of anyone of Japanese descent.

And when I purchased Lucy's record, the store owner seemed gruff. Was it because of the color of my skin and the shape of my eyes or was he just having a bad day?

I left the store with my purchase and rounded the corner. From the paper bag, I pulled out the 78 rpm disc. I ran my fingers over the printed name on the cover: Lucy Heart. The song on side A was "I'll Never Stop Dreaming". Side B's "Will You Forgive Me?" caught my attention as the word *forgive* seemed to jump off the cover and jab at my heart. Lucy's face was not on the card cover, but rather, a photo of her taken from the back. She was in a blue evening gown with a string of pearls around her neck. She had on a glittery hat, the veil from it covered all but her mouth and a few strands of hair—hair that was blonde, cut short. *They don't want her to be Japanese,* I thought. My stomach spun like a ride at the fair. I gripped the edge of the vinyl record and then placed it into the bag.

Back at the apartment, I entered the kitchen where my aunt poured Emi a bowl of Cheerios. As she added the milk, she said, "How was your stroll?"

I muttered that it had been all right.

She looked me over. "You look like warmed death."

"You mean like death warmed over?"

"That, too." She filled the kettle with water. "You need a pep. I have just the thing. *Ocha* that I found in my box."

"From when we had to pack up and leave San Jose?"

155

"Yes. Don't worry, it's not old or stale."

"Are you sure?"

"Green tea keeps. I heard it keeps for decades."

I wondered if that was how long prejudices kept.

After Emi finished her cereal and left the room, Aunt Kazuko poured tea from the teapot I'd bought for her. She said, "Guess what I heard?"

With my aunt, there really was no telling. "What did you hear?" I asked.

"I heard that one family stayed in the camp."

I rubbed a hand over my shoulder where a pain seemed to have developed. I really was too tired for her stories revolving around gossip she heard at the beauty salon.

"This family didn't want to leave camp, so they stayed at Heart Mountain. No place to go. Had to be evicted."

"Are you serious?"

"I don't joke about these kinds of things, Nathan. The family said, 'Where do we go? Our orchard we used to work on is gone, our house we rented is no longer vacant, where do we go? All we have is here at our barracks. We will stay.'" My aunt grinned. "You can laugh if you want. I did when I was told this story." Then she added, "Funny, but it has a sad side to it, doesn't it? Like you want to just hug that family and tell them it will be all right."

I smiled and drank my tea. It didn't taste stale, just hot and soothing to my throat.

I showed my aunt the record then. She took her time studying the cover, turning it over and over, commenting on Lucy's hair color, and repeating the song titles. After a while she said, "You buy this, but we have no way to listen to it."

In my excitement, had I forgotten that we had no phonograph? Probably. I let a sigh fill the room. "Do you think your *wealthy* family has a spare phonograph?"

She laughed. "I think they have at least three."

Emi danced into the kitchen. "Nathan, it's time for my lesson. Nathan, come on!"

"What lesson?" I asked, although I knew what she meant. I had told her that she needed to practice at least once a day in order to get good.

She pulled me out of my chair and led me into the living room. We sat on the bench in front of the piano and she said, "What shall we play?"

"You play something. I'll listen. And remember, sit up straight."

"I know, I know. Don't slouch." She poised her fingers over the keys, took in a breath and then, from memory, played "Mary Had A Little Lamb."

I watched as she intently moved her hands over the keys. The five year old was playing the piano and not just any piano, but Mama's Gulbransen. Years of selling fish had allowed us to have enough so that she and Papa were able to purchase the Gulbransen.

I recalled how Mama would play for us on summer evenings when the windows brought in the outdoor aromas of whatever our neighbors were cooking. She would play while the rice steamed in the cooker and while Papa would fry the fillets of trout or sea bass.

Suddenly I realized that Emi had stopped playing. With her legs swinging underneath her, she looked at me. "Are you sad?"

I tried to shrug it off. "That was good."

"You weren't listening," she said.

"I was."

"No, you know how I know you weren't listening?"

"How?"

"You have that look in your forehead."

"What?"

"It gets wrinkled. You are in another world."

I smiled, noting her choice of phrases. The last one was obviously borrowed from our aunt. "I was listening. You are doing really well." We had to get this piano tuned. If Emi was going to play, we needed to invest in having a piano that sounded as good as it could.

After dinner, I planned to ask my aunt if she knew of anyone in her To the Table group who tuned pianos, but instead, I turned on the radio to see if I'd get to hear Lucy sing. Tomorrow I'd go to the music shop and ask if the owner would let me play my record.

Maybe by tomorrow, his gruffness would disappear.

❀

Her hair was now blonde. No longer black or long. I remembered her as the slim girl in the kimono, the young woman I fell in love with that often wore a silk hibiscus in her hair. Now she was famous. She'd never come back to San Jose. She was gone from me.

Emi asked for a cookie.

Seeing that I was the only one in the house, I realized it was up to me to get one for her. She followed me into the kitchen. The animal cracker box was empty.

She started to whine.

I let her whine, and even wanted to join her.

She pounded her fists on the table top. The tears flooded down her cheeks.

"Hey," I said, "if you stop crying, I can find you a surprise."

But she wouldn't be consoled. Her tears dripped down her cheeks. "I want my mama," she said. "Everybody has a mama but me."

Quickly, I picked her up and held her. *Just cry, Emi, cry. Let it out.*

When Tom got home from school, he spread his homework out on the kitchen table. He said he was thinking about going to college. "I'd like to teach," he said.

"Teach what?"

"History. Or literature."

"What about space adventures?" asked Emi, who like the rest of us, had been subjected to Tom's alien stories. Her tears had dried, and she had joined me at the piano where I'd played a few of Mama's favorites. That seemed to have calmed her nerves, as well as mine. No, we would not be selling this piano.

That night, we had a dinner of baked chicken, mashed potatoes, and grilled eggplant. Aunt Kazuko glazed the eggplant with a soy-sauce-sesame-seed-mixture she recalled from childhood.

After our meal, Emi cleared the plates without breaking any, and Tom and I washed and dried them while our aunt sat at the table writing a letter in Japanese to her mother in Nagano. Emi joined her with a box of crayons and her coloring book.

As I put the last plate into the cupboard, the phone rang.

Aunt Kazuko answered the phone, an old model that was stuck to the kitchen wall. "Hello." After a pause, she said, "I'm very fine. How are you?" Then, "Just a moment." Covering the mouthpiece with one hand, she looked at me. "It's for you, Nathan."

I dried my hands on the tea towel. She gave me a slight smile and handed me the receiver.

Then she shooed Emi and Tom out of the kitchen and even closed the kitchen door behind her when she left.

It didn't take long to understand why she'd done this.

Chapter Twenty-seven

"Hello, Nathan?" The voice on the other end was as soft as I had remembered it.

Within one second, I was back at camp, recalling the curve of her smile.

"So how are you, Nathan?"

I wanted to say, "Great, now that I'm talking to you," but I refrained.

"Good. Good. We got a shop."

"A fish market?"

"No, a general store."

"That's great."

"How about you? What are you up to?" I tried to sound casual, as though I knew nothing about her and had not bought her record, and that if I had a record player I would surely listen to it fifty times a day.

"Well, I'm singing. I made a record."

"Good for you. I always knew you would get there one day."

"It's been a hit."

"Really? What's it called?"

"The song that has been on all the radio stations is 'I'll Never Stop Dreaming.'"

"Lucy Heart? That's you?"

"Yeah."

"I thought you were going to be Meredith Rose."

She giggled. "I remember that. That seems so long ago."

I braced myself. I was sure she had called to either ask about Ken or talk to him. Now that she was Lucy Heart, I was sure she wanted even less to do with me. Me, clumsy, never sure of what to say, me.

"Where's your shop?"

"It's on East Empire. It's a tiny place, but it's a start."

And soon we were laughing and talking like old friends. We talked about the lousy food at camp, the cold weather, the way the wind whipped across us from Heart Mountain. She didn't bring up Ken or

Mekley. It was as though we both knew what could and couldn't be discussed.

"My mother said she saw you a few weeks ago."

"Yeah, at the grocer," I said. "She was buying lettuce, I think. I was buying bread and butter. We talked about Hiroshima and she recalled that Papa has family there."

"Are they all right?" Lucy asked.

"He had several friends and family members die," I said. "Others are now sick from the radiation."

"War is horrible. I hate what it has done."

"Everybody has been affected. This whole country is trying to get back on her feet."

Suddenly she said, "I have to go now. My producer wants me to make another record, and we have to negotiate all that." Quickly, she added, "I know you don't like good-byes so I'll just say, see you later."

When we hung up, I stood in the kitchen and wondered if our conversation had really happened. Perhaps it had just been some fragmented story I had created in my mind. My mind spun back to the day Lucy left camp. I recalled how our mutual friends said she had gotten out of the dreary camp and was going to Manhattan to be a star. She had not told me good-bye then because I had not wanted her to.

And now I felt as empty as I had then. She had pursued a dream, and her dream to sing professionally had come true.

My dream was lagging so far behind.

Chapter Twenty-eight

"We used to have a fish market," I said to Tom and Emi at dinner one night.

"I remember it," said Tom. "I used to walk down to it and help Papa ring up the customers."

"That was Papa's passion. But I'm not really good with fish, so I decided a general store might be better."

"What are we going to call the shop?" asked Emi. This seemed to be the question of the week, and so far, no one had a name we could all agree on.

I debated as I walked around town. Should it be the Mori Market? Mori was clearly Japanese. I wanted it to be a place where everyone could come to shop. Yet what was wrong with a Japanese name?

My aunt was making raisin cookies. She had received the recipe from someone at her To the Table group. As she dropped the dough onto a greased cookie sheet, she asked, "How about The Mori Market?"

"What if we called it by a more American sounding name like Smith or Barrymore?" I asked.

"Smith? Barrymore? It wouldn't be us."

In the end, Papa suggested a name. After dinner, he sat on the sofa and watched the rain coming down, forming puddles in the street. "You want to sell everything there, don't you? People's vegetables and fruit, greeting cards and candy bars. It sounds like it will be a place to get everything but buttons."

The rest of us looked at each other and smiled, like we knew. The name had been decided. We'd go with that.

"Everything But Buttons," I said. It was a whimsical, unique, and cute enough name that everybody should want to shop there.

After the others had gone to sleep, I sat with Papa on the sofa where he was listening to the radio. "I wanted it to be a fish shop," I said, because I felt that I owed him that. "But I don't know enough about fish. The people in the church told me that people need a place to sell their wares. Do you think this is a good idea?"

He put his fingers against his chin and looked me over a few times. "You are so tall now, Nobu. I remember when you were born. I was so grateful that you had at last arrived, safe and sound."

"Mama said I cried a lot."

"You were determined. You never seemed to let up. Always moving, always wanting to see what was next. It was as though childhood was beneath you, and you wanted to be rid of it to move onto more." His sigh was deep and robust, like a strong cup of coffee. "You were your mother's favorite son named Nathan. Do you remember when she used to tell you that?" He almost smiled.

"Yes. Yes." *You know you are my favorite son named Nathan.* I often wished she could have said, *You are my favorite son.* Period.

"She used to play the neighbor's piano before we got our own. She said that playing made her feel the most alive and closest to God. She said that a person should always be close to whatever made her feel alive."

I waited for him to tell me more about Mama and her love of music, but that was all he said. It was as though thinking of his precious Etsuko had drawn him into a silent place, a place I could not go. He turned the radio off, rested his head against the back of the sofa, and closed his eyes.

I thought of leaving the room, but something tugged at my heart, and I knew that I needed to stay. "I want to tell you something," I said. "I hate to bring this up, but . . ." I took in a deep breath.

His eyes were still closed. Perhaps this was the time and place to tell him when his eyes were shut, and I didn't have to look into them to confess that the watch was gone.

"Something awful happened in camp. Really terrible."

Papa remained motionless.

"Papa? Did you hear me? Papa?"

I wondered if he was asleep, but then he shifted his head to the left and said, "What happened?"

"The watch is gone. Our watch was stolen."

His eyes opened. He looked at me, sat up.

"Our watch was stolen," I repeated.

"Did the Americans take it from you in the camp?"

"No. Yes. Yes, they took it from us." I wouldn't tell him that I stole it back and was sent to a cell because of my actions. I wouldn't break his heart even more by telling him that Ken had had something to do with it.

He rubbed his chin. "What a shame."

I had expected him to do more, to lash out, to scream, to blame me.

He searched his pocket and muttered about the whereabouts of his pack of cigarettes. Finding his pack under the coffee table, he pulled out the last cigarette, lit it with a shaky hand, and took a puff.

"I tried to keep it safe. It was in Mama's suitcase." I had vowed to protect it, taken an oath. But none of that had kept our family heirloom secure.

"The war stole much from all of us," he said. "We all lost."

And suddenly, the watch didn't seem important anymore.

I went over to sit next to him, edging as close to him as I could get, like I did when I was a little boy. I breathed in his familiar smell, noted the mole on his neck, the way it felt to be close to him.

After he snuffed his cigarette into the ashtray, he put his arm around my shoulders. "You are my special boy," he said. "You are my special son."

We sat like that for a few minutes, just the two of us Mori men, without a family treasure, but nevertheless, together.

Chapter Twenty-nine

O ur general store was going to be a reality. I made a list of everything we needed for it, including a cash register. Aunt Kazuko asked around at church and came up with an old one that a former store owner was willing to donate. She also brought me a door chime in the shape of a little silver bell.

"A door chime?" I questioned.

"Every store has to have one. It is a good way to alert you, and you need to be ready for all those thousands who come to shop."

Thousands, I thought. Was my aunt that confident about our store?

Opening day was drawing closer. Farmers as far south as Coyote had called to ask about selling produce at Everything But Buttons. Locals from the church called almost every day.

One elderly gentleman with a cane, and a mustache like General Sato's, often walked past our front porch. Each time he saw me, he'd cry, "When does your store open? Will you sell candy bars?"

There were three times in my life where I was so flabbergasted that I wasn't sure what to do. That spring morning in 1947 was one of them.

I was waiting for the coffee to percolate and looking over the ledger to make sure that I had recorded all the non-perishable items people had brought for me to sell for them. I'd forgotten to write down a box of handwoven pot holders, but just as I started to write, my pencil lead broke. While I rummaged through kitchen drawers, searching for the sharpener my aunt had, there was a knock at the front door. Seeing that Papa was not going to make his way to the door, and Emi was too occupied playing with her baby doll at his feet, I walked toward the door.

Just as the knock repeated, I swung it open.

There he stood; at first I had trouble recalling how I knew him.

For one thing, he wasn't in his uniform, but dressed in a pair of khaki trousers and a blue and brown plaid shirt.

Gloom spread over me. What was this man who still tormented me in my dreams doing here?

"H-h-hello. I . . . uh."

Immediately, I sensed something was wrong. At the camp, this soldier never stuttered.

Awkwardly, he handed me a small cardboard box.

I suppose in all the movies, this would be the time I'd opened the box, but I didn't. I couldn't.

"It's there," he said. "Your watch."

My lips were dry. Slowly, as though I was in some sort of slow-motion trance, I peeled back the lid. Inside was the Mori watch. The morning sunlight coated the gold casing for a brief moment. If I turned it over, I would see the bamboo and crane etchings. I felt like a kid again, but I didn't want to give this man the satisfaction of being overjoyed. "Thanks." I prepared to shut the door.

"How have you been?"

"Fine." I was not going to let on that I was caving inside over the fact that our finances were so low.

"I wanted to say how sorry I am." He looked me in the eyes. I had never noticed how crystal blue his eyes were before.

"Sorry?"

"For the watch. For what I did. For all of it."

"Well, thanks for returning the watch." I took a step back and pushed the door to an almost shut position.

"May I come inside?"

I didn't want Mekley in my house. He had no place in my life.

"Please."

Sometimes when you want to do what you want to do, you plow ahead and do it, neglecting to stop and listen. Then there are other times when you decide that it might do you well to listen. The way I see it, when we come to that crossroad of choices—to move ahead or to pause—we are given one second. One second to make a decision. I wanted to plow ahead—to shut the door in Mekley's face. But for whatever reason, I took a breath and listened to that inner voice. Perhaps it was from God. I'd like to think it was. Because it certainly didn't come from my heart.

I let Mekley inside. Papa stood, shook his hand, and then led Emi outside.

"Why do we have to come out here?" I heard my sister cry.

"Let's go over to the Shimizu's house," Papa said.

When she continued to protest, my father said gently, "They have animal cookies."

After I removed one of Emi's blankets, and Tom's hardback of a collection of poetry off the sofa, I motioned to Mekley to take a seat. I placed the box with the watch on the coffee table, and sat across from him.

"How have you been?" he asked again.

"We are fine." Thoughts of the times he teased me flooded over me. My head throbbed from the memories.

Mekley sat on the edge of the sofa, like a sparrow perched on the end of a lonely tree branch. "I was in a small inn in Nice, France, during some leave time," he said.

I wondered if it would be rude to ask him to go. I was not in the mood for some recap of his war days.

"While I was there, I got to wondering about God and life and all those things that seem to be prevalent, especially at two in the morning." He smiled. His smile was different now, not as assured. I noticed that he was missing his pinky finger and his ring finger on his left hand. Seeing that I was staring, he lifted his maimed hand and said, "This happened when a grenade went off in a village where we were stationed in France. Five men in my platoon died that day."

He wanted to talk, the Mekley I had known had always been a talker. I listened as he reminisced about battles and buddies of his who had died. The deeper he got into his memories, the stronger his southern accent became. He spoke of God and how when he was lying in a hospital bed in France, a chaplain listened to him confess his sins. "I made a promise then that I would get that watch back to you. I knew it was important to you, the way you had to have it back and snatched it off the dresser at the Towson Farm."

I regretted that day. It cost me.

"I didn't know how to do right back then. I am sorry."

Of course I wanted to know how he got the watch in the first place. "Where'd you get it?"

The question seemed to make him jumpy. He nodded toward the box. "Your brother gave it to me."

The words stung. All my anger seemed to come back with a rush. How could Ken have done that! What kind of loyalty had he had to our family? *Wait a minute,* I thought. *He's lying. Ken wouldn't.*

Mekley's eyes were cast in shadows. "I'm afraid I used to drink a lot, and often. I was bothering the girls, and so to keep me from them, your brother gave me the watch."

"What do you mean *bothering* girls?"

"Flirting with them. One in particular. I was drunk that night. I'm not proud of what I did."

"But why did my brother give you the watch?"

"You don't know?"

"No."

"Your brother and I had formed sort of a friendship. I would get him cigarettes and alcohol. He had his gang of San Jose boys, and in order to be in the gang, you had to pass an initiation. One boy kept begging to be part of the group. His name was Robert Higashi, a little fellow. Must have been only about thirteen. Ken said he could join only if he stole a watch."

"Our watch?"

"Yes. Ken told him which barracks to enter and where to find it."

"But why?" I tried to hold back my anger that seemed to appear from some dark corner of my heart. This anger had been part of me for a long, long time. "Why would he have someone steal our family watch?"

Mekley looked at me as though I was thick in the head—like Henry Towson—unable to grasp concepts and so was made to sit at a table and draw. "To keep me away from Lucy."

"A watch to keep you away from Lucy?" My voice escalated, thundering throughout our house.

Mekley coughed, cleared his throat and said, "I was drunk. He promised me the watch, and I had to promise never to bother Lucy again."

"But why the watch? Why not money?"

"Look, it was all wrong. I'm sorry. I know it's very valuable. I kept it safe."

"Why didn't Ken just report to the project manager that you were bothering Lucy, or whatever it was that you were doing?" I opened the box and turned the watch over. There were the etched bamboo trees and two cranes. As a child, I had loved any chance I got to touch the watch; it was a sacred piece of history and we—the Mori family—had earned it by our bravery. "Why did he feel he had to do it this way?"

"He was not the brightest man. He reacted on his gut, but then again, so did I."

"You two were friends?"

"I suppose." He let out a raspy wheeze. After a moment, he said, "We both liked Coca-Cola and women and Glen Miller music. But after I was told to stay away from Lucy, it all changed. He hated me. Hated me for ruining things. And then when he wanted to turn me in, he couldn't. I had too much on him. His gang, the empty barracks they used for their hangout, the items I would bring to them." Mekley coughed. "Sorry," he said. "This cough is one I brought home from the war. My doctor said it's like perpetual bronchitis."

I thought of Mama and the pneumonia she had contracted in the camp. Mekley's cough wracked throughout his body, as I tried to push aside the memories of her last days.

"Would you like some water?"

He nodded and cleared his throat. "That would be nice."

If someone had told me three years ago that I would be pouring a glass of water for a soldier who was as ugly and beastly as Mekley, I wouldn't have believed him.

War certainly did have a way of changing us all, I thought. War made the toughest of men diminish into little children. But deep down, I knew that the only one who could make a man as mean as Mekley apologize was the very touch of God. Clearly, this soldier had had some sort of divine encounter.

Amazing grace that saved a wretch like Mekley.

As the water flowed into the glass from the spigot, I thought of the water of baptism that cleanses every wretched one of us.

The watch was back! After Mekley left, I gripped the round heirloom tightly, feeling the cold gold against my palm. Our family heirloom was part of us once again. I wanted to run over to the Shimizu's house to tell Papa, but my feet wouldn't move. I just sat there, stunned, and rubbed my fingers over the back, tracing the bamboo and crane engravings. This watch, this piece of history, this . . .

I didn't want it anymore.

From Mekley's story, I tried to envision what had happened the night Ken told Robert to take the watch from Mama's suitcase. I recalled how Ken had reacted when I told him that the watch was missing, and when I'd informed him that I had found the watch. When I was told, that to settle the worries of the nearby Caucasians, I must pay for my theft, where had he been? What had he been thinking? Why hadn't he stood up and told the truth?

The truth would have gotten him into trouble. The truth would have been a mark against his reputation. Yet he hadn't seemed to care how the lies affected my reputation.

And Lucy, she had at least visited me in jail.

I didn't want it anymore.

I placed the watch back into the box, and opening my closet, set the box on the top shelf. Sprawling out on my bed, I knew that my heart wanted something else. Not one thing, but one person.

The Saturday before Monday's opening day of the general store, Tom made some fliers to post around town on telephone poles and inside the front window of the shop. They read: Everything But Buttons Grand Opening.

We had merchandise, all commissioned. There were embroidered handkerchiefs, plenty of canned items, fresh produce. Aunt Kazuko had done her part, and word of mouth—the best form of advertising— had spread over the town. I had ordered some candy and greeting cards from a catalog at wholesale. Tom helped me arrange these on racks by the counter.

Together, we stood with our backs to the front door, so that we could get a good view of how our products looked laid out for our customers to see when they entered the store. Perishables on the left, non-perishables on the right.

The man from the phone company arrived and installed a new phone, one that sat on the counter. He gave us a number that was ours. Tom walked down the street to the barber's and asked to borrow his phone. When our store's phone rang, I knew it was Tom. I answered anyway.

"Hey," he said. "We are really ready to be in business now."

Tom stayed with me the whole first day of business, which was a warm Monday in June. School had just let out for the summer. He hobbled around the shop arranging merchandise and trying to make the most of the circumstances.

"I wish," he said, "that we had money to buy more stuff to sell. We don't even have any matches or towels."

But when the bell chimed, and the first customers entered, I relaxed. They bought plums and pickled beets and a few candy bars; it didn't seem to matter that we had such sparse merchandise. We were selling and that felt good. And the store was as it was supposed to be—a place for local farmers and craftsmen to bring their products to sell. Just like To the Table, the group at church. Because no matter whether you had ripe plums to sell—fit for the emperor himself—or just a few handkerchiefs, what mattered was that you mattered, and you were welcome to bring it along.

"Do you ever wonder what Ken is up to?" Tom asked, after a customer left with a paper bag of carrots and onions from the Yano farm, located north of San Jose.

All the time," I wanted to say, but my pride got in the way. I decided to play it cool, like I was okay with the fact that I hadn't heard from Ken in over a year. "Sure, sometimes. Do you?"

"All the time," he said.

❀

"I need a pep." As soon as Aunt Kazuko came home from cleaning the *wealthy* house, she was muttering about how tired she was. She fanned herself with a pink paper fan. "I walked all the way." She reached into the cupboard for the box of rice crackers. "Can you turn the kettle on for an old woman?" she asked, looking at me.

I was seated at the kitchen table, looking over the finances from Everything But Buttons. Once I tallied up all our costs versus our profit, I could see that we were in the red. By the time I paid each person commission for their items they had brought to sell, and the shop's rent for next month, we'd have only enough to buy a few groceries and pay half of our house rent.

As if I didn't have enough to worry about, now my aunt wanted me to do something for her. I wanted to balk, but did as I was told. I filled the kettle while my aunt removed her shoes and massaged her feet. Her heels were red, the color of blood. The leather pumps on the floor looked like a chew toy for a pet dog. "You need a new pair of shoes."

"Ah, no, these are fine."

She needed shoes; Tom needed a new brace. We needed. We always seemed to be so needy. We'd been the recipients of other people's charity. It was humbling to think of how much we had been given. The list of items included old clothes, pots, pans, food, and even toys for Emi.

As the kettle boiled, the phone rang.

Seeing that my aunt wasn't going to tend to either, I turned off the burner and then answered the phone.

"Hello," I said.

"Hi, Nathan."

"Lucy!"

"How are you?"

"Great! And you? What's going on in Manhattan?"

After a few seconds of silence, I realized that she was crying. "Things aren't working out well," she said.

"Why not? Aren't you recording your next record?"

"I want to come back to San Jose. Would you talk to my parents? Go visit them and tell them that I would like to come home."

"Can't you call them?"

She sniffed a few times. "I can't. I mean, I did. They are upset with me."

"Why?"

She only sniffed louder.

"Is something wrong at your aunt and uncle's house?"

"I miss you."

She surprised me. As many times as I would have given up my right arm to hear her say those words, now they did nothing for me. "What is it you need?"

"I want to come back to San Jose. Back to home."

"Then do it."

"Do you really think that I should?"

What was the matter with her? I had just told her she should come back here. Why couldn't she just do that? Hop on a train or bus or whatever, and come back.

"I want to know what you think."

Why did it matter what I thought? Why did she feel she needed to ask me now? Why hadn't she and Ken asked what I thought before they'd decided to have Robert Higashi steal the watch and then pretend that they had no idea what happened to it?

"Nathan . . . ?"

"Whatever you want to do." And with those words, I hung up. My hands shook as I placed the receiver back in its cradle. "Why does she torment me by calling me?"

"You are silly boy," my aunt said as she poured us tea. "I don't know why you have to be so hard on her. She cares about you."

"How do you know?"

"Why else would she waste her time and money calling you?"

"She and Ken ..."

"What about them? She doesn't still care about him."

"How do you know?"

"Well, I do know. She wasn't asking if she should go to England. She wants to come here. Here, to be near you."

I wanted my aunt's words to be true, but who really knew? I wondered if Lucy's life was so out of control that she could never come back. I'd heard that it happened to people. People changed. Circumstances changed them.

"Only God is constant," my aunt told me one afternoon, as though she could read my thoughts. "He is the solid rock we have to stand on. All other ground is just sinking sand."

"That's a hymn," I said.

"Yes, we sang it last Sunday. You were there in church. But you were so far away. You need to live now, Nathan. When you live the moment, you are rich. No matter where you are, no matter how little money you have in your pocket."

Chapter Thirty

My sister lived in the moment. She didn't dwell on yesterday or seem concerned about tomorrow. But, even so, there were times I wanted to shake my head at her and tell her to think. She begged me to have a concert here at the house. She wanted to play the piano for the Shimizu family. "Please invite them over now," she said one night at ten when I was trying to get her to go to bed.

"If you want to have your own concert, then let's plan one," I suggested. "We can invite the Shimizus over tomorrow afternoon."

Mr. and Mrs. Shimizu and their two teen boys came over. They sat on the sofa as Tom, my aunt, and I served hot tea and chocolate éclairs from the bakery.

First, there was the usual chit-chat, then Papa went outside to smoke, and when there was a lull in the conversation, I motioned for my sister to take her place on the piano bench.

But Emi didn't budge from her chair.

I tried again to get her attention, but she ignored me.

Finally, when the éclairs were all consumed, I said, "Emi wants to play a song or two for you."

Emi refused to play.

I grabbed her hand and took her into the kitchen. After I shut the door, I cried, "You're the one who wanted me to invite them over to hear you play. Now get in there and play something!"

"What's the magic word?"

I looked at her. Really, did she think I needed to ask her to please play? "Okay."

"Okay, what?"

"Please."

She giggled. "No."

Emi!" How could someone so small cause me to become so exasperated? "Come on . . ."

"Say it."

I sighed.

She hit my arm.

"Mama wouldn't let you get away with that."

"Yes, she would."

"She would not." I used my stern tone, the one I reserved for reprimanding her.

"She would, would, would!"

"No! No! No!" I felt a pain grow in my temple. "Okay, please, Emi, play."

She smiled and marched into the living room. Soon I heard her play "Mary Had a Little Lamb."

The guests thought it was great, but I knew it was a cop out. Emi was far more advanced than this selection. She had become lazy.

The Shimizus clapped when she finished, a flawless piece. They asked for another, but she said she had to go. She came into the kitchen and said, "I did it."

"You can play more than that."

"I want a real teacher."

We couldn't afford a real teacher, that was a fact. "What's wrong with me? I've taught you to play, haven't I?" I asked.

"You aren't a real teacher." She crossed her arms across her chest and let her bottom lip protrude. She looked like the epitome of a spoiled rich child. "You aren't really a teacher."

"Why not?"

"Because you live here. A real teacher comes to your house."

"Okay," I said. I knew that she needed to play at least one more song for our guests who had come over under the pretenses of a concert. I could hear them in the living room, anticipating something more. Facing my sister and looking into those eyes that resembled Mama's, I said, "Here's the deal. You go play another song—a really hard one— one that will make everybody proud, and then I'll get you a teacher."

She smiled and marched into the living room. I watched her pull out a sheet of music from the bench. It was "Silent Night." She positioned herself in the middle of the bench as I had taught her and placed the sheet in front of her. Then she played. She played with skill and only made two small mistakes. I listened from the kitchen and breathed relief that she had been successful. What did it matter that it was a Christmas song, and we were in the middle of July?

Her audience clapped, and she slid off the bench, gave a small bow, and entered the kitchen once more. She found me and said, "Make sure that you get me a good teacher."

After our guests left, she rummaged through the music sheets in the bench. Finding what she wanted, she pulled one out.

I glanced at the title of the piece. It was "Amazing Grace."

She sat on the edge of the bench, slouched over, and started to play.

Was she trying to make me miss Mama even more? Ever since Lucy had sung this song at Mama's funeral, I associated it with the loss of my mother. Yet, Emi didn't seem to care about nostalgia. She pounded the keys.

I stopped her. "If you are going to play, you need to play well. And what did I tell you about sitting up straight?"

"I can't." She swung her legs and wiggled her bottom.

"You can."

"You are annoying me." She sounded just like our aunt.

"Fine, you play alone." I turned to Tom and asked if he'd like to go see a movie with me.

"Are you paying?" Tom asked from the sofa where he was reading some thick book on Shakespeare.

"Sure," I said.

I had never had a nine-to-five job before, and the days at the shop wore me out. On weekends when I closed the store, I wanted to relax and not be bothered by a five-year-old. She didn't know this; she just knew that she could push my buttons, and for her, that seemed to be entertainment.

"How about me?" she asked, as Tom and I prepared to leave the house.

Tom sat on the living room floor and slipped on his shoe that was attached to his leg brace. He worked quickly.

Emi continued to ask, "How about me, me, me?"

"Why don't you just stay here with Aunt Kazuko and play with your paper dolls?" I suggested. The flat paper dolls my aunt had bought for her last week were in a stack on the coffee table, along with their clip-on outfits.

"I want to go with you." Quickly, she found her shoes where she'd last tossed them under the sofa, although our aunt was always reprimanding her for not placing her shoes at our house's front door. "Like we do in Japan," Aunt Kazuko often said. "Take off your shoes and come into the house." To which Emi often replied, "But we are in

America!"

Emi sat on the floor to put on a pair of cotton and rayon socks she dug out of her saddle shoes. "Please, please?" She pushed her little clad-feet into the shoes and stuck out her legs—a gesture indicating that she wanted me to tie the laces.

"All right," I said, reluctance lining my tone, "but you can't be so bossy." I bent down and tied her laces.

"You won't like the movie," said Tom, as he stood, adjusted his brace, and walked toward the front door.

"How do you know?" she asked.

"It won't be one you can understand."

"Then let's just get ice cream. I can understand that."

We asked our aunt if she wanted to join us, but she said she had a stomach ache. Sure enough, she traced it to something she'd consumed. "I eat at that restaurant on the corner of Fourth Street and Taylor. The *unagi* (eel) is so *mazui* (tasteless). I think it can't be fresh."

"Which restaurant are you talking about?" I asked.

"The one the Tateishi family owns. That hole in the wall. He's engaged, you know."

"Who's engaged?"

"Haven't you heard? Jennifer Tanaka and Jeff Tateishi are getting married next April."

"Woo," said Emi. "I wanna go to the wedding."

"Ahh." Aunt Kazuko leaned against the kitchen sink. "I hate to get sick off of food that is too *mazui* and cost too high."

Before we left, she called out to me. "You better find a girl soon. They are all being snapped up!"

"Are you getting married?" asked Emi.

"No," I said, opening the front door.

"He's only nineteen," said Tom. "He's still a baby."

Emi laughed.

"It wasn't that funny," I said.

As we walked to the ice cream shop, I noticed that Tom winced as he hobbled. He seemed to not be walking with his usual gait.

"What's wrong?" I asked.

"Brace just feels a bit tight, especially around the knee."

"He's getting too big for the brace. He needs a new one," said Emi.

"Can't you have it adjusted?" I recalled how we had often frequented a cobbler's shop in San Jose before the war. Prior to the visit, Mama would have taken Tom out to buy a new pair of leather shoes. The cobbler—an elderly man named Mr. Tennyson—would attach the steel piece of Tom's knee-ankle-foot orthotics to the heel of his right shoe. We'd sit on a bench in the front of the store and wait, as he hammered the heel. When the brace had been attached, Tom would slip into the right shoe first, and then the left one as Mama would secure the strap just below his knee and then the one above his knee. Tom would take a few steps. Sometimes Mr. Tennyson had to lengthen the brace, a job that usually required a doctor, but when Mr. Tennyson learned to do it, it saved all of us a trip to the hospital.

"It's also breaking," said Emi.

"Breaking?" I asked.

"The straps are almost gone," said Emi.

I wondered when the last time Tom had been fitted for a new brace. It had been back in camp a year ago when Tom needed new shoes, and Aunt Kazuko had ordered a pair from the Montgomery Ward catalog. Mr. Kubo had found some tools to attach the brace to Tom's new right shoe. But that brace had never been replaced. That brace must be over four years old.

"Show him where it is breaking," Emi said to Tom.

"Nah, it'll be all right."

Tom never complained and that wasn't fair, I thought. Everybody deserved to complain every once in a while. Everybody deserved a day to say what was troubling him or her.

"We'll get you a new brace," I said as I patted his back.

"And a piano teacher for me," said Emi as she skipped along the sidewalk in front of us.

I pasted on a smile. "Sure."

And at that moment a prayer formed in my mind. It was just like so many others I had prayed over the years. *God, you will provide, somehow, some way, won't you?*

Please.

Chapter Thirty-one

A nd then one day at the end of July, when the lavender hibiscuses were at their height in blooms, my life changed again. And it was the fourth time in my life to become flabbergasted. Since getting back to San Jose, Papa's return to us, Lucy's first phone call, and Mekley's visit had all caught me off-guard as unexpected surprises. Another was about to happen.

I was with a customer who was interested in buying a carton of pickled beets. I wasn't sure what one needed with so many beets, but this customer was from out of town and heading east and said she was delighted to see beets for sale. "Beets are rich in vitamins," she said. "Did you know that?"

I did, as a matter of fact, and told her so. I was sure that Mrs. Hirayama, who had picked and pickled the beets in a vinegar-and-onion brine, knew that, too.

"*You people* have been picking sugar beets for a long time, haven't you?"

I knew she meant well, but even so, heat rose from my face. She was a customer; I needed to hold it together. "I think *many people* have been picking all sorts of things for a long time," I said. "And for that, we should be grateful."

"Ah, yes," she agreed. "I am grateful for everyone's hard labor."

As I rang up the woman's purchase, I forced a smile, took her money, and thanked her for shopping at our store. She turned to go, just when the door's bell chimed. I looked at the door and nearly lost my breath.

There stood Lucy! There she was with her hair cut short like it was on the cover of her album. It was not dyed blond, but black, just as black as I remembered it.

She made her way toward me, as I stood paralyzed. Halfway across the floor, she said, "Hello, Nathan. Quite a shop you have here."

I managed to get from behind the counter, and as we met, her arms wrapped around me in a tight embrace.

I found my voice. "What are you doing in town?"

She stepped back and smiled. "You look handsome as ever."

Again I asked, "What are you doing in town? Staying at your folks?"

"Just a visit. Show me around the store. Mom said you had a grand opening."

I showed her the jars of pickled produce, the knitted scarves, the handkerchiefs, carefully stitched with flowers, the rack of greeting cards, comic books, and candy. "Tom said a store wasn't a store without comic books and candy."

"I'd have to agree."

There was something different about her. I watched as she made her way around the store alone. A customer entered to buy some fresh plums; plums brought in from the Yanagi orchard outside of San Jose.

"Nice day, isn't it?" she said to me. She'd been in before, even been at Heart Mountain with us, but I couldn't recall her name.

"Is it Lucy?" the woman asked, as she spotted Lucy looking over greeting cards.

"Yes. Hello, Mrs. Nita."

"Well, when did you get into town?"

"Last night."

"Where are you living nowadays? Still in New York?" She said New York with a slight air to her tone, making the name of the city sound posh.

"Yes." Lucy smiled, but it wasn't one of her genuine ones. She was guarded.

I didn't care how guarded she intended to be. Once Mrs. Nita walked out of the shop with her plums, I walked over to Lucy. "How is it, really, in New York?"

"Oh, you know. Busy. Lots of people. Manhattan is crowded compared to here."

"How are you, really?"

She lowered her eyes and studied the card in her hand. "Get well soon," she read from it. "That's what we all need, isn't it?"

Panic weaved into my throat. "You're not ill, are you?"

With her eyes still lowered, she said, "In a way, aren't we all? I mean, we're all dying."

I grabbed her arm, right at the shoulder. "What's wrong?"

She lifted her eyes then. Looking me in the face, she said, "Nathan."

Something about the way she said it, I knew. She was in trouble.

She had been in Manhattan. All sorts of things went on there. There was the mob; there was high society folk, there was pregnancy. "Lucy?"

Leaning against my chest, she said, "I am home now."

I wanted to ask her all the questions buzzing in my mind. I wanted to tell her about Mekley's visit and the pocket watch, that I knew the truth—that I knew she and Ken had not been honest with me. But for those few moments, I just let her lean close to my heart.

When a truck pulled up and one of my vendors dropped off crates of raspberries and pears, I took inventory. After writing down the number of crates he had on a form—a form specifically drawn up for our vendors—I asked him to sign at the bottom of the page.

Since we had no typewriter, and my aunt needed one, she went to the library. While Emi read picture books, Aunt Kazuko asked to borrow the library's Underwood.

She created a sheet for me to use in the shop. "This will keep everybody in the know," she said when she came home and handed it to me. And of course, that is what we all wanted—everybody to be *in the know*. All kidding aside, I appreciated my aunt's knowledge about accounting and how to keep the checks and balances in place. I wanted happy vendors as they were the heart and soul of Everything But Buttons.

I wanted more time alone with Lucy, but vendors and customers kept entering, needing my attention. As I dealt with them, Lucy stood close by, making it hard for me to concentrate on candy bars and pickled beets.

After a while, she said, "You're busy. I'll come by later."

"Tonight," I called out as she headed toward the door. "Meet me here at five. We can get something to eat."

She came by a little before five, but said she couldn't stay. "I promised my mom I would eat dinner with her and Dad."

"Well, can you talk a bit before you have to go?"

"Sure."

Each weekday I closed the shop at five, and today, when the old clock on the wall ticked toward five, I thought of all the days I stood at the door with the key in my hand, wishing that Lucy were here to walk home with me. Now here she was—here, in the flesh. But instead of feeling euphoria, worry spread over my chest. Be in control, I told myself. *You have to know the truth even if it hurts you.*

I offered her the one chair in the shop, and she sat. I leaned against the counter and then turned a crate upside down and sat across from her on it. "So what have you been up to?" I asked. I figured I would start with the present and let it lead to the past. I was desperate to hear her side of the story with Mekley.

"It's been okay." As she brushed hair off her face and tucked a few strands behind her ear, I noticed a mark just below her ear on her jaw line.

"How did that happen?" I asked.

"What?"

I stood and walked over to her. Placing my hand on her jaw, I saw a jagged indentation—an imprint in her skin.

She pulled my hand from her face. "I was with my record producer. He got mad one night and ... he ..."

"What about Mekley?"

"Mekley?"

"Yeah. In Heart Mountain."

"He was forceful, too. But drunk. Did Ken tell you what happened?"

"No. I haven't spoken to Ken since he left camp."

"I haven't heard from him in over a year," she said. "I hope he's all right."

"Whose idea was it to give Mekley the watch?"

"Ken's." Her voice was low. "I should go."

But she didn't leave. She sat and looked at her hands.

"Lucy, you have to tell me. How bad can it be?"

"What Ken and I did wasn't right, Nathan. But Mekley was a soldier, and he threatened us."

"Threatened you?"

"Yes. He said that unless I spent the night with him, he would tell the camp authorities about Ken."

"Tell them what? They knew he had a gang."

"It wasn't the gang. He was bringing whiskey into camp. He bought bottles of it from Mekley who got it from either Cody or Powell. Then Ken sold those bottles to other internees for about twice the cost. He had a regular business going on."

"Were Mekley and Ken friends?"

"At first they were. It started out that Mekley would get cigarettes and Cokes for Ken. He also let Ken use a room in one of the buildings as a club house."

I wondered how much more of the story she was going to unveil. I didn't have to wait long.

Softly, she said, "Mekley came onto me. 'How much do I have to pay you for her?' he asked Ken one night. And after that Ken was mad at him and wanted him away from me. But Mekley didn't listen."

Suddenly her eyes filled and she said, "Ken and I knew that we had dug a big hole. We were in deep. Really, Mekley was the one who should have been behind bars. He harassed me. I have let a lot of men harass me, Nathan. I'm not proud of that. I am learning to stick up for myself." She wiped her tears, and although I so wanted to rush over to her and tell her that it was all right now, I couldn't. I had to hear the rest of her story.

"Just what did Mekley do?" I asked.

"He approached me one night when he had been drinking. Ken had been drinking, too. Mekley was like an animal, and Ken told him to stop. Ken had to literally pull him off of me. Of course, Ken had no power over an American soldier. So to keep Mekley away from me forever, he promised him the pocket watch. Your family's heirloom. He told the story behind it and how valuable the watch was. Mekley agreed. Ken then had a guy who wanted to be in their gang steal it from your barracks so that it would look like theft. Ken couldn't let on what really happened. Can you imagine? People would be so infuriated with him for trading his family heirloom to a soldier. Especially to Mekley, the most vile of all soldiers. And I certainly didn't want my reputation ruined by letting people know I'd been accosted by a man."

Accosted seemed a strange word to use in this case. "You were in danger. Mekley was drunk." I remembered how Mekley had admitted to me during his visit that he had been drunk. "He could have raped you."

She nodded. "That's why I will always be thankful to Ken."

I wondered then. Did she still love him? Was she missing him, as she had in camp when he'd left to enlist?

"I've had lots of time to think," she said. "I knew we hurt you. I hated that because of us you had to be in jail."

I felt a surge of anger at her, at Mekley, but most of all at my brother. He was family. He should have protected me, stood up for me. But I didn't want this time with Lucy to be consumed with frustration over Ken. She was here. Here with me. How long had I waited for this time? Lightly, I said, "So why Lucy Heart?"

She laughed. "Do you like it?"

I wanted to laugh with her. But laughter was far from me and seemed inappropriate. There was so much I wanted to know, so much only she could tell me. "Why the blonde hair?"

"They said no one would buy an album from an Asian. That's what I was told. So my producer decided that I should change my looks. We went to a hair salon where they dyed my hair platinum blonde. My producer—"

"Does he have a name?" I was tired of her using the words *my* and *producer* together as though she was married to him and calling him *my husband*.

"Yes. It's Donovan. He got me my first record deal."

"So they liked your voice, but not your face."

"Well . . . I guess you could say that."

"Did Donavan like you?"

"He drank a lot. He got angry. He took it out on me."

"Did you love him?"

"Donovan?" She looked puzzled by my question.

"Yes, your producer."

"No, it wasn't like that."

"How many stitches in that cut?" Now that I had seen the scar, it was impossible not to notice it. From my guess, it was about an-inch-and-a-half long.

"Thirty-three."

I hated that she knew the number—that the number flowed so easily from her mouth. Those stitches were going to be with her forever, part of her identity, like her name. If only she'd stayed, we could have left camp together after the war. In my care, I would have kept her safe; there would be no scar.

She left the chair and circled around the shop. "You were so responsible. In spite of everything, you were in charge. Wounded, but reliable."

"Wounded?" The word was not one that held strength or honor. Wounded was what happened to soldiers and baby birds.

"It's not so bad to be wounded. When you really open your eyes, we all are. Every single one of us." She forced a small smile. "I know I'm wounded. I'm really not as serene as my songs. I used to believe that God wouldn't let His people get caught up in situations that would harm them. But now I know that sometimes it's far easier to ignore His still small voice and just plow through. Just do what we want. It's that human will thing. He lets us fall when we insist we want our way."

I had interrogated her enough. When I looked into her eyes, I saw how weary they looked. The liveliness they once held was gone. "I'm glad you're safe," I said at last.

She leaned against me for a second, and then without warning, lifted her mouth and kissed my lips.

Without a word, she turned, and left the shop.

I didn't sleep much that night and by morning I was as confused as ever. Although her kiss had been pleasant, it seemed too quick, too spontaneous, and without any explanation. What did it mean for her to have kissed me? What did it mean to me?

"Who is she?" I asked aloud, just before daybreak. Who was this Lucy Heart? Certainly, she wasn't the Fusou of camp.

But I was not the Nathan of camp either.

Adversity caused us to change, some for the better, some not. How could I hold anything against the girl who had kept me sane with her soprano voice and songs with words that soothed my soul? How could I deny her the attention she deserved?

Yet, I wondered.

Finally, at the end of the day, I asked God what to do. He was silent, as He often is. I waited for Him to tell me to consider a real romantic relationship with her. Perhaps He'd show me by sending me a bunch of hearts or some passage about love. Some sign. Humans are forever asking God for signs. We don't often think that sometimes you just have to step out. Step out like a toddler learning to walk.

Chapter Thirty-two

L ucy was still in town. I wasn't sure for how long, and I didn't want to miss out on a chance to spend time with her. I called her parents' house and asked to speak to her.

"Can we go out to talk somewhere? Grab something to eat?" I asked. I sounded confident, casual. Over the years I had often thought about how I'd ask her on a date. None of my scenarios had been like this. In each one, I was nervous, uncertain of her response. But that Saturday morning, I knew she would say yes.

"Yes, sure we can," she said.

I didn't want to see a movie. I wanted to sit across from her, stare at her, and talk with her. "Can you meet me for dinner at that little hamburger shop near Main Street?" Last I recall, there were no anti-Japanese signs in the windows.

"Barry's?" she asked.

"Is that what it's called?" Hearing Barry made me think of Barry Kubo. I made a mental note that I owed him a letter, and this time I would have lots of good news to fill it with. "Meet me there at six," I said.

I was five minutes early. She was late, apologetic. I didn't care. She was here with me, and as we sat across from each other at a table, I thanked God for this gift.

"I was always mesmerized by you," she said, after the waitress took our orders.

I felt my heart take wings and flutter against my chest. "Really? Why?"

"You were the strong one, always thinking, always taking care of your mom and family. You were the backbone."

"I suppose you're right." Once the words left my mouth, I thought of how old they sounded, like I was some aged man talking, one who should be hunched over, adjusting his hearing aid. Ken had accused me of being old before my time. *Lighten up, Nobu!*

Here she was. Here we were. And all I could think about was that day when I'd approached her and boldly asked her why she had wanted to be called Lucy. "Do you remember when I asked you why you wanted to be called Lucy?"

"Yes. You told me that I should go by Fusou. You told me that Fusou suited me. I have always wanted to know since that time how a name comes to suit a person."

"I guess you become the name. You fit into it over the years."

She reached for my hand. Her fingers felt like silk, like the silk from a kimono Mama had worn on New Year's Day. "I have admired you for a long time," she said.

"Why?" When I looked into her eyes, I was afraid I might see doubt. But her face was serene, beautiful, youthful. Yet the new addition of that scar bothered me. I looked away, pretending that I wanted to ask our waitress for another soda. The truth was, that scar bothered me as well as what it stood for. Being jealous of Ken was one thing, but now being jealous of a man I had never met, now that was something new for me.

The waitress brought us Cokes. I waited till she left our table to ask Lucy, "What did he use?"

"What?"

I gestured toward the scar on her jaw.

"His fist."

"And he's still your producer?"

"Yeah. Sort of." She dropped her gaze and looked at her glass of soda.

"Did you go to the police?"

"For what?"

"To tell them that he hit you."

"No, a neighbor took me to the ER."

"Did they ask what had happened?"

"I told them that I had fallen and hit a rail outside my aunt and uncle's apartment building."

"You lied."

"Yes." Quickly she said, "No."

"Yes and no?"

"When he hit me, I fell and cut my jaw against the brick fireplace in his house. So technically, I did fall."

"What were you arguing about?"

She reached across the table and found my hand. "Nathan, please. It doesn't matter anymore."

When our burgers arrived, we picked at them as though they were old grievances set before us, dressed up in disguises on white platters.

Guardedly, we spoke of the weather, the economy, and candidates for the next presidential election. I thought it was safe to ask her about life in New York City, provided that I didn't ask about her recordings or producer again. Her meticulous explanation of how to get on and off the subway made me smile, as did her attempt at a Brooklyn accent. But after that, she didn't seem interested in continuing to share about the big city life. So I let it go and finished my Coke.

Someone put a coin in the jukebox, and soon the music of Glenn Miller filled the diner. I thought of how Mama and Papa used to dance to "In the Mood" together. I thought of family and courage and how life could shatter in one single second.

When it seemed like we had both had enough of sadness, we looked for something to laugh at. We watched a couple, who had just entered the restaurant, find a table nearby. They were dressed alike in matching blue sweatshirts that had WBO printed in large white letters across the chest.

"What's WBO?" Lucy whispered.

"You don't know?"

"No, what is it?"

Quickly, off the top of my head, I came up with a reply. "White Boys Only."

"Ohh, that's bad." She giggled.

"Or it could be worse. White Body Odor."

"That's worse! How about World Body Odor?"

"I guess that's better. That way we aren't discriminating against anyone. Not boys or girls or any race."

"I hate discrimination," she said flatly.

But I didn't want the conversation to go back to being one that was intense. I wanted humor, laughter, if possible. "Aunt Kazuko thinks we should sell matches and towels at our store."

"Matches and towels? Clean towels, I would hope?"

"None with body odor."

"I like your humor. I always have."

I let her hold my hand and wished the moment could last, but my mind was spinning. Now, with Lucy back in my life, I couldn't help but think of how Ken needed to be back in it, too. He was family. Mama would have wanted me to find him. Had Mama been here, she would have never let him get so far from us.

"What's going on in your mind?" Lucy asked.

"I was thinking about Ken." He was my brother. And Emi's and Tom's. How could I continue to deny them his presence in their lives? Jumping from the table, I said, "Let's go find out about Ken."

Lucy looked confused. "How? He's in London."

"Well, somebody in town has to know more about what he's up to." I grabbed her hand, paid the bill, left a tip, and together we exited the restaurant.

I knew the Hashimoto family had a son in the 442nd regiment. They worked on a farm north of San Jose where they picked strawberries. We could take a cab to their house.

Mr. and Mrs. Hashimoto were in the middle of a late dinner but welcomed us inside as they finished eating. They asked if we'd like something to drink, but we declined, and Lucy apologized for coming for an impromptu visit during the dinner hour.

She and I sat in their modest living room on a sagging brown sofa that must have come from the same store ours had come from. The room held two wing-back chairs, a floor lamp and an oak coffee table with a few noticeable scratch marks. The clock on the mantle ticked loudly, and then when the nine o'clock hour hit, a little bird came out and sang, "Cukoo-cukoo," nine times. Next to the clock was a framed photo on the mantle. Lucy and I decided that it must be Alex Hashimoto. There he was, in uniform, clean shaven and militant, standing by an army tank.

"Isn't he handsome?" Mrs. Hashimoto said, as she entered the room.

"Yes," said Lucy.

"Ken looked just as handsome in his uniform, I bet," said Mrs. Hashimoto.

I cringed. I had no idea what Ken looked like in his army uniform. Only once had he written to us while enlisted, and I'd tossed the letter away after reading about his antics. I knew that, at that time, Lucy was hearing from him, too, and her gushy feelings toward him stopped me from wanting anything to do with him. Besides, he had betrayed me, our family. He had let a connection to our past slide through our fingers. And what made it worse was that he hadn't cared.

Mr. Hashimoto joined us. He was a little man with a chubby face and a dark beard. "You haven't heard from Ken?" he asked me.

"No, not in a while."

"He's in London."

"I did hear that. But what is he doing there?"

Mrs. Hashimoto smiled. "He's in good health. He survived the war, as did Alex. The two of them have a Japanese restaurant in the East End."

From Lucy's response, I gathered that she had no clue that this was what Ken was up to either. "Somebody mentioned something about a restaurant," she said. "but I didn't know that Ken was involved."

"Apparently, they are doing well," said Mr. Hashimoto. "They found a Japanese chef who makes really good *tempura* and *teriyaki*. The local people like his cooking."

"I'm sure you miss him," said Lucy, and I wondered if she said that because she missed Ken.

"We do," said Mr. Hashimoto. "But he is doing what he wants to. We hear from him about every two or three months."

"Not often enough," said Mrs. Hashimoto. "But you know how boys can be when it comes to writing letters."

"Have you seen Alex since the war ended?" I asked.

"He came to visit us at Christmas last year. He stayed a week. Then back to London."

"I would have liked to have talked with him," I said.

"I should have called you to let you know he was here." Mrs. Hashimoto nudged her husband. "Get that review," she said. "You know, the one from the magazine."

He grunted, heaved himself up, and plodded into the other room. When he returned, he had a page which he handed to me. Lucy slipped close and together we studied the paper which appeared to be from a magazine called *London Style*. The article was titled, "New Japanese restaurant offers tasty meals." Under the title was a photo of Alex and Ken, both smiling, in front of their restaurant.

"Do you see the name of the restaurant?" asked Mrs. Hashimoto.

Lucy ran a finger along the curved letters of the front door of the restaurant. "He named it Nathan's," she said.

"You may have the article," said Mrs. Hashimoto. "You take it home and keep it safe."

"Thank you," said Lucy.

I blinked back tears.

Mr. Hashimoto drove us to my house in his truck, and when we arrived, it was almost eleven. I invited Lucy in, and she said she could stay a little while.

The house was quiet, and as I checked the bedrooms, I saw that everyone was asleep. Papa was now sleeping in Tom's room on a bed the Shimizu family had given him.

"I used to check the beds and do a head count at camp," I said, as Lucy sat on the sofa. "Ken was rarely in his bed."

"That gang took a lot of his time."

"What exactly did they do?"

"Oh, they did all sorts of crazy things. They fought the gang from L.A. Went to dances. Tried to appear tough. Flirted with girls."

The Hashimotos had a framed photo of their military son on their mantle. On top of ours, we had only a bare glass vase from some box of donations. I placed the article on the mantle and used the vase to hold it upright. "There," I said proudly, "now we are just like the Hashimotos."

Lucy laughed. "Sit down."

I eased down next to her and put my arm around her shoulders. Here she was, here we were. Ken had named his restaurant after me. What was the next step? I'd write to him. I'd tell him that I had harbored resentment for too long. I'd tell him that Mekley brought the watch back. All was well.

"I'm sorry that you've been estranged so long from your brother." Lucy's voice was soft against the dimly-lit room.

"And you? You used to be close to him."

"Once. But I lost contact with him. Out of sight, out of mind."

"And with me?"

"With you it has always been different. I told you that I admired you. From afar."

"Afar."

"With you, you were much more deep in your heart than Ken was. Ken teased and flirted. He charmed everyone. You," she turned her face toward mine. "You were always thinking. Always seeing life with a pair of realistic glasses. You had this depth. You still have it, Nathan. People like Ken and me . . . we are so much alike. Yet we need people like you to keep us grounded."

Although my arm was around her, and she was here, right here, her mouth just inches from mine, I couldn't kiss her. My mind was still restless with why and how come? Had I been a lion in a cage at the zoo, I would have paced. Ken was safe. Lucy was interested in me. But what about her producer? What about her glamorous life in Manhattan? Was she going to return to it and leave me again? And what did she mean that she and Ken were alike? What was *people like you? Grounded?* What was she implying when she called me *grounded?* The word conjured up a ball and chain in my mind. I was stable, the one people came to after they had made mistakes, the one they returned to so that they could confess their sins and go out again.

As though my swirling thoughts were an energetic force propelling me to action, I bolted off the sofa. "Would you like something to drink?"

"No, thank you."

"Can't I get you a cup of tea?"

"No, I'm fine."

"I just don't get it," I said. "You aren't honest, Lucy. You used to tell the truth. You sang songs that were truthful and good, songs about God and country."

"What are you saying?"

I ran a hand over my face and let it rub against the stubble on my chin. "You won't talk about your life in Manhattan."

"What do you want to know?"

"Are you going back?"

"I don't know. What do *you* want?"

"You said you wanted to be at home. If home is here, then why would you return to New York?"

"I have a contract to make another record."

"So you are going back?"

"I don't know."

"Well, I'm going into the kitchen to get some coffee. While I make it, you can think."

In the kitchen, I opened the cupboard and took out the can of Maxwell. I measured the coffee and water, as I did every morning, only tonight I didn't hum the songs she sang in camp. I didn't hear her slip out either, but she did. When I went back to the living room, the sofa was bare, and she was gone.

Chapter Thirty-three

The next day I called her parents' home, but they said she wasn't there. She had packed up and left in the morning.

"Without telling you where she was going?" I asked.

"Only a note that said she would be back and not to worry about her," said Mrs. Yokota.

"Do you have any idea where she might have gone?"

"Nathan, you can't chase her. Please."

I wanted to say that I couldn't let Lucy go, that I had already let her go once. Too many people had left my life. I wanted Lucy permanently in mine. Didn't they know that I had once been willing to jump in front of a bomb for her? True, I'd been naïve then; I had been fifteen years old. But now at nearly twenty, I knew I needed her.

But Mrs. Yokota just interrupted my thoughts before I could form them into words. "Just run your business, and take care of your family, Nathan. And pray. God will meet her. These things take time."

❀

I had let her go again. She had been seated on our sofa in our house, and now she was gone.

I kicked myself. Had I made her feel shameful? About Mekley? About the producer? About what she and Ken had done?

What was wrong with me? Ken was not coming back. Now Lucy was gone again.

Each time our phone rang at home or at the shop, my heart jumped. But she was never on the other end. I waited a few days and then called her parents to ask if they had heard from her.

"She took a train to Seattle. My sister is there," said Mrs. Yokota.

I begged her for the phone number and, reluctantly, Mrs. Yokota gave it to me.

When I called the first time, no one answered.

I tried to smile at my customers, concentrate on their comments to me about how happy they were to have this general store, and respond accordingly. I calculated how much we had made this month in sales. I counted our money in the cash register and hoped that one day we'd be making enough to open a savings account.

When I locked the door at five-fifteen, I took the opportunity of being alone to make a private phone call.

Lucy's aunt answered and passed the phone to her.

My words tumbled out. "Come back. Work in the shop with me. If living with your parents is too hard, rent an apartment."

"Nathan, I can't. I have no money. I spent the last of it on the train ticket to Seattle."

"I have money," I blurted. "Come back. You can make a record here. You can go to L.A. to cut one and then come back to San Jose." I knew I was making it all too simplistic because I wanted it to be, because I wanted her in my life.

"Oh, Nathan," she said, "I had my day in the sun. I tasted the small amount of fame. I had to fight and deny my own roots in order to get a contract. I feel like I sold my soul to the Devil. I lost a part of me; the me that I used to be."

Why was she talking this way? This was not how she should talk. She was talented and beautiful and had a godly soul. "What is it you want to do now?"

"I want to find home," she said. "I want to share it with the people I love. I want to know that I am right where God wants me to be."

For a few seconds we were silent.

After a moment she asked, "How about you, Nathan?"

"What?"

"What do you want?" she asked.

What did I want? I let a moment pass as I thought. I had been so busy trying to take care of everybody. I wondered if I had any desire that had not been worked to death out of me.

So much of what I had wanted was lost . . . Gone was any hope of having a normal life like others got, a life with Mama, Papa, Emi, Tom, Ken, and me—all together as a family. I had felt broken, lost, confused. But with Lucy in my life once again, it seemed as though something right had been restored.

"Come home, Lucy," I whispered. "Come back to me."

Chapter Thirty-four

Ken took it upon himself to give Mekley our watch so that the soldier would keep away from Lucy. I wanted to pawn the watch so that Lucy could be helped once again. But I had learned from Ken's mistake. He acted on impulse. I wouldn't make the same mistake. There are times when families need to do the right thing, and that often means bringing other members into the picture.

So I went to my aunt. She was looking over Everything But Buttons' revenues and expenses.

"I have something to tell you," I said.

She glanced up at me through her reading glasses. "Okay, but make it quick-quick."

"It's a long story."

She looked at my face and then closed the ledger.

"I know you are busy."

"Never mind that. I have time. Put on the kettle for tea. And, oh, get the cookies."

Scanning the pantry, I saw no cookies.

"Behind the jar of jelly," she said. "In a paper bag."

"You hid them?" I saw the bag and pulled it out. Opening it, sure enough, there was a tin of chocolate cookies.

"With all of you vultures in the house? I have to hide. What else is a poor woman to do?"

Over cups of hot tea and chocolate cookies, I told her about Mekley's visit. I included how he'd stuttered and been apologetic.

"I remember that soldier," she said with disdain. "He never do any work. He only look at girls. I can't imagine him stuttering or saying he was sorry."

I told her how in a bar in France, Mekley was convicted of his wrongdoings. "He asked God for forgiveness."

"Repented?" Aunt Kazuko's eyes widened. "That is the power of God's doing," she said. "That is how God operates when He opens your eyes. God opens, and you see. You look at truth and after that, you know you must act in truth." After having said that, she seemed pleased with herself for sharing, fluffed her hair with one hand, and waited for me to continue.

At the end of my story, my aunt had finished all but two of the cookies. "I ate too much," she said, patting her belly. "Hide the cookies from me, will you?"

"What about the watch?" I said. "Don't you think it would be okay to let the money from it help us? Don't you think we could all use some money to make a better life for us now?" I took in a breath before asking one last question. "Don't you think I could get a train ticket to bring Lucy back?"

"Talk to your Papa," she said. "He will tell you what to do."

I found him on the porch with his cigarettes, the grey fedora on his head, and a slight smile against his lips.

"Papa, I need to talk to you." I sat on the porch railing facing him and saw the lines in his face, the creases that I had never noticed before. "It's about the Mori watch."

He drew in a lungful of smoke and let it out. "Did that soldier return it?"

"Yeah. I have it now. It's safe." The last time I had checked it was still on a shelf in my bedroom closet.

"A few years ago I had a dream that it was lost."

"It was, remember?"

He continued as though he hadn't heard me. "At first the dream scared me, but then I realized it was only a watch."

"The watch isn't lost. I know I told you that it once was. It's here. That soldier did bring it back."

"Good, good."

I excused myself and left him to go and fetch it. When I returned, I sat next to him and placed the opened box with the watch on his lap.

He snubbed out the cigarette butt into an old coffee can he kept under his chair and used as an ashtray. Carefully, he took the box in both hands. Running his fingers over the back and front, he opened the casing to see the face of the watch. "6 o'clock," he said. With fingers wrapped around the chain, he lifted the watch to his ear. "Stopped ticking."

"It just needs to be wound up a little bit. Like you do." I studied his face for a smile, but there was none. Perhaps I could get him to talk like he used to about our family treasure. "Tell me the story of the watch again," I said.

Papa leaned back in his chair. He sighed a few times, as though the action was helping him to remember. "A young girl slipped into the river," he began. "She couldn't swim. She was sure she was going to die."

I closed my eyes, letting the sound of his voice take me back to yesterday, back to when I was a boy, back before the terrible war, to a sweet season when Mama was with us.

"She was going under. The water was cold and . . . she knew . . . she was going to die." Papa paused. Abruptly, he said, "Did she suffer?"

I waited for him to continue, but after a moment of silence, I opened my eyes. I saw that he was looking right at me. He was waiting for me. "Uh, yes, the girl suffered. A bit, but she was saved." Had my papa forgotten the family story? Or did he want to make sure that I knew it? This was unlike him. In the past, he never asked questions when he recalled the special Mori family tale.

Suddenly, Papa's hand left the watch and gripped my arm. "Did she suffer?"

My mouth turned dry, and a lump formed in my chest. Papa was not talking about the girl in the story.

"Did she suffer when she died, Nobu?"

I saw Mama's pale face, my memory even heard her cough and her frail voice asking me to take care of everybody. "No, she died quickly," I lied.

Papa relaxed his fingers against my arm. He closed his eyes, and I closed mine.

We sat like that until the moon rose above us, shining like it does no matter where you are in the world, no matter what you are going through or have been through. We breathed in the sweet aroma of nearby roses, roses that clung to thorny stems before winter whisked them away.

A neighbor's barking dog brought us out of our thoughts, and then we knew it was time to get ready for bed. Together, we stood. Together, we entered our home.

❀

While brushing my teeth, I realized that I hadn't asked Papa if it was all right to sell the watch.

The next morning at breakfast, the more I chewed my toast and thought about telling him about Lucy and her need for money, I concluded that it was a bad idea. I watched him read the headlines of the paper, watched him spread strawberry jam on his toast, watched him stir his coffee. And all I could hear was the sound of family history, of tradition, of the value of the watch and how it had been in the Mori family for three generations.

Sell it? Papa wouldn't go for it. What if I just sold it behind his back? He was so lost in his muddled thoughts that he would probably never ask where it was.

But I had made too many mistakes about this watch. Now I needed to tell Papa that while it had once been a noble treasure for us, this watch had become a source of frustration for me.

As I walked to my store, I prayed for wisdom.

When I reached Everything But Buttons and unlocked the door, my prayer was still unanswered.

Aunt Kazuko entered the store that afternoon, greeted me, and while I talked with a customer, she dusted off the tops of some canned plums before flopping onto the chair. "Business good today?" she asked.

"It's been okay."

When the customer left with a pack of Wrigley's gum and two greeting cards, she said, "What did your papa say about the watch?"

"I didn't ask."

"Why not?"

"I'm afraid he'll say no."

"I saw Mrs. Yokota today at the grocery store. She is worried about Lucy. I told her that you love her and that you want to pay for her to come back."

"You told her all that?"

"Yes. And I will tell your papa the same thing."

I knew I needed to do this. "I'll do it. I'll tell him." *Tonight. After dinner.*

"You can do it now."

"Now?"

"He went to the cigarette shop but after that he'll be coming here."

"You set this meeting up?" I gave her a quizzical look. "Why are you wanting to be so helpful?"

"I'm always helpful to you. And I will help you with some advice now."

"What's that?"

"You tell your papa how you feel about Lucy. He loved your mama very much. He understands love."

"Do you think he'll ever get over Mama's death?" I asked. It pained me to remember how he'd asked last night if my mother had suffered.

"He will always walk with a hole in his heart." She stood and began dusting off the tops of cans again as though the action helped her voice her thoughts. "You tell him you love Lucy, she is the one for you, and that you want to bring her back here from Seattle, and that you need money to do that. You say all that. You hear me, loud and clear?"

The door opened, the bell sang, and in walked Papa.

"Say it like I tell you," my aunt whispered as Papa made his way toward me.

I grabbed my courage. I wasted no time. Now while the shop was without customers. "Papa, can we sell the watch?"

My aunt shot me a look that told me I had done it all wrong.

Papa rubbed his chin. "What's this about?"

Then I told it just as my aunt had instructed me. I spoke of love, and how I needed money to bring Lucy back to me, that by selling the watch we would save Lucy. I even added that the watch had been presented to our family because my grandfather had rescued a girl and that now it could also be used to rescue a girl. I must have talked ten minutes without taking in air.

Papa looked out the shop window. "The watch has been in our family for three generations."

"I know."

"It's the only tangible inheritance I have left from my parents."

A customer entered, creating a gap in our conversation. I wanted the customer to leave, but she was enjoying browsing.

"Are these beets?" she asked, as she picked up a jar. "I love beets."

Aunt Kazuko walked over to Papa and said to him in Japanese, "If Nobu doesn't bring Lucy here and marry her and have children, then there will be no more Mori generations."

Papa nodded. I wondered what his nod meant. After several minutes, he said, "Do what you must." Then he left the shop, leaving my aunt and me to exchange grateful smiles.

❀

After Papa and my aunt left, I walked around the shop with new energy. My smile wouldn't leave my face. I was planning my trip to Mr. Rizzardi's when a silver-haired woman from Aunt Kazuko's To the

Table group entered. She handed me a small wooden sign made of the same material blackboards are made of.

"I came here on Saturday and you weren't here," she said. "I wanted to buy some canned plums for a pie I planned to make for Sunday's dinner." The woman seemed disappointed. She wore bright red lipstick and her lips formed into a pout.

I knew that she was telling me that I needed to show my customers what my shop hours were. That was a good idea, one I would consider. "I'll have to make a sign with the hours posted," I said. "Or perhaps the landlord will let me paint the hours on the door."

She pouted even more. Her lips were so red against her powered white face.

What was wrong with her? Did not being able to buy plums really make women that upset? I'd have to ask Aunt Kazuko.

Taking a piece of white chalk from her pocket she thrust it into my hand. "This is for you to use on that blackboard!"

I held both the blackboard and the chalk, one in each hand. "I will use them," I said, hoping I could appease her.

"You can write your store hours on it." With a sharp fingernail, she pointed to the blackboard.

At last I realized that her gift to me was to serve the purpose of a sign. I apologized for being thick in the head. And then to make her happy, I wrote out our store hours on the board in my best penmanship.

Once I finished, the lady nodded in approval. "You need to hang that sign up now," she said.

I searched the shelves for a nail.

"There's a nail here," she said, finding an abandoned one sticking out of the storage door frame.

I wiggled the nail out of the wood as she stood close by, watching me. The top of the chalkboard had a hole and so I strung a piece of string through it. "What do you think?" I asked. "This string should hold it well."

Together we walked outside. I pounded the nail into the wood at the very top of the door, just above the windowpane. I used my fist, although the heel of my shoe would have been a better choice.

Then I hung the string on the nail, and watched the blackboard dangle against the glass. Now everyone could read our shop hours.

As we stood outside the shop looking at the blackboard, she said, "Anyone could take the sign down or mark on it."

I wish she'd told me of her concern before I'd hung the blackboard. I scanned the street as cars sped past. She was right, of course. A little blackboard hanging on a door to a shop run by a Japanese was sure to give all those who wrote about the Japs being menaces to society reason to tamper. I could see myself coming to work tomorrow to find this gift destroyed or slanderous words written across it. I removed the sign, and pulled the nail out.

"Can you hang it inside so that it can be safe and yet be seen by passersby?" she asked.

We entered the shop and I shut the door. She watched as I banged the nail into the wood that surrounded the top of the door. This time I used the heel of my shoe. Then I strung the sign from the nail. Now it hung inside where it was protected and yet could be seen through the glass from the outside.

The woman exited the shop, and through the window, I saw her viewing the new sign. The bell rang when she entered once more, a smile on her face. She picked up two jars of plums. "I'll use these in a pie for this coming Sunday," she said. "There's nothing like a good plum pie."

"Thank you. Thank you for buying plums and for the blackboard."

The miniature blackboard and chalk spoke to me of kindness. I appreciated this Caucasian woman's thoughtfulness. With all the hatred toward Japanese, it was nice to get some encouragement and affirmation.

When Tom came to see me before I closed the shop for the day, he erased what I'd written and wrote the days of the week and the hours in his neat penmanship. We both agreed that his writing was easier to read than mine.

Chapter Thirty-five

The pawn shop was quiet, just me and Mr. Rizzardi. I walked over to where he stood behind the counter reading the newspaper. Placing the box with the watch onto the counter top, I took a deep breath. With shaky fingers, I removed the watch from the box. The sun streaming in from the window made it glisten. Opening the hinge so that the watch face was exposed, I said, "I want to sell this."

"How much do you want for it?" he asked, as he picked it up, pulled on his reading glasses. "It's heavy. Gold." He looked at me.

How much? Over the years, I clearly remembered Mr. Kubo telling me that he thought it was worth about three-hundred dollars. With all the boldness I could produce, I said, "I want three-hundred dollars."

"I can give you one-hundred."

Without another word, I turned and walked out of the shop onto the sidewalk.

I heard the bell on the door ring and his voice behind me. "Sir?"

I took in a breath, but did not turn.

"Sir, please come back inside."

"Three-hundred dollars," I said.

"Two-hundred." His tone was firm.

"Three." I tried not to flinch, hoping that he would not see my fear.

"Come back inside," he said.

With my back still to him, I said, "Three."

"I will give you three."

Back inside, he gave me the money. I pressed the bills into my pocket. I thanked him, and rushed outside. It was the first time I had run home, because I didn't want to get mugged.

❦

And now we had money. Tom went to the doctor's and was fitted for a new brace. Emi said he walked taller now. Aunt Kazuko went to the ladies' shop on First Street and bought a new pair of shoes. And a new dress and a new pair of white gloves, because all the ladies at church had a pair. Emi got piano lessons from a *real teacher*. A lady from the church came over every Monday afternoon to teach her. For the shop, I ordered as much as I could, even boxes of matches and towels of all shapes and sizes.

I bought Papa a new recliner so that he could relax whenever he read the newspaper. I encouraged him go to the doctor's to get a check-up. He refused. I expected that he would.

Then one evening he entered the kitchen where Tom and I were washing and drying the dinner dishes.

"I have low iron," he said.

"How do you know?" I asked.

"The doctor told me." He filled a glass with water. From his trousers he removed two tiny brown bottles.

"What are those?"

"Some medicine the doctor gave me today." He took one pill from each container. After downing the tablets, he muttered something; I wasn't sure which language it was in.

"What was that, Papa?" asked Tom.

"If these pills don't kill me," he said, "I think I'll live."

"It looks good," Tom said one afternoon when he came to help me at the shop. He perused the tables; one section was for commissioned items and the other for wholesale products I'd ordered from a catalog. "Like a real five and dime."

But we both knew that our objective was not to become a five and dime. I wanted to keep my first goal in mind that this was to be a place that Japanese-Americans—no, make that all Americans—could sell their wares and feel a strong sense of dignity about what they had to offer, and who they were as Americans.

It was Christmas again, and the town was lit up with decorated trees and lights. Emi played at her kindergarten's Christmas concert. She was excited that, at last, she was in a real concert.

Lucy and I talked by phone at least once a week. She'd found a church with a choir. Between choir practice and helping her aunt and uncle with their business, her days were full.

"Do you plan to make another record?" I asked.

"It's not that easy," she said.

"You did it once."

"Yeah." After pausing she said, "But that's not the life I want now. I told you that before."

"I want you to come home," I said. I'd told her that before, too. "I'm going to buy you a train ticket so that you can come back to San Jose."

She was silent for a moment, and then I realized that she was crying. "Really, Nathan? Really?"

"Yes, I can wire you the money."

"Oh, Nathan, I know you are struggling financially."

"I sold the watch."

"Sold it? But why? It is your family's treasure."

I didn't want to talk about treasures. "If I send you the money, will you come here?"

I heard her sniff, clear her throat. "I need some time . . ."

"Time for what?"

"You know that I've made so many mistakes in the past. I'm at a good place now."

"A good place?" *Without me?* "What do you mean?"

"I have obligations here. I can't just leave."

In that moment, I hated the word obligations. If she loved me, why couldn't she abandon everything in Seattle and come to me?

"Good night, Nathan," she said before I could speak my mind.

That night I pleaded with God. Please, let her come back, stay here, and be happy. And as for loving me, oh, dear God, you know I need her to love me.

❦

Each day at the shop, I hoped to see her standing there as she had that day in July. Tom told me that hope is the word which God has written on the brow of every man. I thought he was brilliant to come up with that saying. Then I saw that very line in one of his literature books with Victor Hugo's name beside it. Tom might not have written those words, but he was brilliant to know that I needed to hear them.

Chapter Thirty-six

S he came back in March when the hibiscus on our street were the most beautiful.

I was at work, arranging items on shelves and thinking of her. It had been months since I'd sent the money for her train ride back to California. When the money arrived, she'd phoned the store to thank me. I told her that if she couldn't come back to stay, to at least come for a weekend visit. I didn't care that I sounded desperate to see her.

After closing the shop for the day, I leisurely walked home. A neighbor on an evening stroll stopped to ask about the shop. Neighbors, I had learned, like to inquire about business and offer their suggestions—whether you ask for them or not.

As I stepped onto our porch, I heard a familiar sound, Emi playing the piano. But there was also singing. Wildly, my heart beat. There was no mistake; no one else sang "Blessed Assurance" like she did.

Midway through the last verse, I couldn't wait any longer. Swinging open the front door, I rushed inside, into the living room.

There she was, seated at the piano bench beside my sister.

"Nathan's home!" Emi cried when she saw me.

Lucy turned from the piano and smiled, just as Aunt Kazuko emerged from the kitchen.

"Emi," she said, "I need your help with dinner, please!"

Emi didn't want to help, but my aunt bribed her with a few grapes.

As the two of us were left alone and the kitchen door closed, I took Emi's place to sit beside the most beautiful woman in the world. "Hello, stranger," I said. "I'm Nathan Mori. I was wondering if you would like to sing while I play a song?"

I played a few notes, and then she nodded. With her hands poised in her lap, she started to sing the lyrics to "My Dreams Are Getting Better All the Time." It was a song I had practiced ever since she said she liked it when we'd talked on the phone one night. As she sang and I played, one thing became clear—her voice and my music belonged together.

"Well, what do you know? He smiled at me in my dreams last night. My dreams are getting better all the time," sang Lucy.

When we finished, I put my arm around her shoulders and drew her to me. It felt like the most natural thing to do; gone was my clumsiness. The scared boy of yesterday had left me. "We make a good team," I whispered.

"I have missed you," she said. Her breath caressed my neck. "I want us to be happy. Together."

"I want that, too."

"We should dance," she said.

Since the only records we had were hers and Bing Crosby's, and since I had yet to get us a record player, I searched for a radio station that played danceable music. My mind tempted me to go back to camp days, those days when I so wanted her to like me, those days when I didn't see what she saw in Ken. I tried to push those days away. I didn't want Ken to once again interfere. Not with this dance.

I turned to a station just as one song ended. We waited for the next song, and when the D.J. announced that it was going to be "My Dreams Are Getting Better All the Time," we laughed and then slipped our arms around each other.

"It's a sign," she said. "We are meant to be."

But I didn't need the coincidence of a song playing on the radio with the lovely Doris Day singing the lyrics to tell me that. I already knew it.

❦

Lucy helped me at the store, and as my aunt said, it certainly was a good thing, because the shop needed a woman's touch. She suggested that we paint the walls a light blue. Jonathan Jones said it was fine with him as long as we supplied the paint. So one Sunday afternoon, we painted. Tom helped, and my aunt helped by keeping Emi occupied so that she wouldn't get covered in paint. Papa stopped by and told us that we were doing a fine job.

I asked him later how he asked Mama to marry him, and he reminded me that it was no Bacall and Bogart story; Mama had been a picture bride.

"This process took some time," he said. "I saw her picture and she was sent mine."

"And then?" I asked.

"I said yes right away. She said yes after three months."

"And then she came over here by ship?" I wanted to hear him tell the story.

"That was a beautiful day when she arrived. She was dressed in a Western dress so that she would look more American. Later we laughed about how her family had to rush around to find the perfect Western dress for her in their little town in Nagano." Papa smiled, and I was glad to see that the memory was a pleasant one.

It was indeed a beautiful story, but he still hadn't answered my question. How did one go about asking a woman to marry him?

I suppose I should have been listening better when the adults sat around the camp telling their stories about engagement. If I'd been more attentive, I would have heard how it had been done. I watched a few movies and saw how Humphrey Bogart and Cary Grant wooed the ladies. They were dressed in suits and had hats. I had never liked the feel of a hat against my head and hair. Not even as a child when we would go up to San Francisco and Mama would insist that I wear a wool cap so that I wouldn't get an earache from the wind. So without looking a thing like Humphrey, what was I to do?

"Nobu, just be yourself." Mama's words spoke through all my confusion.

One evening on my walk home from work, I tried to come up with the best way to ask a woman to marry you.

As I neared our house, I looked around, and, seeing that I was alone on the sidewalk, I practiced. "Lucy, will you please marry me?" No, that sounded too formal.

"Hey, baby, let's get hitched." Too much like a country boy.

"May I have your hand in marriage?" I laughed aloud at that.

"Why don't we tie the knot?" That choice would never make the cut.

When I reached home, I just wanted to take a shower. Get the stench of the shop off my skin. Stick my head under a rush of hot water and let the shampoo flow down my hair and over my shoulders. Lather up with some of that soap I'd bought and sold in the store. Ivory was the name of it; it was so good that it had been floating in America's bath water since 1879, according to *Business First* magazine. Yet the Mori family had never washed with a bar until recently.

Through the opened windows, I heard Lucy singing from inside the house and the steady flow of piano music. Her song was about God's faithfulness. I recalled Him in the dusty camp, in the cold barracks, in the dining hall when food seemed bland, and in the jail. He had carried us through. He had never forsaken us, even when we had felt forsaken by our own nation.

I hadn't planned on Lucy being at our house. I had planned on getting cleaned up, putting on some aftershave and a change of clothes. Then I had planned on walking over to her parents' house, knocking on the door and, on a bended knee, asking her to marry me. But it seemed that my plans were often skewed.

Inside, Lucy hugged me and kissed my cheek.

Immediately, fear set in. Why hadn't she kissed my lips? What was up? Perhaps she didn't care about me after all. I felt the familiar surge of fear creep into my veins. If she wouldn't marry me, what would I do? I'd be forced to live the rest of my life as a hermit. I'd grow old and scaly, like the pet toad named Bogart. I'd be undesirable and would be reminded of my bad luck every night as I sat alone eating a bowl of cream of chicken soup.

"Read to me! I said please!" Emi's voice broke into my thoughts, and I realized that she was talking to Aunt Kazuko and to Tom in her bedroom. She didn't want to go to bed and said she would go only if both of them read to her. "Two stories," I heard her adamant voice through the walls. "I want two stories, and then I'll go to sleep."

Lucy smiled. "At first she had no problem getting ready for bed, but then she overheard the three of us talking, and she didn't want to miss out."

"That's Emi. She doesn't want to miss anything."

"I remember when she was born."

"You brought a blanket your mom knitted."

"It was yellow. Your mother was so pale and weak, but she thanked me for it. She was always so gracious."

I swallowed hard, and hoped that my eyes would stay dry.

"How was your day at the store?" Lucy asked, pulling me from the past. "I was going to come over to see you, but I got a phone call from the minister of music at Second Street Church. Mr. Raymond is his name, yeah, I think that's right. He wants me to sing on Sunday. So I came here to practice with the piano. Emi played while I sang. She really is doing well with those lessons you got for her."

I agreed and then said that I needed a shower.

"What's wrong?"

"Nothing. I just need to get clean."

"Before you take one, I wanted to ask you something." She put her arms around my waist.

I was so aware of my smell, the perspiration from a long day's work. I didn't want to get too close to Lucy. She always smelled so nice, like some sort of flower garden.

"I've been thinking."

"Yeah?"

"You know Sadie and Harold got engaged last week."

"Oh, really?" I had no idea who they were.

"And Bert and Maryanne are getting married in September. And Jennifer and Jeff. Do you know them?"

The discomfort from my date with Jennifer filled my mind. That had been a waste of a night. Ever since my aunt had told me that the two were engaged, I had been glad that it was Jeff God had in mind for Jennifer and not me.

"What about us?"

"Us?"

"Yes. What are we going to do?"

"I . . . well . . ."

"Yes?" She gave me a sly smile.

I wasn't exactly sure what was going on. I had never been in such a situation. Yet, something told me that I was about to enter a very good situation. If I was hearing correctly, what Lucy was saying was actually exactly what I had in mind. "We should. Of course." I mean, after all, I had been practicing how to ask her to marry me for several days.

"Should what?" She was trying to coax it out of me, but what if . . .? What if she wasn't thinking about marriage? What if she thought we needed to wait or that I was too young? Suddenly, all I could think of was how I needed warm water and soap. "I need a shower."

She stood right under my chin and looked up at me. Had there ever been such soulful eyes, such flawless skin, such—

"So, Mr. Nobu Nathan Mori, will you ask me to marry you?"

Did she say marry? Quickly, before she could take back her words, I stooped down on one bended knee. "Will you . . . ?" My mind was a nervous blank. This was not the man who had practiced what to say all the way home. I cleared my throat and in a bold tone said, "Will you, Fusou Lucy Yokota, never leave me again—"

"Yes!" she interrupted.

"You will never leave me again?"

"Yes, and I'll marry you, too."

Laughing, I stood. "You made that easy."

She wrapped her arms around me tightly and whispered, "See? That wasn't so hard now, was it?"

"It went pretty good. I mean I got the answer I hoped for. That's what matters in the end, right?"

"I just want to be with you. We've been apart for much too long." She lay her head against my chest and for a few minutes, we just held each other and breathed.

And it didn't matter that I needed a shower. This goes to prove that even a stinky man can get engaged.

Then we smiled into each other's eyes and kissed, just like they do in the movies.

And I knew that this was how it would go down in the Mori family history. Our children would grow up hearing, "Mama proposed to Papa, and you know what he did after that? He took a shower."

Chapter Thirty-seven

After church on the Sunday before our wedding, we were all gathered at our house for dinner. Aunt Kazuko made a roast with mashed potatoes and gravy. "I am becoming so American," she said. "My friends in Nagano would be amazed at how I can cook."

The meal was certainly an improvement over when my aunt made a meatloaf that no one could eat. She'd misread the recipe and thought it said to bake for two hours when it had only needed to bake for one hour. That had been about a week before we were shipped off to the assembly center. Our lives had been turned upside down then. Aunt Kazuko had most likely been so distraught that she hadn't even been able to read correctly. That's what we'd said to console her. Now she had a cookbook, *The Modern Family Cookbook*, given to her by a woman at our church. My aunt had followed many of the recipes in the poultry section and last Thanksgiving had made a flavorful dressing by using slices of stale bread.

"We have dessert," said Emi. "It's a cake I helped make." Her smile was so wide that I thought it would stretch off her little face.

Papa said he was sure that the cake would be delicious, but he wanted to slip out for a smoke first.

Aunt Kazuko wanted to know what kind of flowers we wanted at our wedding. "My To the Table group wants to arrange the bouquets for you. What kind do you like?" she asked Lucy.

"My favorites are hibiscus," said Lucy. "But I think most people have roses."

"Roses," said my aunt. "They are overrated. Hibiscus is good choice."

"Can we have dessert now? What is taking Papa so long?" Emi squirmed in her chair.

"He probably fell asleep," I said, because I couldn't say the truth. The truth was that lately I'd found him holding thin sheets of paper in his hands and gazing out at nothing. Those pages were letters from relatives who gave horrible accounts of other relatives who were now dying from the radiation of Hiroshima and Nagasaki. I had to take Papa's word for them; they were written with many Chinese characters (*Kanji*) I had never learned. I stood to walk to the front door.

Although Emi wanted to tag along, I told her to carry some plates into the kitchen. "You are such a big helper," I said.

"What would you do without me?" she said, her smile still playing across her face.

"Stand up and carry," said Aunt Kazuko. "But no dropping anything on the floor."

With Emi occupied, I made my way to the front of the house. I hoped Papa wouldn't have tears on his cheeks. I hoped he wouldn't want me to listen to him again tell how his cousin, whose wife had died immediately when the bomb exploded in Hiroshima in 1945, was now at the point where he couldn't keep any food down and was throwing up every night, just a skeleton of a man. "At first, he had been okay. This radiation is a poison that doesn't leave," Papa had said, the pages of the recent letter rattling in his hand. It had been such a good lunch, and I was excited about Lucy and my wedding. I didn't want sadness—just for once, I wanted to see Papa smile like he meant it, like he used to.

As soon as I approached the door, I heard voices. When I looked out the screen door, I thought my heart would stop.

Papa was hugging a tall man dressed in a pair of tan trousers and a navy shirt. His white hat covered his head, but that didn't stop me at all from knowing who it was.

"Ken! You're here!" It's amazing how quickly tears can fill your eyes. I rushed out the door to him.

"Hey," he said. "Just visiting for my brother's wedding." He smiled and then we were hugging each other in tight bear hugs as though we never wanted to let go.

Inside, he hugged Tom first, then our aunt, and then Lucy.

"I am so flabbergasted," Aunt Kazuko said. "Flabbergasted." She laughed, and then repeated it again.

Ken reached for Emi, picked her up in his arms and said, "And who is this big girl?"

Emi squealed, gave him a kiss, and then pulled his hat off his head and scrambled out of his arms. Ken walked over to Lucy and gave her a hug.

"You are taller," observed Aunt Kazuko. "And you look thin. Too thin. Do you not get enough to eat?"

"I eat," Ken said. "I just work a lot."

I recalled in camp how frustrating it had been to get Ken to do any chore. Now he was responsible for a restaurant.

"You need some dinner?" Aunt Kazuko asked. "I make plenty. Plenty for you."

Ken said, "Thanks, but I don't need anything. Traveling always takes away my appetite."

"Did you ride a ship here?" Tom asked. He wanted to know what riding in a ship was like and as Ken shared, I sat back in my chair and noted how time had been kind to my brother, helping him to grow up and become more of a man.

Aunt Kazuko brought in a carrot cake that she and Emi had made. It was covered in white frosting that had taken half an hour to beat into a creamy consistency.

"I am so glad we made this cake," said Emi. "Because today is a special day."

"It's very special," said Ken, and he went over to Papa and hugged him again and then pulled me into a hug.

As we all sat down again, I looked around the table and thought, here we are, all of us together. Mama, it finally happened.

Tom was eager to ask Ken questions about the war. "What kind of gun did you get to fire? Did you kill anyone?"

Ken answered the question about the gun, but never expanded on the latter. From his eyes, I knew he had seen and experienced heartache. You can usually tell those who have suffered; they carry this look in their eyes that can't be erased.

After we ate cake, Ken even having a sliver, Emi wanted Ken to hear her play the piano. We crowded around the Gulbransen and listened to her play "Blessed Assurance" from the Second Street hymnal. Ken complimented her, and that gave Emi the courage she needed to play another song and another.

"Sit down," Emi told us. "This is like a concert."

I knew that there were a bunch of dishes and pots that wouldn't wash themselves. I headed into the kitchen and was surprised when Ken followed me and said, "You wash and I'll dry."

As the sink filled with hot water, Ken gave me a wide smile. "You seem happy."

"I have a lot to be thankful for."

"I can tell that you and Lucy are good together."

"How about you? I heard you have a girlfriend. Or many of them, in fact."

He laughed, a laugh that I well-remembered. "Some things never change, huh? I can't imagine settling down with just one. Not yet anyway."

"I can't imagine you ever settling on one girl either." I scrubbed a plate, rinsed it, and handed it to him to dry.

"You'll have to come to London to see our restaurant."

"Do you really serve real Japanese food?" I asked. "How about *natto*, those nasty fermented soy beans Aunt Kazuko loves?"

He grimaced. "No one would touch those. But the tempura and *katsudon* (pork over rice) people love. Next to fish and chips, of course."

The suds in the sink had disappeared; I squeezed more detergent into the water. A soap bubble rose in the space between my brother and me. When I looked to see where it was headed, my eyes met Ken's.

The smile was gone from his face. "Look at you," he said, his voice breaking. "You are the real hero. You've held everything together."

I wanted to tell him that wasn't true. That it was only through God's saving grace and mercy that I was able to do anything. Like Mekley, I was a wretch. I opened my mouth, but the words wouldn't come. A tear formed instead, and seeing it, Ken drew me to his chest.

"She'd be so proud of you," he said, hugging my smaller frame close to him. "You were the one she could count on."

I was about to say something about her—our mama—but something told me not to interrupt this moment. This was the first time in my life that I felt Ken's tears. As they dampened my hair, I thought, here we are, two Mori men, crying. Here we are, making our own history.

We were back to washing and drying dishes when Lucy came into the kitchen. She put her arm around my waist and kissed my cheek. To Ken she said, "It's good you're here. Nathan has missed you."

I listened carefully and purposefully to hear the way her voice sounded when she spoke to him. I had listened all afternoon. But it seemed that whatever those two had between them before was not there now. For me, this brought gratifying comfort.

Lucy lifted the clean plates Ken had stacked on the counter and placed them in the cupboard. "My friend Mary wants to sing at our wedding, and Emi wants to play. What do you think?"

"Emi's good," said Ken. "She should play. Not sure how Mary sounds. But I bet that Emi could do a swell job. She—" He stopped in midsentence. "Nathan, what do you think?"

"I don't think you've ever asked me what I think."

The three of us laughed. And as we laughed, I had this sense that I bet we could all get along together. God's forgiveness was suddenly larger than any rift that had once been there. God's forgiveness never seemed to end either; it was endless, fresh and life-giving. There was enough of it to bask in for everyone I needed to forgive and for everyone who needed to forgive me.

When the sink had drained, and all the water had been wiped from the counters, we entered the living room. Ken spotted his photo on the mantle. "Where did you get that?" He seemed happy and also amused that we would have a picture from a magazine—his picture.

"Lucy and I went to the Hashimotos, and they gave it to us," I said.

"Nathan was very concerned about you," Lucy added. I knew she was trying to put me in a good light in front of my brother, and I loved her for it.

"We should get a picture of all of us. Together," he said.

"Oh, not right now," Aunt Kazuko protested. "My hair is a mess. Wait till after Tuesday when I go to the beauty salon. Or much better, wait till the wedding when we will all look our best."

I wanted to show Ken the shop and tell him about the watch and how Mekley had told me the whole story and how Lucy had confessed to it. I wanted to tell him that I had Papa's permission to sell the watch at the pawn shop, and that had been a great decision, although a difficult one to make. I had given Mama my word that I would keep it safe; I had failed, but never mind that. I wanted to say that a family heirloom is only as valuable as you make it out to be, and just because it's no longer in the family anymore, doesn't mean it's really gone. The story of the gold pocket watch would still be part of the Mori family heritage. Future generations would just have to rely on their imaginations to know what the watch looked and felt like. I wanted to share those things and more with my brother.

But as the music from Emi's concert filled the room, and the warm June breezes blew into our house through the opened windows, ruffling the cotton curtains and bringing in the scent of freshly mowed grass and summer roses, none of that seemed important to me right then. The past seemed long ago and far away, like a distant cousin. And I wanted to keep it that way.

Ken was here after having been gone from us for nearly five years. We were all together again. We were family. Papa was even smiling like he used to, like he meant it, like he couldn't stop.

I envisioned Mama smiling, too. Since they say Heaven is somewhere above us, I pictured her smiling down. Some say Heaven's nearer to us than we think.

"You do know that you are all my favorites, don't you?" I heard her words as though she was right with us in the living room. It was as though if I reached out, I could touch her hand.

Yes, almost.

The End

Recipe for Aunt Kazuko's Oatmeal Raisin Cookies (1946)

1 ½ cups all-purpose flour
¼ teaspoon salt
1 teaspoon soda
1 teaspoon ground cinnamon
½ cup shortening
1 cup sugar
1 egg
1 ½ cups rolled oats
2/3 cup buttermilk
½ cup chopped nuts
1 cup seedless raisins
Cream shortening, blend in sugar and add egg. Beat until smooth and light. Sift flour with salt, soda and cinnamon. Stir half the flour in with egg mixture; add milk, the rest of flour, and then oats, nuts and raisins. Stir till well mixed. Drop from a teaspoon onto a buttered baking sheet and bake at 400 degrees F. for 10 minutes or until nicely browned. Yields about 36 cookies.

ABOUT THE AUTHOR

A lice J. Wisler was born and raised in Japan as a missionary kid. She is the author of *Getting Out of Bed in the Morning,* and five novels—*Rain Song* and *How Sweet It Is* were Christy finalists. Ever since the cancer death of her four-year-old son Daniel in 1997, she has found solace in writing from heartache and teaches *Writing the Heartache* workshops across the country at conferences and seminars. She lives in Durham, NC with her husband and children where they have a wood carving business, Carved By Heart. Visit her website at http://www.alicewisler.com.